SINGING ALL THE WAY UP

PRAISE FOR STEPHANIE SANDERS-JACOB

"This is an excellent novel about truth, lies, and how one incident can consume a life, losing yourself in the process... It's just a fantastic story that you'll relish and talk about once you've finished."

HORROR READS, GOODREADS

"This novel is beautifully written and you will feel for Laura as certain things come to light and, eventually, the truth is revealed. But at what cost?"

DAVID R., GOODREADS

"...I really loved this book, and I was surprised to find that this is Stephanie Sanders-Jacob's debut novel! She's a pro already. I am excited to read more from her in the future."

WILLOW O'GRADY, GOODREADS

"Stephanie Sanders-Jacob debut novel, Singing All the Way Up, was an interesting read for sure. I love the author's note, speaking on the author's own experiences with aliens/UFOs."

CYNTHIA, GOODREADS

"…. absolutely fantastic! Really, pick up this book if you want a good read."

K.R. CERVANTEZ

"I loved the use of UFOs and how this book still has a cast of realistic people. The plot worked overall and it left me wanting to read more from the author."

KATHRYN M., NETGALLEY

"If this is the first step in the staircase of progression for Stephanie Sanders-Jacob as an author then she'll be climbing to the moon her future books, and I'll be along for the ride… singing all the way up!"

JUSTIN BROWN, GOODREADS

CONTENTS

To my dad, who almost died twice during the editing of this book. He's everything Laura's father is not.

"The mind of a person coming out of Fairy-Land is usually blank as to what has been seen and done there."
-Walter Evans-Wentz, <u>The Fairy Faith in Celtic Countries</u>

FAME

CHAPTER 1
SILENT SHIP

I NEVER THOUGHT I'd say this, but things were better before I killed my father.

For all his scheming, my mother floundered, withered without him—turned into a pale, gaunt thing with watery eyes. That's when things really got bad for me. My mother could barely hold herself up, let alone me and my Incident.

She sent me away to the freak show—did you know they still have those? Where else would all those hungry, voyeuristic eyes go? I stood before them all, arms outstretched, and sang some quavering song in a language I didn't understand. And I didn't do it particularly well, but they still wept.

"I felt your pain," once gasped a man after. I was huddled against the building we'd just performed in, hugging myself, shielding my body from the wind and the cheap coats of the people streaming home. "It felt like I was right there." He wobbled on his feet, but I knew he wasn't drunk. I know what that kind of belief can do to you.

"You were there," I said, relishing the wonder in his eyes.

"What was it like?" he asked. "The craft, I mean."

I sighed, the question too concrete, not enough about me. In truth, I did not remember the alien craft that supposedly plucked me from my childhood home. I don't remember seeing the thing. I don't remember the beings onboard, and I don't remember singing. They said I was singing all the way up, caught in a shimmering beam that held me completely still except for my jaw. I sang. Something no little girl should know—operatic, orgasmic, an aria perhaps, and my parents lay crumpled beneath me, screaming, begging me to come back down. But I wouldn't. I couldn't. I slipped into the ship, and only then did my singing stop.

They said I reappeared earth side that night, smiling dementedly through the sliding glass door until someone noticed me and screamed. My parents ran to me, enfolded me into themselves, and found me much renewed from the sullen little seven-year-old I was said to be. I sparkled. I was more. I was special.

Except I can't remember any of that. There's a point where everything washes out to black—a day, otherwise normal in its onward grind, now dipped in dark acid, partially eaten away. I was there, playing beneath the table, my dolls dancing on stiff legs, and then my parents were screaming. They pulled me through the door—a threshold I didn't realize I'd stepped through. I cried because they were crying, a strange glint in my daddy's eye.

All details of The Incident, as it has come to be known both familiarly and internationally, have always been reminded to me by my parents, namely my father. Before every interview, TV appearance, trip to the grocery store, he'd remind me of how rapturous that moment was, when I was hanging there beneath the bulking, silent ship.

"You were singing," he'd say.

"All the way up!" I'd reply, our little call and response.

The papers, the radio shows, the conventions, all the fans say it happened, and that it happened to me. They say my voice was beautiful. But I can't remember—twenty-five years later, and I still can't remember. So, I collect stories like trophies—stories about the unusual, the weird—searching for truth in other people's words, other people's heartache. I need to know what happened. I need to know if, despite the fame and worship, I'm alone. There are stories here—consume them, gnash them between your teeth. When you spit them back out, study the splatter as if they were tea leaves in a porcelain cup. Can you see me in that mess?

I follow the thread back from where I am—fire–freak show–Daddy dying–interviews–TV special–parades–conventions–book deal–radio shows–concerts–local paper—I follow it back, and it begins in a fray—nothing. There's nothing at the beginning of my rope—just dark, dizzying black. And when I see it, I don't feel much like singing at all.

———

Here's the first story, dizzying and uncertain.

Frederick Valentich disappeared.

First, he was there, flying over the Bass Strait, and then he was not.

He was on his way to King Island to meet his friend for seafood; when you're a pilot you can do such frivolous things. Never mind he couldn't pass the commercial exams or get into the Air Force—he was a pilot one and the same.

He left at dusk when the air was calm and easy. The ocean below him sparkled with the sunset, and he felt at peace—something he never experienced when his feet were on solid ground.

But soon the quietude was shattered; a gleaming, metallic thing buzzed his plane, sending the whole craft shivering. He dipped lower to avoid it and wiped at his brow. "Crazy," he spat.

He picked up his radio and reported it in, hoping to hear it was someone he knew from back home, messing with him.

But it wasn't. No one could move that fast, maneuver so deftly.

It flew before him, then above him, flashing a green, hypnotizing light.

"It's playing games with me," he radioed to the base. And it was—looping by again and again, doing great circles about his plane.

"My engine's gone funny," he shouted into the radio. The engine sputtered and choked whenever the craft was on top of him.

Alarmed, the men on the other end asked him to describe the plane.

"It's not a plane," he said. "It's—"

And then came the sound of metal being beaten. The transmission was gone.

Neither he nor his aircraft were ever found.

Some speculate that Frederick, a rookie pilot, had become disoriented—was flying upside down, and the craft he saw above him was his own plane's reflection, distorted by the waves.

CHAPTER 2

MOON-EYED

THE DAY AFTER MY ABDUCTION, a nice, bumbling man in big myopic glasses came to quiz me on my experience. I ate ice cream and kicked my legs at him underneath the table and said things like "I dunno" and "mm-hmm" when my mouth was too full to say the other.

"It's the damnedest thing," my Daddy said. That made me put down my spoon—he only cursed when he was angry. "She doesn't remember a thing after the beam. I think they wiped her memory."

"Could be. Could be," said the reporter, who scrawled notes on a bent-up legal pad whenever my Daddy spoke but stayed rapt and still when I made some small comment. "It wouldn't be the first time I've heard of post-abduction amnesia."

Abduction? Was that the word for what had happened to me? I thought it was a normal day—a day so usual it wasn't worth remembering. Until it wasn't. Until my mom and dad were screaming and throwing their arms around me there on the back porch, and I didn't know why. I thought I had been underneath the dining room table, playing with Barbies. I thought I was staying up past my bedtime because I'd been extra good.

I do remember savoring the way the night glowed simultaneously gold and blue and I'd basked in the faint moonlight that came in through the sliding door. I loved night. As I spun my Barbies, I had been imagining I could feel the rays of the moon—ticklish and cold— across my skin. And then my parent's hands were on me, checking me for injuries and rubbing away their own snot. I guess that was a type of abduction, but maybe not the kind the man wanted to hear about.

"I don't remember it at all," I said, spooning more melted chocolate ice cream into my mouth.

My dad said, "Sure you do, honey. You just have to try."

I was trying. I was trying so hard.

"Don't you remember the beam? Big and golden? Earlier you said you remembered the beam."

I shut my eyes. I wasn't sure what I had agreed to remember in order to get the ice cream. A beam. "Like a light?" I asked.

"Yes! Light! You were floating up in it."

I remembered rolling across the carpet so I could better see the moon through the slider. "I was in the light of the moon. A moon beam."

"God that's good," said the man from the newspaper. "Why was it like the moon?"

"I—" I looked to my dad for support, but his face was blank and faraway. "I guess it was from the moon, the light—er, the beam, I mean."

"And this moon, did it move?"

I liked the reporter, but he was a bit of an idiot. "Of course the moon moves."

"But this moon, I mean. The one with the beam."

"Well, sure."

The man nodded. "This is good stuff. Good stuff. You're doing a great job, Laura. And did it glow?"

"Yes—golden blue."

"Beautiful," he whispered. "That's really gorgeous. Were there people onboard the ship?"

"You already asked me that," I said. "I don't remember a ship."

"I mean, on the moon. Were there people there?"

I had seen the pictures—the grainy video of the flag raised above gray lunar dust. "Yes," I said.

We stared at one another, and I watched sweat trickle down his forehead. "Tell me more about the song you sang."

"Umm-well, Mom and Dad said it was the best I've ever sang. Loud and clear and I hit all the notes. But they hadn't heard the song before. It wasn't anything they could have taught me, and nothing they remember hearing on TV. And they said it was a different language, I think, I mean, I'm not sure what language it was. I—" I drove my spoon hard into the middle of my bowl. "It's hard to understand." My voice broke—I wasn't doing a good job repeating what Daddy had told me to say.

"I think I'd better let you get back to your ice cream." He smiled wide and slapped my dad on the arm, knocking him out of his reverie. "Great kid you got here, Sam."

"Sure is," Daddy said. "Did you get what you need?"

The reporter mopped at his forehead with a paper towel. "Everything and more. With a little luck and a lot of coffee it'll be in the morning paper. I'd better get back to the office to type this thing up."

The men shook hands, and my dad escorted the reporter out of the house.

"Why'd you go on about the moon?" my dad asked upon returning. "We didn't talk about that."

"I didn't! He wanted to talk about the moon, not me. And I remember—I remember the moon last night is all."

Daddy rubbed a hand over his face. He looked older, tired.

"But I did good about the singing," I said. "I told him how you all thought it sounded so good but weird."

"But how did *you* feel?"

"I don't remember."

"It'll be a miracle if that article comes to anything. Poor Steve. He needs to break a big one. I thought of him right away. We went to school together, you know."

"I know," I said, even though I hadn't known.

But the article was gorgeous. Breathtaking, even. You've probably seen it, reprinted a thousand times. It won Steve awards and became an essay in his own book on the subject of UFOs. Even now I can't read it without sobbing—he made me into something ethereal and pure, swept up in a moon beam, singing my rapturous song.

I remember the article looking real strange sitting there among the livestock auction and Sheriff election news, but that's why it took hold.

The best part of the article, everyone said, was how Steve pointed out that there was a new moon that night—pitch dark, black.

———

This is the story of something winged and impossible.

William ducked close to the ground to see the tracks better in the early morning darkness. They were big, bigger than any man's he'd ever met and spaced far enough apart that William had to leap to get from one snowy imprint to another. He pulled his coat tight around him, breath fogging. He should have kept to the barn, he thought.

The goats had been agitated, pushing themselves against the bars of the pen, and William worried a coyote was hanging about. So, he'd picked up his lantern and gone out into the cold. That's when he saw the tracks—big bare feet stalking away from the forebay.

Now he was somewhere beyond the property, back into the pines. The prints weaved between the trees as if left by a drunk man —a big man, a colossus.

It was darker here in the forest, but looking up, William could still see a smattering of stars. He stared up at them, trying to orient himself in the dizzying dark. Recognizing the constellations was soothing, even if he didn't know their names.

A black circle, spinning in out of the north, eclipsed the stars, and William stumbled backward into the boughs of a tree. Snow fell onto his head, his shoulders, and he shook it away. He squinted up into the dark, at that vast shape blocking out the constellations and felt dread.

The dark mass continued on overhead, becoming obscured by the tops of the pines. William ran, determined to see the thing. He forgot about the prints and trampled them in his desperate pursuit.

Stopping, he came to a spot where the trees grew thin. He had a good view of the disc now and could see it descending, dipping into the dense forest beyond his vision.

He put his hands on his knees and took big, gulping breaths, thinking he definitely should have kept to the barn.

Then there came a great flapping of wings, as if a roost had been disturbed, and William straightened, once again looked to the sky. A man, eight feet tall and with the angular wings of a bat, flew over the treetops. With every beat of his wings, the man dipped and floundered as if the appendages were new to him, had just sprouted from his back. William shouted, but the man was far away now, slipping from view.

A cold, thicker than the winter cold — supernatural and strong - settled upon William when he realized the creature was flying back toward the barn.

He stood in the clearing for a long time, afraid to return to the goat pen and what he'd find there.

CHAPTER 3
MEN IN BLACK

THE PHONE KEPT RINGING. The only respite I got from its shrill call was when my mother slipped the handset off the hook. But Daddy always noticed the silence, always dropped the phone back on its cradle with an unceremonious plunk. He'd wait there a beat, maybe two, before the ringing started up again, and then he'd smile.

"You've really stirred something up," Daddy said, happier than I'd ever seen him. "You've woken up this town." I didn't know a town could sleep, but it made sense, I guess. If any town could sleep, it would be ours—all dusty and slow.

On our first outing after the article was published, Daddy coached me in the car. "Judging by the calls, I'd say there's a mighty lot of people who want to talk to you," he said with a wink. "If anyone wants a picture or an autograph, you just smile, and do as you're told."

"What's an autograph?" I asked.

"You don't have to smile," said my mother.

Daddy looked at her for a moment, it was a loathsome look, before turning back to me. "An autograph is just writing your name. You can do that, right? He tapped his breast pocket and said, "I have a pen right here. I'll give it to you when we get into the store."

I ducked between my parents and the grocery cart while we shopped, pretending to be interested in the same old cereal and junk food we always bought, careful not to acknowledge the sharp way my parents looked at one another, their terseness.

I held my mother's hand even though it hurt, her grip was so tight. She didn't like the way people stared, the way the bravest of them came over and asked me questions in front of the meat counter, blocking the aisle so a crowd started to form. Mom glowered over it all. I wasn't sure why she'd even come. To protect me, I hope, but more likely it was to prove something, to darken my daddy's day like a laden cloud.

My father, however, was oblivious to her. He loved the attention. He'd smile at the ravenous-eyed, offer up autographs to anyone who stopped to talk, all while my mother burned.

I was scared, though I tried not to show it. Up to this point, my world had been quite small—just my mom, Daddy, and me. And I was happy that way; I didn't know there could be anything more. So, the constant buzzing interaction dizzied me, tired me out. I clutched a pint of ice cream to my chest, hoping to feel its coolness all the way to my heart. It would be melted and lukewarm by the time we exited the store, a slurry of sticky candy pieces and milk.

It wouldn't have been so bad if the people who wanted to talk to me were kids, but they only stared at me; shy or disgusted I couldn't tell. It was mostly men and teenagers who pried their way into our triad, desperate to know just where I'd gone.

"What were the aliens like?" asked a girl with black lipstick not only on her lips, but teeth.

I opened my mouth to speak, but my daddy was already answering. He shoved a newspaper on top of my ice cream, fished a glittery pen out of his pocket and told me to sign. I wrote my name in big looping letters, enjoying the way the ink glided out. I underlined my name twice, just to use the pen a little more.

"She has no recollection of any beings on the ship," said Daddy.

"Maybe it was un-piloted. Just a scout. A drone ship."

"Maybe," my father said patiently.

The moisture from the ice cream made a blob on the picture of my face. The girl didn't seem to notice, didn't even look at the cryptic assemblage of characters I had scrawled on the page. Her eyes were only for my dad. "What do you think they did to her?"

"Sam," my mother said, a warning.

He held his hand up toward her, a previously fatal gesture in our household. But he had power now, so my mother just vibrated darkly beside me. "It's impossible to say for sure, but she wasn't injured when she came back to us, and in fact, has been showing improved cognitive and behavioral functions."

"Like, she's smarter now?"

"Calmer, too," my dad confirmed.

The girl looked at me for the first time, her grey eyes watery from stray mascara flakes. I tried my best to stand up straight under her scrutiny, but I had to twist away from the heat of my mother, from the weight of the girl's stare, and I knew I just looked bent and little.

"Huh," she said. "That's trippy. I wonder what they *did* to her. Like maybe a chip in the brain?" She talked like I wasn't there, like I couldn't be addressed directly.

Go away, I thought. *Go away.* I squinted my eyes and held my breath. A smothered squeal escaped my lips—an oddly melodic sound that made my mom jump.

She grabbed my elbow and pulled me toward a greeting card display, leaving my dad to preside over the black-lipped girl alone.

We pretended to read condolence cards until my father remembered us.

After that first trip out, I was sure the excitement would abate, but it only grew. Reports of lights in the sky, some from that very night, dominated the newspaper and soon everyone was convinced that not only had I been abducted, but there were witnesses to the ship, to the faint sound of my singing ringing through a distant wood, to livestock acting up, refusing to leave the shelter of lean-tos and sparse trees. Something, everyone agreed, had happened that night, and I was the key. Getting close to me was like getting close to an answer, even though I wasn't sure if I knew the question.

———

This is the story of the deaths of two men and a dog. This is the song of the slag.

Days before the Roswell crash broke the headlines in June 1947, there was the Maury Island Incident.

Harold Dahl, his son, dog, and two crewmen were sailing across Puget Sound. It had been an unremarkable trip but for the cresting of a slick black whale off their port bow. Harold thought the whales lucky—always bringing something with them, it seemed. Last time he saw one, he'd won three dollars at pinochle, all spent now. He sighed, turned his eyes to the horizon, and saw six donut-shaped UFOs streaking beneath the clouds.

His heart caught—a snag in the rigging. He raised a trembling finger and gasped out something incomprehensible, but the men understood and lifted their own eyes to the improbable stars racing above.

They were directly overhead when one exploded in a silent burst of light. Harold buried his head in the crook of his arm and cried out for his wife. His skin was burning, melting. Someone was screaming —an unholy sound that hurt worse than his skin. The scream slid into a breathless whine, and someone called out, "The dog is hit!"

Harold raised his head and took stock of the surrounding men, all singed and pale but still standing.

"The dog," said one of the crewmen.

Harold turned and saw his dog lying there on the deck panting, twitching. He knelt and laid a hand on its ribs. He felt the rise and fall of the dog's lungs, at first rough and ragged, fade into nothing at all.

He stared down into the wet, red pits pockmarking the dog's flesh, cauterized wounds ringed in burnt fur.

"What is this stuff?" asked a crewman.

Harold pried his gaze away from what was left of the dog. His son was toeing a metallic blob, gently prodding it with the tip of his boot.

"Don't touch it," Harold gasped. "Could still be hot."

There was slag everywhere, pooled all over the deck, cooling from a blinding red to a dull gray. Specks of it clung to his shirt where it had melted the fibers, enmeshed itself into the very fabric.

"Stuff's everywhere. Can't help but touch it," said the crewman. He held his arm away from his body at an awkward angle—he had been hit.

Harold said nothing when the man bent down, pried a piece of the stuff loose from the planking with his good arm.

Harold accepted the slag with trembling hands. He slipped it into his breast pocket, felt the warm stone heavy against his heart.

At home, he stared out the windows, eyes trained on the sky. He was afraid. He couldn't do it again—the burning, metallic rain, the smell of burnt flesh. Though his skin was healing, the slag had knocked something loose in him. He turned the piece of rock over in his hand and squeezed it tight.

He was still standing in the window when a black car rolled to a stop in front of his drive. Harold tucked the stone back in his pocket. It was then that Harold received the first known visit from a "Man in Black."

The Man was tall and thin. He didn't blink.

"What do you want?" asked Harold. He wasn't impressed by this man's dark suit, by his impeccable hair.

"What you saw," said the Man. "Out there on the water."

"You a reporter?" asked Harold. He had put in a few calls to the police. It wouldn't surprise him if he ended up in the blotter.

The Man's eyebrows raised. "Have you talked to the press, Mr. Dahl?"

"No," said Harold. "I have not."

"Good," said the Man. "What you saw out there, it's between you and me now. Tell anyone else, and you'll have major problems on your hands."

"Oh?" said Harold. He was so tired. He shut his eyes for a moment.

"Bad things will happen, Mr. Dahl. Do you understand that?"

"Sure," he said.

The Man in Black left, folded himself back up into his shiny car. Harold stood in the window even though his eyes kept drifting shut.

Harold only told a few people at first—the police, his wife, a neighbor who saw them burying the dog in the backyard. But the story tumbled out into the world, and he began to comment on it from time to time. When asked, he'd produce the slag from his pocket and tell those interested all about the exploding star. When nothing happened, when the promised problems didn't appear, he grew bolder, began speaking to the press. It seemed the Man in Black was bluffing—no one could keep him from singing the song of the slag.

J. Edgar Hoover, intrigued, sent two airmen. They arrived in a black car, just as the Man had, but these two were clumsy, sweating.

"Give us the slag," said one airman.

"Why? What slag?" said Harold, who kept the stuff in his pocket all the time now. He was reluctant to give it away, this thing that had scarred him and struck down his dog. Its familiar weight in his shirt was comforting.

"Don't you want to help your country, sir?"

"Well, I don't know."

"It could be Soviet. You know that, right? It could be Soviet, and we've got to get it tested." The airman dabbed at his brow with the cuff of his sleeve.

Harold hesitated, patted the lump at his breast. His exploding star story was one thing—it marked him as an outcast, sure. Maybe people hung back before approaching him, talked about him behind his back. But to deny the US government their right to investigate the Soviets? That would mark him as something else entirely. He fidgeted. "And if I do give it to you, can I have it back? After it's tested?"

The airmen looked at one another in silence.

"Sure," said one. "I don't see why not."

The other airman frowned.

Harold pulled the thing from his pocket and deposited it in the airman's outstretched hand. "Be careful with it," he said. "I want it back."

"Sure thing. It's got its very own flight to Dayton," smiled one of the men. "It can sit right up front."

Harold wept when he heard the news that the plane had caught fire, killing the airmen and sending the slag plummeting to Earth once more. It was lost among the wreckage.

Harold recanted his story; told the world he was a liar. He denied the slag ever existed. But, until his dying day, he stood in the window, waiting for black cars.

CHAPTER 4
RADIO FREQUENCIES

DESPITE ALL THE attention at the grocery store and the way the phone rang, things were mostly normal at home. I still played with my toys, still ate all the same things, still watched all the same shows, but there was a current in the air that shifted things ever so slightly— just enough so you could never forget that everything had changed. Sometimes it was carried by the new tempestuous way my mother looked at my father, or by the number of times someone knocked on the door, or just by the way my daddy looked—somehow younger now, invigorated. But I tried to ignore it. I hoped with enough neglect it would all go away, be buried in time.

Nevertheless, it grew.

My daddy arranged for me to talk to reporters in other towns. Towns so far away I hadn't even heard of them on the nightly news.

All of this I accepted with grim lassitude, but there was one event I looked forward to with true eagerness: going to the radio station.

I had always wondered what, exactly, a radio station looked like. I yearned to know what they did inside, what those buttery smooth voices sounded like in person and if they matched the faces of their speakers. So it was under this buoyant atmosphere that I agreed quite readily to go, delighting my surprised father, and disappointing my mother thoroughly.

We bounced along in the car, listening to the radio station we were soon to visit. It wasn't one we normally played, but Daddy and I decided it would be good to get to know it on our way in. It was mostly a talk station, though they did play a few country songs as we drove—Shania Twain and Tim McGraw. Between songs, the host, his sonorous voice guaranteeing the truth, talked about all kinds of things —how to repair your car, how to get stains out of your shirt, how the government was about to get us all killed; I can't say I understood it all, but I couldn't wait to find out what that voice looked like behind the microphone.

We lived outside of town where they grew corn and warehouses, but it wasn't too long of a drive—soon we were turning into a little lot where a small shack crouched beneath a towering antenna. "That's it?" I asked, expecting something a little more formal.

"I guess so," said Daddy. "I guess you don't need much room to broadcast." He seemed cheerful despite the general unimpressiveness of the place.

"I thought it'd be big."

Daddy unbuckled his seatbelt. "What you're doing is big, honey. It doesn't matter where you are. This will reach so many people, change so many lives. That's what's big."

I reluctantly slid out of the car after him. "Okay," I said.

"And remember," he said. "You were singing."

"All the way up," I said, wary.

The inside of the building was even more disappointing than the façade. The dark space inside had been divided up into four tiny soundproof cells—one in each corner of the room. Each door was lit with a glowing "ON AIR" sign.

At first, we were alone in the middle of all these rooms, not daring to speak, not trusting whatever soundproofing protected the sacred voices within, but soon a door opened and a tall man with big, coifed hair stepped out of a cell, the glowing light on the door now extinguished.

"Sam! Laura! I'm so glad you could make it. I hope you weren't waiting long?" He cleared the room in big easy strides and offered us his hand. His deep voice—familiar and yet so different in person—made me shiver. I let my daddy touch his hand first.

"Not at all!" said Daddy. "Just got here."

"Great, great! I'm Ray, Ray Trout. You're listening to Ray—Ray Trout in the Mornings," he said, voice booming in that little cavern. He laughed at either his own hilarity or my flinching and said, "C'mon, this way. We have five minutes until we go live."

We crowded into the closet he had just appeared from. It smelled like old coffee and aftershave. Close your eyes and try now to grasp it—the stale scent of morning breath, of someone's cluttered bathroom, the fetid mingle of cologne and toilet water. Can you smell it? I remember feeling sick, like I was breathing in the fumes of Ray Trout himself.

"Alright, go ahead and have seats there, right. How this is going to work is I'll introduce you, tell a little synopsis—that's, like, a story," he winked at me, "of your experience. Then, Laura, I'll ask you some questions. If you don't know or don't understand, the best thing to do is to just talk about anything else related to your story. The worst thing we can have is dead air. Do you know what dead air is?"

With the way the room was smelling, I thought I knew. But I shrugged just to be on the safe side.

"Dead air is when no one is talking. People get bored and turn the station, or think we've gone off air. What we wanna do is fill up the time with sound. Any sound. Do you understand, Laura?"

"Yes," I said.

"Excellent. If things get quiet, Sam, or it doesn't seem like she can handle this, I may pitch things over to you. Is that alright?"

"Absolutely. Despite the abduction—she was changed, you know —she still sometimes goes blank." He winked at Ray. "In fact, I've prepared a—"

"Laura, see those lights over there?" Ray Trout gestured to a row of dead bulbs atop a gray contraption. I nodded. "Those are the phone lines. What we really want, what we really, really want to see is one of those light up. That means we have a caller, and we can talk to them. That'll really help fill the time."

"Yes, sir," I said.

Ray Trout put big headphones on our heads. Mine kept slipping off, the band falling over my eyes. Ray didn't seem to notice or care that I clutched the headphones to my ears, so worried I'd miss my cue.

Suddenly it was happening—the headphones pouring sound into my head, corny spiraling intro music, Ray Trout's big thunderous voice, even louder in the headphones than in real life. "And this one's for you late night sky watchers, you paranormal investigators, you who ask, 'are we alone?' With me today I have Laura Statley, a little girl just about to turn eight years old, who was—I kid you not—abducted by extraterrestrials. Laura was attacked by an alien ship in her own backyard. Her poor parents watched helplessly as she was sucked into a real-life flying saucer. But, get this. Laura wasn't scared, oh no. Laura was *singing* as she was pulled from this earth. That's right—singing. Damn well too, I'm told. Her parents use the terms 'operatic' and 'rapturous' to describe what they witnessed. Laura, are you a big singer in the best of times?"

"Umm no, sir," I managed, but my mind was whirring: attacked? Ray Trout said I was attacked. Didn't attacks hurt? Weren't attacks scary? I had never heard that word used to describe The Incident before. It seemed every new person had a new way to describe what had happened to me—all revelatory, all possibly true.

Ray Trout was saying something for a second time. "What's that?"

I said, forcing my eyes to focus, pressing the headphones tighter against my ears.

"I was asking if you ever read or watch movies about aliens." Glancing over at the bulbs on the machine, I noticed they were still dead, dark in the room.

"I mostly only watch cartoons."

Ray chuckled. "There's always Marvin the Martian. Anyway, Laura, I'm told you can't remember anything from that night, is that true?"

I shrugged then realized no one but Ray Trout and my daddy could see it. Shrugging again, I said, "I guess not."

"So, all of that time is just gone?"

I thought of my Barbies doing splits on the dining room floor, pirouetting in the moonlight. "I guess I just remember something else. It's something else now." Still no lights, still no phone calls. I closed my eyes so tight little flashes erupted behind my eyelids like strobes on a dark night. I could make lights in my head, commune with lights in the sky, but nothing lit up in Ray Trout's cell.

"Fascinating," said Ray. "Implanted false memories, perhaps."

But they were there. I was there. The moon was there. I was making the dolls dance and then they were laying on the floor and I was being swept away. If only I could remember if the dolls were still there in the morning. Where were they? Where were they even now? Did my Barbies still exist, or had I imagined them?

"Honey," Ray, was saying. "What do you think?"

I thought they were there. I could feel the cool plastic in my hands, feel their tangled hair against my cheek. I thought that we were all there. But maybe I was wrong. Maybe I had been abducted. And people wanted to hear that story, not the one about my Barbies. I felt dizzy, lost.

"Mr. Statley, I can't imagine your fear, the helplessness you felt when you saw your daughter rising up into that thing. Do you mind describing a bit about the ship?"

Daddy was opening his mouth, puffing up his chest, but it was me that people wanted to hear from. Not Daddy.

So, I sang. It wasn't operatic, whatever that meant, and it wasn't anything special: just some song they teach you in Girl Scouts. But I drowned him out. I snuffed out the light in his eyes. I knew I'd have hell to pay for it later, but I sang loudly and kept him from telling MY story. Now the only lights shining, other than me, were the ones for the phone lines popping on in perfect order: one, two, three, four, five. I remember the satisfaction—the pride. If anything glowed, I wanted it to glow for me and me only.

———

This story is about greed. It's about the fallibility of "proof."

The Big Ear radio telescope in Delaware, Ohio was grinding away, picking up its usual static and nothingness as it searched for evidence of extraterrestrial life. It'd been scanning outer space since 1973, picking up only background noise.

In August of 1977, Jerry R. Ehman was looking over the print-outs of unremarkable 1s and 2s and sometimes 4s when he came across the following transmission: 6EQUJ5. It stood out like a sore thumb against the rows and rows of baseline nothingness. "Wow!" he scrawled in the margin in red pen.

It was a seventy-two second signal coming from the direction of Sagittarius, unlike anything ever detected before or since.

Some see this rarity as proof of extraterrestrial life and others see this lack of repeatability as failure. What, exactly, do we require as we search the skies for proof?

The Big Ear telescope was disassembled in 1998 to make way for a golf course.

CHAPTER 5
INTRUSION

I BEGAN to miss the way things were before my Incident. There had been slow summer mornings alone with my mother. She and I would stay home daydreaming, listening to the soft murmur of lovers on television, sharing the housework while Daddy went to the factory. I was still too young to understand what he did there, but he'd come home smelling raw like pennies and lightning. I didn't want to hug him until he showered all that stink off.

But after the radio show, Daddy started staying home all the time too. At first it was temporary—just a few days to help answer the phone and set more interviews, he said—and then it was permanent, his new role as my manager suddenly more lucrative than whatever foul smelling task he performed at the factory.

Our gentle morning world was shattered. All was movement.

The phone continued to ring, my daddy shouting into it. The TV stayed primed on the breaking news, which to this day makes me feel on edge, even when nothing particularly worrisome is happening in the world; it's the idea that it might, and that I'll have to witness it there in real time, no filter between us.

My daddy paced through the house, his steps loud and reverberating, while my mother was relegated to a little seat in the kitchen where she sat and smoked and chewed her lip in silence. My head took to rattling, something I had never noticed it do before.

People came, too. More interviewers and reporters, of course, but also photographers, agents, scientists, writers, curious neighbors hiding under the guise of delivering a stray piece of mail (couldn't they have just put it in the box?). Even a state representative paid us a call.

For this last visit my parents donned hideous matching pantsuits and stuffed me into a puffy dress better suited for Christmastime than a summer meeting. We stood in a row, all lined up along the driveway, waiting for this important person. Sweat pooled around my collar and bugs nipped at my ankles. We waited in silence. When he at last arrived, when he climbed out of the back of the car, he looked so small I almost laughed. His teeth were bright white, and it hurt to look at them directly, but he just kept smiling. He handed me a certificate for being abducted and shook my hand. I wanted to ask him if he had anything else for me, but he was very busy, and had to go. Even my mother behaved for that visit; she smiled and nodded and held Daddy's hand. I stared at the entwined knot of their fingers, somehow knowing it would be the last time I'd see their affection.

I missed my toys and my quiet. I missed my mother and how she used to be with her soap operas and quiet chores.

I realize now, my mother long gone, that I never truly got to know her—she was occulted by the bright star of my father long before I ever thought to think of her as a person, someone knowable.

———

Here's something more recent, one about missed opportunity and foresight.

The first interstellar object detected in our solar system was discovered in October 2017. By the time we noticed it, it was already hurtling away—too fast to catch up with and properly photograph. All we could study was its shadow, which revealed that it was either a weirdly shaped lump of rock (rather turd-like in nature) that defied the laws of gravity while tumbling past the sun, or a thin saucer possessing its own means of propulsion. Scientists much prefer the turd theory, just a weird rock, though it is just as unlikely as all the rest. Its name, 'Oumuamua, means "scout" in Hawaiian.

DADDY LUMPED people into two groups: True Believers and Not. There was no middle ground—no room for those who had yet to make up their mind or just didn't care. If you weren't wholly invested in my abduction to the point of near-worship or, at least, passing over a few dollars, you might as well have been the enemy.

I was eight when my first book came out. I write "my" like I had anything to do with it; in reality, someone had written a book and put my name on it. But it was a good book, or so I'm told; by that time, I'd missed so much school I could barely read, and I refuse to read my book now, in its entirety, for fear of finding my father in the pages.

After the book came out, I travelled around to different bookstores and alien conferences signing the title page with my pink sparkly pen. Sometimes I even read aloud a little, which was always hard because I was never quite sure what it was going to say. I stumbled over words, lost my spot. But people didn't seem to mind. They lined up all the same.

It was at one of these readings in a big bookstore that a Certified Enemy made himself known to us. I had just read part of my book that went on and on about how greatly expanded my views of the universe had become since my experience (not a total fib—I had seen corners of my limited world I had never known existed after The Incident) when my daddy asked the crowd if there were any questions. Hands went up. Most people were nice—their questions not even questions, just thinly veiled praise, and astonishment—but I knew this guy would be trouble by the way his hand shot up and stayed up even as the other people were called upon. There was an urgency to him that unsettled me.

His hair was dark and close-shaven, a pair of wire-rimmed glasses perched on his nose. He had the air of an old man, despite looking quite young—younger than my daddy. He held his arm up ramrod straight until, at last, my daddy gestured his way.

"Yes, I have a question," he said, his words fast and percussive. People around him winced at his voice. "How can you do this? Spread these lies? Involve that little girl?"

A gasp went up among the crowd.

"Now, now," said my daddy, who had probably rehearsed for a moment such as this. "Let him ask it."

The people in the audience fidgeted. I sat stock still, not even daring to breathe. The man stared straight into my eyes and made me burn.

"I know it's hard to believe, our story, and we never set out with any agenda to make you feel one way or the other. We are spreading awareness of an event that has implications beyond our little family," said Daddy. "Even refusing to believe is spreading awareness. It's a valid response."

Polite applause filled the room, which had relaxed under my daddy's confident tone. But the man wasn't pleased, he glowered and twitched. "I'm not so sure you've answered my question," his voice boomed out, snuffing the remnants of applause. "Why are you lying?"

I looked up at Daddy, standing beside me and my little table piled high with my book. He was a short man, but he felt so tall then, towering above the crowd, his back straight, his new clothes pressed flat and right. He looked godly, I realized. Like someone you'd see in church. We rarely went, but when we did, I savored the way everyone tried so hard, just in that one little room. I liked to wonder what they were like outside of church; if I would even recognize them at all. Daddy was that way all the time now. A man of God. All pressed clothes and slicked hair. I wondered what altar he knelt at, and if it was me or if it was the small flame of fame that had burst into our lives. I wondered if it mattered.

The crowd was a bubbling, boiling mass now, murmuring and writhing. The man who'd confronted my daddy stood in the midst of them. He shouted, finger aloft, pointed at me. I couldn't hear him over the clamor and Daddy stuttered and raised his hands. It was spiraling away from us, this moment. Daddy couldn't maintain control no matter how godlike he looked.

I grabbed the cuff of his sleeve, and he glanced down at me, face red, eyes wild. I had to do something to make it stop, to quiet all those voices. Pressure built up in my head, panicked and painful. I had to do something.

I sang softly at first, the first line of "When You Wish Upon a Star" nothing more than a whisper. Only my daddy could hear. He frowned, a look of sad incredulity. I inhaled and my voice grew louder, purer. The people in the front row turned away from the yelling man, settled in their seats.

Calm rippled across the audience, a tiny wave turning them about, silencing them. Even the shouting man lowered his finger, quieted his voice.

He looked about him, at my worshipers, mute mouth opening and closing. No one paid attention to him now, and no one paid attention to my daddy.

"You can stop it now," Daddy whispered, pulling his sleeve from my hand. "You can cut it out."

But I had to see the song through to the end. I had to see what else I could do.

So, I stared into the man's eyes, partially hidden behind the glint of his glasses, and jutted out my chin. I sang just for him. I wanted him to go away. I willed him to blink out, to disappear.

And with my song, he drew his arms to his chest, folded in on himself. He seemed smaller now. Pushing through the crowd, he stumbled toward the aisleway. The people drew away from him, pulled up their knees.

I only stopped singing when the doors swung shut behind him. He'd been expelled by my voice. It felt good to have banished him, to have done it all with this strange new power. People were listening, listening to only me. I wondered where this talent had come from— within or above? In either case, I had made something shift, and it thrilled me.

The room was silent for a beat or two, then the people stood and came toward me. They formed clumsy lines, wanting more from me, my book clutched to their chests like shields.

———

One of the earliest and best-known abduction stories is that of Barney and Betty Hill.

Barney and Betty were driving home through rural New Hampshire in 1961 when they witnessed a bright sphere moving erratically in the night sky.

They left the car at a picnic stop and peered at the strange star through binoculars, wondering just what it could be. Both agreed it was no normal aircraft. It descended toward them, forcing them to run back to their vehicle.

They continued their drive, all the while keeping their eyes on the peculiar light that seemed to dance and stalk alongside them. When it swooped again, Barney stopped the car for a second time.

Barney exited the vehicle with his pistol and approached what he could now discern to be a saucer. Inside, through a giant window, the silhouettes of beings beckoned. "Just keep looking," they said inside his mind.

He was shaken from his trance when part of the craft began to open, and he ran back to Betty and the car, screaming that they were going to be captured and taken. But the craft was now above their vehicle. *How?* His heart was exploding in his chest.

He dove into the car, and they sped away. Betty rolled down the window and peered upward—the craft was still there. And then the world was buzzing and burning and beeping and their flesh tingled, and they found themselves thirty-five miles away.

They wondered if it happened. They wondered if they'd simply drifted off together, gotten lost. But Barney's watch was stuck, the hands wouldn't budge even when wound, and Betty's nightmares took on a sharp new realness that stayed with her long after she'd woken up. They went to hypnotherapists, to doctors, to the press. They wanted someone to grab them by the shoulders and tell them they weren't coming apart at the seams. Like so many abductees, they wanted someone to say, "me too."

Modern interpretations of this event remind us that Betty and Barney were an interracial couple at a time when such a thing was considered immoral. Therapists claim all of Betty and Barney's experience—the dreams, lost time, words spoken under hypnosis, broken watches—all of this was some kind of stress response generated by living through all that hate. But then so is the perfect star map of Zeta Reticuli, Betty, a housewife with no knowledge of the stars, drew from memory. Another woman, an elementary school teacher named Marjorie Fish, would be the one to recognize the map for what it was.

SOME OF THE better events we did over the years were the conventions. There are conventions for anything you can think of: cat groomers, baseball card collectors, and yes, alien enthusiasts. At first, we only went to events I was scheduled to speak at, but I developed a fondness for the strange, wide-eyed people who frequented them, and we started attending as spectators, too.

There was a warmth at the conventions—the excitement of finally not having to explain yourself when initiating conversation, the thrill of common language. I enjoyed watching it blossom up between people who looked like they got no other outside interaction —it was a pure, good feeling.

The truth was I was becoming more unusual every day. I was the type of person you'd smile at sadly because you knew this convention was their one and only reason for being—their annual foray into the world.

I couldn't remember the last time I had played with another kid my age. I was either too busy or too weird—the other kids loved to stare but wouldn't dare to get close enough to play. Sometimes I'd see their screwed-up faces at the grocery store—they knew all about me, but I could only just barely remember them. Daddy had me start going to school on the computer, which was great for traveling but I never met anyone after that.

I spent most of my time out-of-school playing alone, researching UFOs, or joining Daddy at conventions, interviews, and book signings. Soon, I would start staring up at the sky, desperate for a beacon, a sign, some sort of answer.

By the time I turned ten, the abduction consumed me. I was no different from the others who had read my book or listened to my interview. The rush of their excitement was my own, and I didn't need my father anymore when people came up to me, desperate for information; I had my own theories, my own emotions to push forth into the world. Perhaps by taking a more active role in my story, I could grasp the threads of it more tightly, yank myself back to the source. I just had to know: did it happen? Had I truly been abducted?

As my obsession grew, my doubts intensified. I spent countless nights in bed staring at the ceiling, begging myself to remember The Incident. Every time I tried to imagine myself suspended, singing, transported away, I felt nothing. There was no fear, no euphoria, no weightless memory. Just chasmic nothingness. But isn't then my inability to imagine the scenario also proof that something may have happened? It's like part of me was wiped away, somehow. And I can't get close to the part that's gone.

That's why I loved the conventions so much. They were full of abductees who spoke about their experiences with such conviction that it made me ache. They knew what it meant when I said I didn't remember, why I hurt when everyone around me remembered and retold what should've been my experience. I hung onto every word of probings, strange languages, flashing lights, looking for a part of myself there. It was the closest to the truth I could get, even if it wasn't my truth.

And then I met Sylvia.

Even back when I was twelve, she was a grandmotherly woman—all warm smiles and white, properly set hair. I thought she looked out of place at the convention, thought maybe she was there to support her grandson or had wandered down to the hotel conference room by chance. But when I saw her seated at one of the panels, pink reading glasses on and notebook in hand, I knew she was someone special.

I followed her out of the talk about lucid dreaming and establishing contact and into the next event she chose, determined to sit beside her. I lost my dad in the rush between rooms and would be scolded for it later, but for now the only thing that mattered was figuring out this woman.

To begin with, there weren't all that many women at the conferences. And the ones that did come usually came with their husbands or sons or had wild, knotty hair and basement smells. But she was so kempt, so poised. Maybe she was a reporter or a writer, I thought—that would explain the notebook. Well, if that was the case Daddy would forgive me for running off after her. He was always looking for new people to write about my story.

At the next panel, I closed in behind her, and we sat down in unison. I must have startled her because she jolted a bit, a ripple across her serene exterior. "Oh, hello," she said. Her voice was just as honey sweet as I wanted it to be. "I didn't see you. I almost sat on you!" she laughed.

"No way," I said, beaming. "Not at all. I'm Laura."

She grasped my hand in hers—warm and soft. "Well hello, Laura. I'm Sylvia."

"Are you really here for the abductee convention? Are you an abductee?" I couldn't help myself. The words came spilling out, all clumsy and fast.

Sylvia smiled, her teeth perfect and shining. "Of course I am. I come every year—wouldn't miss it. And what about you? Are you here with your parents?"

I paused. She didn't know me. Didn't know my story. This was rare in this circle, so information-deprived and eager to paw at and pass around every new encounter. "You haven't heard my story yet?" I asked.

"You haven't heard mine?" she said. "This is a lucky meeting."

A man with his hair pulled back in a ponytail stooped down between us and I recoiled. "You're Laura?" he asked.

"Erm, yes," I said, trying to see around his head. I didn't want to lose Sylvia, to let her out of my sight. I caught a glance of her, all smiles and winks.

"Wow," said the man. His breath stank. "Can I get your autograph?"

I was barely listening, my mind on what Sylvia had said about having a story, about luck. I accepted the pen into my hand without looking down, scrawled my name across the page.

"Wow, man, thanks," he said, straightening himself. "I wish I had my tape recorder with me. If I could just get a tape of you singing, that would be something else. I heard you sang at a reading a few years ago? And you caused a whole crowd to go catatonic? Man, I'm sorry I missed that."

Catatonic—I didn't know what that word meant, but it sounded good. It sounded powerful. I nodded. "I remember."

"Do you think you could, like, make my brain stop buzzing all the time?" His voice was quieter now, a trace of embarrassment there.

"Maybe?" I said. I wasn't sure what I could do, or why I could do it, but it seemed, in that moment, sitting next to the bemused lady in pink, like I could do anything.

"How much?" asked the man. He pulled out his wallet.

"Well, I mean, maybe I could but I'm not going to do it. Not right now," I said, frowning. This conversation had already dragged on for too long. I wanted to get back to Sylvia.

His face fell. "Oh," he said. "Okay. Maybe next time?"

"Maybe."

He took a nodding bow. "Uh, thanks for the autograph. I mean it. I'll look for you next time?"

I chewed my lip, waiting for him to leave.

"Oh my," said Sylvia when the man had gone away all reluctant and slow. "Does that happen to you often?"

"Sometimes," I said. People were always asking for autographs, begging me to sing, but it never felt right. It never felt organic. No matter how hard they pleaded, I wouldn't do it. But this catatonic thing was new. So was the buzzing head. I didn't know what either signified, but something exciting was beginning to coalesce in my mind. I shook out my hair. "So, you're really an abductee?"

"Sure am," she smiled. "Have my own book to prove it." She made a vague gesture in the direction of a merch booth, and I resisted the urge to jump up and go check.

She pulled two wrapped candies from her little white purse and handed me one. "Let's be friends."

I popped the strawberry candy into my mouth and swirled it around with my tongue. I couldn't believe such a nice woman had a *story*, a complicated, messy, unbelievable story. A tear-yourself-apart, doubt everything you've ever learned, lose everything you ever had, story. I felt cleaner, more good for sitting there beside her. She was so put together.

As the sugary sweet melted on my tongue, I vowed to someday wear my hair white and curled in the front. If you saw her, if you could wear my odd and lonely eyes, you'd understand.

———

Here's the story of a lie, albeit a beautiful one.

George Adamski, grandfather of ufology, is best known for his most likely faked, but dramatically beautiful photos of UFOs. He claims to have seen hundreds of UFOs, sometimes all at once, passing in front of the moon like a fleet of clouds. He lectured and wrote about his experiences, establishing a name for himself in the field.

In 1952, well into his obsession and study of the crafts, he went into the desert with some friends, as one does. Sure enough, like fate, a large object hovered above them, beckoning George on. Of course, it was there for him, chosen one that he was, so he left his friends behind on the road and strode into the high desert to meet the thing.

A scout ship carried down a young man, lithe and blond. This is one of the first accounts of the Nordic breed of aliens we see so often in encounter tales—they're elven and pale, so purely white. Other than his pale skin, eyes and hair, George says the only thing that marked this being as an "other" were his strange clothes.

The alien, Orthon the Venusian, communicated via telepathy to let George know that nuclear war was not so great. When Orthon left, he trailed further messages in the dusty prints of his boots, which were spangled with symbols and untold meaning.

George did manage to get a photograph of Orthon's ship, but it would later be debunked as either being a lamp used to warm chickens or a surgical light.

His friends claim that, through the waving mirage of heat, they saw two people standing in the desert.

George says he went on to have a great friendship with Orthon's race, even getting to take a joyride in their ship to the moon.

It was so nice to be chosen.

THE MOMENT I got home from the conference, I typed Sylvia's name into *Ask Jeeves* and began reading. Her book came up right away; the cover was white with raised gold lettering—the kind of thing you'd see on pulp romance novels. The color choice looked holy—pure. I wanted to read it so badly but was scared to ask my parents to buy it for fear of exposing our friendship and getting it taken away.

After I'd read and reread every word on her website, even the boring copyright stuff at the bottom, I opened my email and started typing. I told her everything: the story of The Incident, the doubt, my father's weird pride in the whole thing, my mother's reticence. I told her that I wasn't sure if my experience had even happened. It was the most I had ever told any one person, and I knew my parents would kill me if they found out; I was supposed to be always professional regarding my story at all times. To express any shortcomings was to shatter the illusions put forward in my book, in the television programs I'd been on and the hundreds of interviews in magazines, radio shows, and in newspapers. It was almost like I had to be inhuman myself—a super-evolved creature who never stumbles. The Incident had remade me, after all.

After I pressed "Send" I was sick. I had never opened myself up like this before—it wasn't like I had any friends—and I immediately regretted it. What would bright, bubbling Sylvia think of fault-ridden, crumbling me? I searched online to see if there was a way to unsend a message—there wasn't. I quickly typed up another email explaining away my first, but deleted it. Perhaps it was better to say less in cases like these.

That night, I lay in bed, hot and sweaty, waiting for Sylvia's reply. I imagined I could feel her reading it—a hot flush creeping up my neck, fizzling into my boiling, pounding head. What if I ran into her at another conference? I could never go back—she'd know me for the fraud I was. And what if she told other people? Well, it'd all come tumbling down, and we'd lose everything. Daddy would have to go back to work. I'd have to go back to that school, with the stares and low whispers and "take me to your leader" boys.

I had ruined it all.

Yet there was another feeling too. To destroy it all was a massive relief. There was a promise of normalcy there, despite the damage already done to my reputation. Could it get any worse? I wasn't sure it could.

When I was positive my parents were asleep, I crept from bed, careful to avoid the floorboards that moaned when trampled. I tiptoed through the house to the computer desk in the living room and winced at the roar of the machine as it fired on. I had to check. I couldn't wait.

Junk mail. School stuff. And there it was—a reply from Sylvia shining bright among the ads and trash. And then I was inhaling it. I read it two, three times before realizing she wasn't disgusted. She wasn't appalled. She was that same kind lady I had sat next to at the conference, but now she too was cracked open, laying out before me her abduction story.

The parallels between our stories made me gasp. I knew she had been abducted, but as a little girl? Sylvia had been playing near the woods with her friends when a large cigar-shaped object came to rest above the tree line. The other children, knees quivering, begged to go back, but Sylvia was entranced: she refused to return home just yet. She wanted to explore the thing.

Her friends screamed as she walked toward the dark green maw of the forest directly beneath the object. She crossed the boundary between field and forest, expecting to feel the cool dampness of the woods, but instead was engulfed in a hot, white light. Her head steamed and whistled like a teapot coming to boil, and she couldn't get enough breath to scream.

And then it was over. It was night. The roaring in her brain was replaced with the hum of crickets. She stumbled out of the woods to find her friends long gone. She walked home alone, dazed and tired.

When she got to her house, her parents were all in a tizzy. And there it was: the familiar gathering up in arms, the tears, the smell of ozone.

She couldn't remember what happened to her in the ship, or even if she'd been taken at all. But something had to have happened to have whittled away all that daylight. Sylvia had tried regression therapy, hypnosis, dream journaling, all which she called "hocus pocus," to no effect. It was just white, hot terror. Too hot to touch.

Therapy, hypnosis, dreams—I wrote these things down. They hadn't worked for Sylvia but maybe they could for me. I was willing to try anything, even hocus pocus.

I pressed "reply."

———

There's a lot of misdirection in ufology—so many ways to be lead astray. Here's the story of someone who dove in and never resurfaced.

Paul Bennewitz began seeing strange lights in the sky in 1979. He could sit on his porch and watch them zip and dive and blink. It alarmed him that all of this was happening right under the Air Force's nose; he lived across the way from Kirtland Air Force Base, after all.

When he started picking up strange transmissions on his amateur equipment, he'd had enough. He contacted the Air Force and was promptly visited by some military men who took much interest in his telescopes and electronics.

"We think you're really on to something here," they said. They told him to keep an eye out—they could really use his proud American expertise.

They gave Paul special software he could use to decode alien transmissions and soon he was learning about downed craft and upcoming invasions. Paul dedicated himself to this task, and the government kept rewarding him with longer and longer glimpses behind the curtain, even once guiding him to the site of a secret base. It was addictive, it was rapturous. It was all Paul wanted to do. He lost himself to the work, which was, in truth, all a misinformation campaign perpetuated by the Air Force to hide their next-gen technologies and to make fools of the ufologists on their tails. They had even created props for Paul to stumble upon, to write about, to lecture on. It was a cruel joke.

Paul ended his UFO mission not in the lairs of some secret base, but in the psychiatric hospital. Sometimes it hurts to be chosen.

CHAPTER 9
ENCOUNTERS

I WAS BRAVER NOW with Sylvia on my side. It was easier to withstand the lonely days spent pecking my schoolwork into my computer, the overbearance of my father, the moodiness of my mother. I even considered the idea of living with my doubt like a bedfellow—letting it curl and settle around me, carrying it wrapped around me like a sad, bedraggled boa. None of it mattered much in those days. If Sylvia could harness all that unknowable miasma, so could I; I would have to if I wanted to be anything like her.

We exchanged emails every day, sometimes multiple times a day. At times, the emails were ebullient and light—about her pets, her son, my favorite songs, little inconsequential things—and at others, sometimes in the same message, we grappled with the meaning of life, the taunting push and pull of the universe.

"I've never met anyone like you," she wrote, and I felt proud. The truth was, I had never met anyone like her either. I had never had anyone talk to me like she had.

We made plans to meet up at the next conference, to attend all the same panels and talks. I couldn't wait to be close to her.

We struck out a deal to exchange books; I'd finally get to read her work, and it wouldn't cost my parents a thing—just a dusty copy of my own book that got lugged around with fifty others in a dented cardboard box. They wouldn't even notice. I was embarrassed to show her mine—it wasn't me, after all—but it would be worth it to get to read her words, absorb more of her than I already was. It was the first time since The Incident I could say I truly felt optimistic.

I began to love Sylvia, but dared not tell my parents—I was so afraid they'd take her away from me. The age difference alone would upset them. If they were to find out I was sharing my innermost thoughts—my complaints, my doubts—with this stranger, it would all be over.

So, it was really very awkward when they arranged a "play-date" with another girl my age—I didn't have the heart to tell them we were too old for playing, and that I already had a friend. There was no need for the bossy church girl they locked me in my bedroom with one Saturday evening.

"So, you go to Living Word?" the girl asked, her voice snide and prying.

"Sometimes," I replied, aware of the scrutiny I was under.

"Why haven't I seen you there?" She picked at the scabs on her knees, flakes falling to my rug.

I winced. "Well, we're always on the road," I said. She raised an eyebrow. "But we usually sit in the back."

She didn't seem impressed. Her name was Bethany, and she was the kind of person you knew of, but didn't directly know until all of a sudden, you're forced together in your dingy little bedroom by parents who worried about your socialization skills.

"How old are you." Every question she spoke was an accusation.

"I'm twelve. How old are you?"

"You don't look twelve. You look littler. I'd say you were nine or ten. I'm thirteen, of course."

"Sure," I said.

"When I turn fifteen, I'm allowed to get highlights in my hair."

I ran a hand through my own mousy brown hair, dim and tangled. I didn't see why Bethany would need highlights—her hair was already shining gold and curled in perfect spirals. "That'll be really nice," I said, trying.

"I got my ears pierced for my thirteenth birthday. Look." She pushed back some glossy hair to reveal perfect little purple rhinestones in the middle of her slightly reddened earlobes. They looked sore.

"Wow that's cute," I said.

"Do you have your ears pierced?" she asked.

"No."

"Why not? Don't you want them done? It doesn't hurt. Not really."

"I guess I've never thought about it," I said, and it was true. It had never really occurred to me to alter my appearance or try to look any certain way. My parents took care of all that. They dressed me for events and photographs and the rest of the time I was alone with no one to see me. I didn't really think of my body as something I owned —something I got to customize and beautify; it was more of something that things happened to, violently and at random.

"I can give you a makeover. I brought my stuff!"

Before I could answer, Bethany was unzipping a small tote and pulling tubes and glittering palettes of eyeshadow and brushes from its depths. "I think we should go with a fall-toned look," she said. "To bring some warmth to your complexion."

I nodded, dumb.

Bethany was strangely gentle as she padded and swiped at my skin with her powders and tints, yet I couldn't get the image of her prying the scabs off her knees out of my mind. She was using those fingers to pat color on my cheeks, my eyes. She cooed and mumbled quietly to herself as she worked.

At last, Bethany held a miniature mirror in front of me—so small that I could only view a few inches of my face at a time. She hadn't done a particularly good job; the eyeshadow was lopsided, the mascara had somehow ended up on the bridge of my nose, the lipstick was way too dark. I looked gaunt and sickly, but that wasn't her fault.

This is not one of those moments when the teen girl realizes she's got potential and can have it all: boys, friends, the spot on the cheerleading team if only she took off her glasses, shook out her hair, and used a little rouge. No. There was no revelation here. I was still me, bubbling up, spilling over, occluding any makeup I wore. I just smiled weakly and thanked her for her work.

When she left, I didn't bother washing it off. I fell asleep with it on, and it melted down my face, making me look old and tired. I liked it better this way, drooping and lived in. It looked like I had done more than plodded around the house in my pajamas and read my schoolbooks—I had been somewhere, done something. There was a dark imprint of my eye on my pillowcase to show for my existence.

———

Here's a story that sparked a thousand others.

It was a late summer night. Dog days, they call them in that desolate part of Kentucky. Hot, stagnant days when you don't let children swim in still ponds for fear of catching something, despite the cool it brings. The Sutton family was gathered inside their three-room home, not watching television, not listening to the radio, not doing anything of the sort because they didn't have any of those luxuries in this corner of Kelly—not in 1955. Instead, they were listening to the dog bark—frantic, staccato bursts.

"He sees something out theers," they said. And the eleven of them piled against one another to squint through the rare windows and see what they could see.

"Billy Ray did say he saw something fall, Ma. He did say—"

"Stop it."

There would be no talk of what Billy Ray saw, bright and silver, tumbling from the sky earlier that evening. They had laughed at him then. They would laugh at him now; they must laugh at him now.

But there—you could just make it out, a glow up on the rise, right where Billy Ray said the thing had fallen. The dog snarled at the light. Ma rubbed at her arms, urging the hair to lay flat.

And then they were coming—small greenish men, coming down the hill right into the dark of the holler where the house sat nestled and vulnerable. Ma was screaming then. The babies were screaming too. And someone grabbed their gun and fired, fired, fired. But the little men just flipped backward, landed on their feet, and shifted back into the darkness.

They kept coming back, hour after hour.

The little men dangled their tiny, hooked hands down from the porch roof and stroked the family's hair, got shot at and floated like leaves to the ground.

The little men leered through the windows, they lingered on the doorstep. Thank God for the .22.

The Suttons shot holes through the walls and listened to scratching on the roof until they burst from the house and ran to their cars and drove like hell to the nearest police station. They were told they probably encountered great horned owls.

This, in 1955 Kentucky, is one of the earliest references to little green men.

CHAPTER 10
PARALYZED

I HAD to phrase it just right, at the perfect time, or I would be yelled at, berated. So, I waited until Daddy was bright with laughter. A new edition of my book was coming out with an updated cover and glossy pictures wedged in the middle. Mom flipped through the advance copy, declared it "very nice," and never picked it up again. But it was all Daddy talked about.

"Waldenbooks has already promised us our own display. Cardboard cutouts, bookmarks, all of it. We'll do a tour of some of their stores, but it should fit in our schedule. Honestly, we have them by the balls. We can do it whenever." He was talking fast, moving his hands in time with his voice.

"I was wondering," I began, "I mean, maybe it would be alright if—"

"What?" he said. "Spit it out."

I blinked. This already wasn't going well. "Well, I was wondering if I could get hypnotized." The words came out in a breathless shout—a jumble of syllables rammed together.

"What?" he said, eyebrows bunched. "Hypnotized?"

"Yeah. I was just thinking I could get hypnotized and see if I remember anything. From The Incident, I mean." My face felt hot, red.

"Why would you want to do that?" asked Daddy.

I winced, ashamed of his incredulity. "To know the truth," I explained. "I want to know the truth."

"You do know the truth," he said, turning from me. "I told you what happened and there's nothing else to know."

He was walking away, ending the conversation before it had even started.

"Wait!" I cried. "Please!"

He whipped around, so fast, such a violent motion that it caused me to draw back, put my arms out in defense. "You do not talk back to me."

"I—I wasn't talking back, I was just—"

"You think I'm going to waste money on some shrink to put you to sleep? I can put you to sleep." His voice was a snapping bark.

Tears rolled down my cheeks as he looked me up and down in disgust.

"Don't ask me for anything like that again," he snarled before stalking out of the room.

I stood there, crying softly, unsure of what to do next. I wanted to know what happened. I wanted this to work. I wanted to at least try. Hypnotism, while it didn't work for Sylvia, seemed like my best bet at remembering. I had encountered it in many of the cases I researched and there didn't seem to be harm in trying.

"He just doesn't want you to be disappointed, honey." My mom was suddenly there before me, brushing the hair out from my eyes. "Stuff like that—it never works."

"Sometimes it does," I said. "Sometimes people see things, remember things. I don't know why I can't try."

She sighed, put her hands on my shoulders. "I don't even know if there are still people out there who do that. I mean, how do you find a hypnotist?"

"I'll figure it out," I said, knowing Sylvia could lead me in the right direction. "All you and Dad would have to do is drive me there. I'll do the rest. Please?"

"I don't know." Her face was contorted with emotion—confusion, worry.

"I just want to remember."

"Maybe some things are better off forgotten," she said.

I frowned. "What do you mean?" I couldn't imagine any scenario worse than the yawning dark of not knowing.

She shook her head, flustered. "I'm just saying that things are fine the way they are. You've got your new book to worry about. Let's not take that for granted."

I opened my mouth to protest, but she was drifting away, back to wherever she had perched, listening.

I wiped the last tears from my eyes and retreated to my room. I should have known better. I should have worded it differently. I should have lied. There was nothing I gained—absolutely nothing—by being vulnerable, being honest.

Next time I wanted something, I wouldn't ask.

———

There are different breeds—some are strange, some are reflections of humanity seen through a warped mirror. Here's a story about standing helpless before terrifying features.

Some people put sachets of lavender beneath their pillow to help them sleep, but never consider there are beautiful, vast fields of the stuff growing somewhere. They're gorgeous—rows and rows of hypnotic purple-like amethyst peaks.

Maurice Masse owned one such field in the south of France and was tending it one day when he noticed a pilot had landed in the midst of it, crushing multiple rows of plants. He wasn't pleased. He understood that sometimes planes needed to land on short notice, but here? In the middle of his crop? He pulled his pants up higher and went to have a word with the folks.

As he approached, he realized this was no ordinary plane. Instead, it was ovular and stood on small tripod-like legs. Perhaps it was some sort of prototype? Two pilots crouched on the ground nearby and examined a sprig of lavender, holding it up to the light of the sun, rotating it in their thin fingers. They didn't seem distressed.

Then, they turned, and Masse was faced with the horror of their countenances: human eyes set in large, bulbous heads; clean slits for mouths. Masse opened his own gaping, fleshy mouth to scream, but one of them had pointed some sort of tube at him and no sound came. In fact, Masse could not move at all.

The creatures gargled and growled at one another as they stared at Masse, their eyes full of familiar human curiosity. This reassured the farmer, though paralyzed, and he could not access his fear as they studied him.

The two "men" climbed back aboard their ship, which hovered above the ground for a moment before flashing away, too fast to see.

Then Masse knew true horror: he remained stranded in his field, incapable of movement. He could breathe, he could see, and he felt his heart beating violently in his chest. But he could not move. He willed his fingers to bend, and they would not. The lavender swayed around him, taunting him with the ease at which they bounced in the breeze.

At last, like a lopsided house of cards, he fell to the ground, inhaled the rich scent of dirt and plants and something new, something metallic and bright. He pushed himself upward. He was free.

Or, at least he was free in movement. A drowsy tiredness stayed with him for weeks and he slept, and slept, and slept, and dreamed of clean slit mouths, and human eyes in giant heads.

CHAPTER 11
RESEARCH

BECAUSE I COULDN'T UNLOCK the answers I needed from my own mind, I turned to the minds of others. I accumulated a small library on alien encounters, stuff like Jacques Vallée and Whitley Strieber, books you could find with corners all bent up at used bookstores and convention booths. My parents, usually unwilling to buy me the slightest thing, happily purchased these types of books.

"It's nice you're showing an interest in your work," said Daddy as he pulled crinkly bills out of his pocket and carefully counted them out on bookstore counters.

"I'm glad you like reading," said my mother as she eyed my purchases. "I used to love reading when I was your age." She had a wistful look in her eyes, and I wondered why she had let the habit lapse.

I sat on my bed with the books at one hand and a dictionary at the other. They were enormous books, complicated. I often needed help to decipher the pages. Sometimes I flipped through, looking for the dark blot of a picture. I liked the pictures the most—lights seen through blurry lenses, drawings of UFOs. I would study them for hours.

Someone had given me a second-hand folder—a rainbow mess of unicorns and kittens—in which I stored the most important alien accounts. Sometimes they were things copied verbatim from books, TV shows, and convention speakers, but often I retold the stories, took them and smooshed them between my hands, made them my own. Rewriting the stories in this way probably wasn't the best method of conducting research, but it made me feel powerful. I couldn't change my own circumstances, but I could reshape someone else's.

Sometimes I got so absorbed in this task that the world melted away, seeming as distant as a star. I was in one such trance, pencil poised above the wide-ruled paper, when something struck my head, sending my whole body sideways.

I cried out in pain and lifted a hand to my ear.

Daddy stood at the side of my bed, a red, angry look on his face. "I said, go pick up your shit in the living room."

"What?" I asked, voice cracking. I hadn't heard him come through my closed door.

"Are you deaf?" he roared.

I stared up at him, confused. "I didn't hear you. I've been writing."

Daddy snatched at the pages before me. He grabbed them from their middles, crinkling them irreparably.

"Don't!" I cried.

He stared down at the pages in disgust. "What is this?"

"It's my UFO stuff," I pleaded. "My notes. It's important." I thought that if I could make him see that I was studying, working on something related to my role, he would ease away, but he just sneered.

"Nothing is more important than listening to me." His voice was thunder—a growling rumble. "Nothing is more important than doing what I say. And if this research means your ears are broken—" He ripped the pages in half and then half again, sending slivers of paper floating to the ground. I stumbled off the bed and collected the pieces, plucking some from beneath Daddy's foot, crawling beneath him. I was suppressing a cry—a wail. Days worth of transcription lay sprinkled around my floor.

"Clean this shit up," said Daddy, kicking at a particularly crumpled piece.

"I am," I whispered, clutching papers to my chest.

I could feel his anger on my skin, scalding and scarlet. "You're so lazy," he spat. "You're so—"

I sang. Catatonic—a state my followers said I could engender. If I could lull my daddy into some sort of stupor, fix his raging heart, maybe he would just let me be myself.

"What the hell are you doing that for?" Daddy looked redder than ever.

I squeaked the first two lines of "When you Wish Upon a Star," my voice wavering.

"This again? What is wrong with you? Stop it." He stepped on my foot.

"Ow!" I cried, pulling my foot from beneath his heel.

"Pick up the mess," he said.

"Okay! I said I would."

He shook his head, repulsed. "I don't want to hear you for the rest of the day."

"Okay."

He left and slammed my door shut behind him.

Had it worked? Had I done anything at all? I had been scared, unable to sing with any conviction, unable to concentrate. But he had left. He had gone. Next time I would harden my wish, make it something undeniably clear.

I laid the papers on my bed. I would rewrite them later, after I'd seen whatever mess was waiting for me in the living room, and I'd rewrite them again after that, washing the anger from the first draft.

Though I've now graduated to an intricately nested series of folders on my computer, I still keep these stories. I still rewrite them. These are the interesting ones I've included between the pages of this story—the story of my undoing.

I often wonder what my Daddy would say about these retellings, about putting them in this book. Sometimes I think he'd shake his head, tell me I'm wasting my time. But, then again, I can hear him laughing, head thrown back, teeth sharp and white—he'd be proud of me, profiting on someone else's nightmare, slipping my way between their stories like some infernal snake.

———

This one's about culpability.

Many have weighed in on UFO's significance to the human psyche, but none greater than Carl Jung and Jacques Vallée.

Jung, the famous Swiss psychoanalyst, was keenly interested in the phenomenon and proposed that everything about the UFO, from abduction experiences to the vessel's shape, were archetypes embedded in the collective human unconscious. He proposed their typical round shapes are emblematic of man's hopes and fears. Drawing comparisons between the mandala, an ancient symbol of the universal, and the disc-like UFOS, he suggested UFOs are not a physical phenomenon, but rather an omnipresent psychic one, thus explaining away the uncanny coincidences between various encounters and abductions.

Jacques Vallée, on the other hand, believes UFOs are physical, but are also elements of the many myths and legends humans have shared throughout the ages. From faeries to Bigfoot, Vallée believes aliens are responsible for our most fantastic tales. Vallée also asserts that myths allow humanity to understand herself.

UFOs, by this view, are symptoms of societal stress. In ancient periods of strife humans saw winged angels, had their children stolen by faeries; today we have big-eyed aliens, silver UFOs. We process and shape ourselves through these symbols as they become part of our art, our TV shows, our books, our discourse.

I'm partial to Jacques Vallée's interpretation—that aliens are real, flesh and cold metal. That they've been here forever is a strange comfort. I'm not alone in my suffering—the beings have always visited us.

Jung's insistence that they're our own creation scares me. It means I am responsible for the tales of horror, of abductions, and mutilations. It means you are responsible too. Why do our dreams, combined, make something so monstrous? As a child, I only wanted soft things, happy looks. Yet Jung says I am complicit in creating something terrifying. Now, perhaps, in adulthood as I spin and warp these alien encounter stories, I am a bit more to blame.

MY THIRTEENTH CHRISTMAS was a rare one in that we actually left the house—crawled out from the gloom and stale air and into the frost and cinnamon-scented world. Christmas morning, we usually sat in the dark living room, tree blinking haphazardly, and exchanged our meager gifts in silence: usually books and clothes for me, something domestic for Mom, like an iron, and ties and shoe polish and other things to make you look good for Daddy. Then we'd have carry-out Chinese food and go to bed. A flat, dim day.

But that Christmas, Daddy was feeling "cooped up," he said. He said it was time we bring the greatest gift of all to the world and then gestured vaguely at me and then the sky. Mom rolled her eyes, but put on her best festive sweater and little jingle bell earrings all the same. They put me in a collared black velvet frock—something for a much younger girl, I thought. It made me look shapeless, obscene somehow, but I didn't fight; I didn't want to spoil our chances of going somewhere unrelated to aliens, and doing something I had seen all those Lifetime families do.

We piled into the car and began the long trek to Harrisburg, where Dad's family lived. I fidgeted in the back seat, wondering if my second cousins would recognize me, if they'd brought gifts to exchange. I hadn't brought a thing. I scavenged the back of the car for an offering, a dog-eared almanac, an empty french fry container, and found nothing I could give.

I couldn't remember meeting anyone in our family, but I did know a little about Daddy's side. He'd talk about them occasionally—his estranged cousins, an elderly aunt. They'd pop up in stories about things and places he'd seen as a boy. Mom's family was never discussed. She had no stories, no past it seemed, and I was never interested enough to ask. It was as if my mother sprang from thin air, nothingness, whereas Daddy came from flesh and blood—sweating and shouting and ruddy faced.

I could tell Daddy was nervous on the way over—he was tapping his fingers on the steering wheel, flicking through radio stations indiscriminately, never landing on any one long enough to make out what sort of thing they were playing.

"Stop," Mom said, laying her fingers on my father's, still grasping the tuning knob. "Just focus on the road." Her voice was steely, hard, unlike herself.

Dad flapped his arm, shaking her off. "Don't tell me what I can and can't do in my own car."

Mom sighed, a sound like all the air rushing out of a two-liter. "I just want to make sure you're paying attention, is all."

"You don't think I'm paying attention? You don't think I can drive?" The tips of his ears were turning red, and I knew his face was all knotted up.

"No, no," Mom said quietly, and I could almost feel her folding into herself, forcing herself to become smaller in her seat. "You're a fine driver."

"Damn right I am," he said, but he didn't touch the radio dial again.

It was almost a relief when they fought. When their attentions warped toward each other, I was free to do as I pleased. It was a pity, I thought, that such a moment was wasted with me tethered in the back seat of the car. I'd have loved to sneak off, read a book, pretend to have normal thoughts because I was just another child whose parents tore into one another every now and then.

Eventually they remembered me, and Daddy's eyes peered at me through the rearview mirror. "You're going to behave yourself now, aren't you?"

"Yes, of course," I stated.

"She's always polite to strangers," Mom said absently, looking out the window. I tried to see what she was watching, but it was just fallow fields covered in blankets of snow on either side of the road—nothing interrupted all that blank whiteness.

"Sure," Daddy said. "But I want to make sure she's respectful to Aunt Jean and Uncle Ray—they're in their eighties you know."

"I know, Daddy."

"And none of that shy shit, if I ask you to tell the story, you—"

"What if we left all that out this year?" Mom said. "What if we just enjoyed each other, without talking about—" She gestured up at the sky, the universal symbol for my encounter.

I thought he'd be mad, I thought he'd turn beet red again, but he surprised me with his restraint. "That'd be nice, but we have an obligation, Marie. That's what they want us there for anyway, to ogle. So let them ogle."

Mom tutted. "They do not want to ogle you, Laura."

"Sure, they do," said Daddy. "We should charge admission."

"At your cousin's house?"

"Sure, why not?" he chuckled. "Imagine that. It's not like they can't afford it."

We turned into a driveway already lined with cars and SUVs—fancy ones, gleaming like jeweled ornaments against the snow.

"Remember," Daddy said, bumping against me conspiratorially as we shuffled toward the door. "You were singing."

"All the way up," I said, the memorized call and response evoking resignation.

Daddy rapped on the door, and we waited. Laughter and the thundering sound of small feet running across hard floors could be heard flashing past, but it still took nearly a minute before someone approached the door. Daddy twitched impatiently beside me.

But he stilled when the door swung open, releasing a warm, candle-scented puff of air in our faces. I blinked against it and the man that stood there. "Sam!" my dad's cousin exclaimed. "Glad you could make it."

Daddy mumbled in response.

"Marie, Laura," the man said as we edged past him, as if he were naming us for the very first time.

Mom nodded graciously. "Greg, thank you so much for inviting us." Her voice, though kind and warm, wobbled with nervousness.

Now that we had all acknowledged each other's names, Cousin Greg seemed more relaxed, as did Daddy—I wasn't sure if it was better this way or not; sometimes it was best to keep Daddy off-kilter.

"Of course," Greg said. "Wouldn't have it any other way." He smiled a white, gleaming smile.

We shuffled into the house, squeezing past Greg. My puffy coat made me twice as wide, and I wasn't sure I'd fit.

"Been a while since I've been here," Daddy grunted. "When was it, Marie? '89?"

Mom's face flushed. "It's so hot. Greg, where can we put our coats?" She was already pulling hers off, so I followed suit.

Greg gathered them up in his arms. "I'll just put these in the spare bedroom. No problem." He didn't come back to us after depositing the coats in a big, unceremonious heap on the bed, and we slunk our way to the living room alone. I clutched Mom's sleeve, feeling suddenly younger.

An old woman sat in a tufted chair, staring off into the middle distance while a crowd of small children roiled and screeched at her feet.

"Aunt Jean," Daddy said, voice full of reverence.

We pushed our way through the squabbling kids, Mom leading the way. She squatted down next to the old woman's chair. "Aunt Jean," she said, nearly yelling in the woman's ear. "Merry Christmas! It's Marie, Sam's wife. How are you?"

The woman grunted, still looking ahead at nothing. A boy fell into me, almost knocking me off my feet. He didn't apologize—just dove back into the brawl.

"We have Laura here with us." Mom reached out to me as proof, and I grabbed her hand; it would steady me if another kid rammed into me. She reeled me in close, into the woman's line of vision, but still I don't think she saw me.

Closer now, I could see the deep fissures in her skin—the velvety white hair spread across her upper lip. I looked away.

"Where's Uncle Ray?" asked Daddy.

"Dead," the old lady grunted.

Mom gasped, pawed at the old woman's gnarled hand. "We're so sorry to hear that, Aunt Jean. That's such a shame. He was an incredible man."

"No one told me," Daddy said. "Didn't even get an invite to the funeral."

"Wasn't one," she said.

"Let's go grab a snack," Mom said, clambering up awkwardly. "Let me bring you something, Aunt Jean. What would you like? Anything to drink?"

The old woman just stared. The kids streaked from the room with a scream.

We followed them, eventually finding our way to the kitchen. It was abuzz—timers beeped, women laughed and yelled and wiped red wine from their lips. Mom swiped a bacon-wrapped something from a plate and handed it to me.

"Marie?" a woman said. "My God, it's been years." She set her wine glass down and circled Mom in a hug.

I turned away, stuffed the bacon thing into my mouth. It was juicy, hot, and salty with a zing of spice—the best thing I'd ever eaten. My mouth tingled with pleasure. I was determined to find the roving band of kids—to see just what rowdy game they were playing. I licked my lips and crept from the kitchen, but not before swiping another bacon thing and stuffing it into my mouth.

The dining room was empty, but the long table was already set for the coming meal: crystal and silver everywhere and an over-flowing centerpiece. I don't think I had ever seen anything quite so fancy. I felt one of the petals of a red flower—it was soft and damp —real.

There was a whoop from an adjoining room and went in search of the source. I found a great mass of children seated in a playroom stuffed with toys and climbing sets and miniature chairs. "Who are you?" asked a blond boy.

"Shhhh, that's Laura," said a girl with a severe haircut. "She's our cousin."

"We're all our cousins," said someone else, and a giggle burbled out of the group.

My cheeks reddened at all the attention. It seemed like a hundred-eyed creature squatted before me on the floor and regarded me with suspicion. It inched closer. "Hi," I said.

"Laura, huh?" The blond boy broke away from the pack, circled me like I was prey. "Aren't you the alien?"

Another laugh rippled across the group.

"She's not an alien! She only met them."

"Yeah!"

"Be nice," said the girl with the dark hair. "Can't you see she's shy?"

"Maybe she doesn't speak our language. Zorp zoot," said a boy who stood and began walking like a robot, stepping on fingers and toes wherever he turned.

"Zorp zorp!" cried someone else.

"Zorp!" said a baby.

Tears welled in my eyes, but I was determined to make a friend. The girl with the dark hair seemed a promising candidate. Though she smiled now at all the zorps and zootings, she had known my name. "Can I play with you?" I asked.

"Sure," said the blond boy. "We're playing spacemen versus aliens. You can be on the alien's side."

"I'm a spaceman!" someone screamed.

"Me too!"

"I want to be an alien. They get ray guns."

"So do the spacemen, then," someone else said.

The blond boy pointed his finger at me in an approximation of a gun. "You better start running."

My breath caught in my chest, and I turned to run. My hair lashed across my face, obscuring my vision, and I ran straight into an adult's hip. "Laura," said my mom, grabbing my shoulders. "We have to go."

"What? Why?" The mass had piled up behind me now and was making all sorts of strange ray gun noises.

"Daddy made Greg mad. We have to go."

"What?"

Then I could hear it: the shouting from the kitchen, the sound of someone stomping through the house.

"Of course, it's Christian!" my Daddy howled. "It was an act of God!"

"Sam!" Mom yelled into the cavernous kitchen. "Car! Now!"

"It goes directly against His teachings. The Bible—"

I heard the dull *thwap* of flesh hitting flesh. Someone cried out and the kids, silent and gawking, floated into the kitchen as if in a trance. Adults sprung from their chairs, wine glasses tipping, ruby liquid soaking into plush rugs. They piled into the kitchen, and those who couldn't fit craned to see over shoulders and heads.

"Stop!" screamed a woman.

Glass shattered, and cutlery clanged to the floor. A feral grunt punctuated another blow.

"Help!"

"Damn it, Sam. Get off him!"

My stomach hurt as if I had been the one punched. My heartbeat quickened and seemed to rise into my throat. I wanted to shrink into myself, to disappear. "Mom, make it stop," I whispered.

"I can't," she said. "I can't."

She steered us toward the bedroom where our coats lay and then out the door.

The cold air bit at my face, my hands. When we got to the car, Mom tried all the doors but found them locked. Daddy had the keys. She sighed.

We waited in silence for what felt like a millennium before Daddy at last tumbled from the house, coat crumpled in his hands. "It happened!" he yelled at the closed door. "Just like I said."

"Please, Sam," Mom begged. "Open the doors."

Daddy tramped toward us through the snow, leaving big, deep footprints in the pristine yard. Even from a distance, the red blooming across his face looked swollen and painful. "Those fuckers —those idiots. I—"

"Doors," Mom said, cold-reddened fingers already on the handle.

"They're heathens," he said. "No manners at all." He fumbled with the keys, and at last the driver's side door swung open. He got in, shut the door, and turned on the car before remembering to unlatch all of our doors too. I was nearly frozen by the time I climbed inside.

I didn't speak the entire way home, nor was I spoken to. I was so ashamed, so hurt by what he'd done; I couldn't imagine ever speaking to him again.

The smell of blood filled the car—the iron scent overwhelming, pushing out the cinnamon smell of Christmas. *Good*, I thought. *Let him bleed.*

———

Sometimes I wonder if the star seen by the wise men was truly a star, or a visitor from another place.

CHAPTER 13

ESCAPE

I HAD RUN AWAY BEFORE, but never with any serious conviction. I'd pack a backpack full of stuffed animals and go hide behind a shrub in the yard. Then I'd retreat to the house when I was hungry or had to use the bathroom, much to my parents' amusement.

But it was different after Christmas. I was older now and angry in a way that felt real and urgent. I had been embarrassed by my daddy —the way he always got into fights—even with family—and how he had to involve my Incident into everything. I didn't want to be near him. And my mother? She was an accomplice—silent and allowing. By leaving, I was taking away the one link Daddy had to the golden and glittering world of the supernatural.

I knew Sylvia lived in Grand Oak and that couldn't be all that far. I had a MapQuest printout folded into my pocket promising me only two and a half days of walking. So, I packed a real bag: packages of Pop-Tarts, bottles of water, clothes. I put on a double layer of socks and snuck out into the cold while my parents napped.

It was exciting at first. I walked along the ditches, peering into them for any signs of life. Sometimes I saw animal tracks, a deer's cloven hoof deep in the snow or the pitter-patter of rabbits with their uneven gait. I stumbled into holes and across stray rocks, but I didn't dare walk on the road—it was coated with black ice, and I was sure I'd fall, end my adventure before it really started.

I stared into the fields surrounding me and thought about how I could be anywhere—the shorn, snow-swept fields here looked the same as the ones around my house. They glowed ominously with dazzling snow—so like the stars—surely a sign I was on the right path.

When I got thirsty, I pulled a water bottle from my bag only to discover it had frozen solid. I stuffed it back inside, embarrassed even though no one was around to see. It felt like a childish thing to have done—packed something I couldn't use. Instead, I stooped and shoveled up a handful of snow in my gloved hands and ate it. It was vaguely salty, and I thought maybe I should have ventured further from the road.

I continued on and eventually found myself along a road cutting through a large wood. My eyes savored the relative dark after the gleaming fields. Here, another sign made itself known: the human creak of wood against wood, bare limbs scraping against hollow trunks. It was an eerie sound, but a good omen, I thought. The world was showing itself to me at last.

A car crept by, going slowly to gain traction on the ice and to gawk at me, I assumed. I tensed—it wasn't our car, but maybe it was someone we knew sent out to look for me. Or maybe someone who would stuff me in the trunk, take me somewhere else—easy prey. But the car didn't stop.

In reality, all my parents had to do to find me was to follow my clumsy footprints in the snow. A real trail of breadcrumbs. I didn't mind having left such a simple path to follow—I almost wished they'd come after me, fold me in their arms like they hadn't done since that night so many years ago.

I hadn't emailed Sylvia that I was coming. As I walked, I thought about this. Maybe I should have—but Sylvia was so righteous, she would have probably notified my parents and my escape plan would have never come to fruition. I wasn't even sure where in Grand Oak she lived—my plan was to find the library and email her from there, hoping she'd see my message and come get me before the place closed.

But what if she was away on vacation? At a convention I didn't know about? Wasn't checking her email? Had issues with her internet? True, she hadn't mentioned any such thing and had just replied to one of my messages that morning, but I couldn't stop my mind from fretting. I tried to focus on the white of the snow, the dark of the forest, the distant thrum of a tractor or snowplow. It had to work.

The sky turned orange and red with the setting sun. It was beautiful, the greatest portent of all. But when it ended, the world was the darkest I'd ever seen it, and colder, too. I shivered, suddenly aware of the wet patches on my legs where the snow I'd trodden through had melted against my skin.

The stars flickered on. I saw the luminous smudge of the Milky Way and shivered harder. I did not want to be beneath all that vastness—it was too much. There were so many stars above, each one harboring planets, maybe even life, maybe the life that had taken me, if anything had. I couldn't stand beneath them, imagining the horror of one coming unfixed from its place in the firmament, of shooting across the sky. Every blinking airplane brought me close to screaming.

I needed a roof above me, a barrier between myself and all that space. I didn't want to see. I didn't want to be seen. Home would hurt —would punish and beat and destroy me—but at least it was a known pain, one I knew I would survive.

I turned around then, aware that the sky could swallow me whole.

The truth was, and still is, that I feared another abduction. There are stories, though I neglect to recount any of them here, of people once abducted visited again and again. The takings become routine, something expected. I'd studied a few of these, but they scare me too much to rewrite. I don't want to spend too much time in those pages for fear of inviting something in.

———

Here's a story about somewhere warm.

It was hot in Phoenix, even in March, and Bill Greiner had the windows of his cement truck rolled down. The barrel rolled and thundered behind him, but it was a soothing noise to him, and he hummed as he drove.

He was going slow—his task was to drive down a mountain pass, full load behind him, pressing him on—but he wasn't stressed. Bill was a master at wheeling the awkward truck wherever he needed to be. It was almost like they were one massive body and Bill was the nervous system, subtle, but in control.

The sun had set, and he could see the stars. He was among them, up there on that mountaintop. In moments like this, Bill felt truly happy.

But then the lights came: five of them traveling in a V formation. He slowed to a stop and pulled the brake. They were there, just hovering in front of him.

The truck suddenly felt too small, claustrophobic, so he flipped on the hazards and climbed out. Squinting against their glow, Bill tried to see open air between the lights, but couldn't. Whatever hung there was solid, boomerang shaped. He bristled. Later, when telling his story, Bill told the press he would never be the same.

The Phoenix Lights stayed above the city for hours—thousands saw them, documented them, dreamt them, and theorized about them.

CHAPTER 14
RETURN

MY PARENTS WERE angry when I returned early the next morning. Mom pulled the snow-soaked pants off my body with furious strength, and Daddy paced the floor, repeating, "What are we going to do with you?"

My skin was red and cold, and I wished someone would offer me a blanket or a warm bath, but no such nicety came. So, I shivered under their ruthless glares, allowing myself to feel pitiful and small.

"Why would you do something like that?" Mom asked.

"I don't know," I said. But I did know. I knew, and it was frothing and thrashing within me—it filled my eyes, my ears until it finally shot out of my mouth. "I don't know if you love me."

Daddy ran a hand over his bruised face. "You could have died. Gotten abducted. Hit by a car. What would we do then?"

Abducted—there was that word. There were so many ways to be taken. A shiver coursed through my body. "Did you look for me?"

"Of course we looked for you," chided Mom.

Dad kicked the corner of the couch. "We called everyone we knew. We stayed up all goddamn night."

"But did you go? Did you come look for me?"

"Yes," Daddy raged. "Almost slid into the ditch doing it, too."

"So, you went out?" My heart leapt. They'd risked themselves for me. They went slipping across the ice, into the cold, for me.

"Don't you ever do anything like that again," he yelled, ignoring my question, my wonder. His voice seemed far away, buffered by the hope I had dredged up from somewhere deep.

"You're grounded," Daddy said.

"Now, Sam. Maybe that's too much just yet. I think she needs to talk to someone or—"

"She's grounded." Daddy stalked out of the room, footsteps loud and reverberating.

I gulped down a great wail. "What does it mean?" I asked Mom, blinking back tears. I had never been grounded before, and I was tired, worn thin. I couldn't think, let alone brave anything less than softness.

"It means no TV, no computer, no sweets. At least for a little while."

"For how long?" To not have access to the computer meant I didn't have access to Sylvia, my lifeline, my everything. It was a shame we were still on winter break at school—I had no excuse to use the computer until after January began. Tears rolled down my cheeks.

"I—I don't know," Mom said, clearly flustered by my show of emotion. "I guess we have to see what Daddy says."

"Can't you do anything?"

Mom's eyelids fluttered. "No."

I went to bed as the sun rose, bathing my room in gray. But I did not sleep. Instead, I stared at the ceiling, let the tears run into the divots of my ears, an epiphany coming to me. My Daddy would always put himself first and, after all that self-idolization, there'd be nothing left for me. I kept remembering a show on PBS about scrapbooking. An old lady cut colored paper into interesting shapes, layered them with stickers and photographs and memories. It was bright and beautiful and alive.

My scrapbook would have burnt and blackened pages from ruined dreams and hopes. No color, no photos, just dark memories, usage, and subjugation.

Some time after I'd finally fallen asleep, Daddy flung open my door, stepped close to my bed. He knelt down. I thought perhaps he'd apologize but instead he whispered, "Do you know what would happen to us if you left? If you were gone? We'd go broke—destitute. You'd ruin us all."

So that's all I was to him—a piggybank, all chipped and bloated. I wanted to rip the cork out, send all my guts spilling across the floor. I could hurt myself—it would be so easy—but my pain never made him pause. He never saw me as a victim, as someone deserving of empathy, of love. I needed to spite him, to curse him, to ruin everything. I needed to hurt him.

I stared at the purpled skin where Greg had hit him. It looked sore and swollen, ready to burst.

He pushed himself away from me and turned toward the door.

"I wish you'd die," I whispered.

I'll never know if he heard me, but I hope he did. Still hope to this day. I hope he stayed up all night replaying the words in his head, turning them over like a tarnished, blackened coin.

I hummed to myself. A lilting, quiet tune. I hummed until I fell asleep.

———

This is a story about being left to rot.

Snippy was a beautiful mare—strong and sleek and came when

called. She was young, but had the soul of a much older horse; they said you could see it in her eyes.

But she was struck down all the same. They found her dead a quarter-mile from the house. Her head and neck were nothing but bones while her body still held flesh. No blood could be seen around her corpse, and her bones gleamed white in the Colorado sun, perfect but for the fact they weren't on Snippy's insides anymore.

While the mare's bones shone white, the surrounding grass was burned black in a great dry patch. Bushes were flattened and strange indentations pocked the ground around Snippy. The earth was marked with the trauma of her passing, all disturbed and kicked up, poor Snippy.

If you touched her remaining fur, you'd itch for days.

Doctors and reporters and veterinarians came to look at her mangled corpse. "Maybe her head got caught in the barbed wire," offered one.

"Then where's the blood? The flesh?"

A reporter posited that perhaps ants had fallen the great mare, who may have been sick to begin with, not so strong after all. They ate her flesh, drank her blood, made the scene so clean and tidy that they left only the radiation to be unexplained. It was particularly high in the area Snippy lay, they said.

The villagers took her bones, reassembled them in homage. They ignored the bullet holes in her thigh, propped her up outside the veterinarian's office as a novelty. No one else in town had something like this.

When Snippy's bones went up for auction on eBay in 2006, no one bid. The dead horse went into storage. She's been there ever since. I've never been a horse person—never collected the velvety figurines, never dreamt of braiding a lustrous mane—but I know a thing or two about show ponies, about being locked away.

AFTER I WISHED my father would die—the night spent hoping and humming—I got good at sneaking, at maintaining a straight face when I lied. I would allow myself to be tucked in, swaddled like a baby, then would stare at the ceiling until the last of the noise in the house had died away. I would untangle myself from the blankets and creep through the house like a burglar.

I emailed Sylvia in the middle of the night—desperate pleas of rescue, angry rants about the unfairness of it all, meticulous dissections of my parents and their every flaw. Typing slowly, it took work to avoid making a constant clatter among the keys, and I'd be exhausted at the end of it.

Sylvia always replied. She met my rage with eloquent sense, which was sometimes maddening, but always read and read again.

"Remember," she wrote. "We're extraordinary people and we're capable of doing extraordinary things."

I didn't feel extraordinary, but I did have something in common with the best person I knew and that heartened me. I sent Sylvia stories of alien abductions found on the internet, of people who claimed to have metallic chips implanted in their calves. She sent me any such news in return in addition to articles on mindfulness, of escaping from the maw of the great bleak monster bearing down on me.

Sylvia worried I was getting depressed. "Tell your parents you'd like to talk to a therapist. It would be so nice to talk to someone other than your parents," she wrote.

I knew my parents would never consent to something like that— something that would open us raw to another person. I had already tried and failed with the hypnotherapy suggestion. And to be honest, I didn't feel like I needed or could trust a therapist—especially one hired by my parents.

"I have you," I wrote back.

"You always have me. But sometimes your feelings are bigger than the both of us. I'm not a professional. I'm just words on a screen, Laura."

These were the few messages of Sylvia's I ignored the contents of —I didn't want anyone else. They wouldn't understand, couldn't understand. To have been touched by the slender, gray fingers of the unknown was to be rendered unknowable yourself. No one but another abductee could come close to comprehending the miasma of grief, terror, and beauty that swirled about inside me. I wanted only Sylvia.

A convention came and went, and I was barred from going, my parents unwilling to drive me the five hours while I was still grounded. I briefly considered running away again, so desperate was I to see Sylvia, but the memory of icy air and pitch-black skies was enough to deter me. I begged my daddy—told him I'd even do a signing or a talk, that I'd earn back the gas money with book sales—but he shook his head. "You enjoy them too much."

The night of the convention I cried until the veins beneath my eyes burst into little red nebulae. Mom made me tea and laid a sympathetic hand on my head, but Daddy rolled his eyes and sneered. "This is what you get for running away, Laura. Being grounded isn't about having fun."

I wanted to rip all of my hair out. I wanted to rip all of his hair out. I wanted to stab him until his blood ran over my hands and spilled to the floor. I wanted him dead.

And then a few nights later he knelt beside my bed once more. His breath smelled yeasty. "I know you've been on the computer at night."

I stared at the ceiling, unwilling to meet his gaze. How? How did he know? Had I forgotten to close a window, typed too loudly, been too distracted to hear his footsteps in the hall? I had tried so hard to make myself invisible.

"How dare you tell that woman anything about me?" His fingers wrapped around my arm, squeezed tight. "Going behind our backs, talking to some bitch on the internet. I don't even know you."

I began to shake. It started as a quiver and grew into a violent quaking.

"You're never going to another convention. Not under my watch. I ought to ground you for the rest of your life." His thumb pressed hard into my bone.

Nausea rippled through me, and my face burned hot. I squeezed my eyes shut as his grip tightened even more.

"When your mother hears what you said about her, oh just you wait. It'll break her, Laura. You'll have broken your mother."

At last, he released me from his grasp, and I realized I hadn't breathed in a very long time. I took a big gulping breath.

"I'm disconnecting it," he said from the doorway.

"But school. I—"

"I'm your school now."

I was too scared to ask him what he meant by that, and he'd already gone away. The empty space where he had been in the doorway seemed to throb with energy. I looked away, buried my head in my pillows.

When at last my parents were asleep, I floated out of bed, dizzy with the new harsh life I faced. Instead of tiptoeing to the computer, I carefully slid the back door open, wincing at the sound of the breaking seal, and stepped outside.

I wasn't dressed for the cold weather, but I didn't care. I carefully climbed down off the deck and pushed my bare feet into the snow. There should have been pain. But there was nothing to feel—I was completely empty.

I walked a ways through the yard, creating dragging footprints in the snow.

When I was far enough away from the house to feel truly alone, I turned my head upwards. Stars upon stars upon stars glittered back at me, and I felt the dawning horror again, felt myself grow incredibly small there among the pines and snow and distant house, all insignificant now. The house felt so far away—too far to reach, to see. It was as if I was in a different world, one of hushed whispers and dancing lights.

I willed for them to take me. To come back. The aliens. The abductors, the ones that forced me to sing, to forget. To rip me from this Earth and tear me apart like a laboratory frog. I cried and steam rose from my hot tears. I cried a long time.

Why wouldn't they come?

I sang—I opened my mouth and a warped note escaped, and then another. I was singing the same old bullshit song from a Disney movie, and I wasn't sure why. The final notes fell flat out of my mouth and the stars stayed stationary.

It wasn't working.

I decided I would take off all my clothes, lie naked in the snow until I froze to death beneath the stars. They would find me in the morning and perha—

An orange-red light moved steadily across the horizon. My heart leapt. "Yes!" I screamed. "Yes!" It was slow, unblinking, and left no tail in its wake. It wasn't a plane, those were different. This light crackled with energy, pulsated with it. I reached out, trying to grasp it, trying to connect, as it disappeared into a constellation I couldn't name.

Then it was gone.

"Holy shit," I said aloud. My body vibrated with excitement. I had never seen anything so beautiful, so terrifying. And I had made it happen. I had willed it into being. My breath came fast and shallow. What else could I move? What else could I do just by wishing? By singing for it?

I replayed the moment in my mind over and over until a familiar layer of doubt began to settle upon me. Maybe it had been a shooting star—I hadn't seen one of those since I was little. What did a shooting star even look—

And an unfixed star rocketed by, shot across the sky in a pure white arc. I closed my eyes, sang my childish song, and focused on my wish. I didn't struggle to come up with one—it was a hope I'd carried for some time. It was a bloodstained, rotten, pulsating hope, and I smiled as I let it unspool in my mind.

"Thank you," I whispered before running back to the house.

I tread snow in through the door, but I didn't care. Nothing my Daddy could say or do would hurt me ever again, because I had been acknowledged, at last.

Have you been inspired? Do you want your own story to brandish when you feel inconsequential and ordinary?

There's a man named Steven Greer who will teach you, for not an insignificant sum, to summon them. Through meditation, intention, and peaceful invitation Mr. Greer claims you too can make luminous orange orbs dance through the sky. CE-5, he calls it: Close

Encounters of the Fifth Kind – human initiated contact. They'll come when called, he says.

They could be flares dropped by conspiring aviators, or pure coincidence.

They could be ultra-dimensional, coming from within as well as without.

He tells you to open your mind, to receive the message. To wish, to pray, to plan, to hope.

But sometimes all you can hear is static. That's a message, too.

I WOKE up early the next morning, heady with the events from the night before. Pulling on a pair of thick socks, I left my room in my pajamas, a vulnerability I hadn't indulged since I was little; I usually felt the need to be unscrutinizable and plain in a t-shirt and jeans—nothing my family could comment on or even notice.

My joints felt loose and free and I hummed a tune as I rounded the corner into the kitchen.

I froze. At first, I didn't comprehend what I was seeing. I was registering something out of place, something not right, but my brain was tripping over the source again and again. Maybe it was an unwillingness, I'm not sure.

Finally, my eyes focused, and I saw Daddy writhing on the floor, spilled coffee, shattered mug bits lying about him. He kicked and pushed, making a sad, brown approximation of a snow angel in the coffee on the tile floor.

He clutched at his chest, bared his teeth.

I took a step backward. The contorted inhumanity of his face was disgusting. His pain was disgusting.

His eyes flicked upward, met mine. They bulged out of his head in panic, but they still saw me.

I peeked down the hallway—the door to my parent's room was shut. Mom couldn't hear; she was still asleep. I was the only one who could help him, I realized with pleasure.

I wouldn't do it. I never would.

I ran back to my room, his eyes following me, begging me.

I closed the door and threw myself on the bed, pulled a pillow up over my head, for I could hear a baleful moaning now and the subtle clink of broken mug as he thrashed. I squeezed my eyes shut, willing it to be over. *Please, please, please,* I chanted in my head. If Mom came out of her room before it was over, it would ruin everything. *Please.*

At last, there was quiet, and I fell back to sleep, at peace with what I'd accomplished.

There was a scream to wake me, my mother wailing and shouting and pounding through the house, tripping over something, falling to the ground, and scrambling up again. I winced at her stubbornness, her emotion.

I pushed myself upward—I'd have to do this right, or it might be bad for me.

I burst from my room. "Mommy?"

"Laura!" she cried. "Don't look. Go back to your room."

But I crept along the hallway, shaking with the intensity of it all. "Mommy, what's wrong?"

She stumbled into view at the end of the hall. Her hair was hanging in front of her wet and shining face. "Don't look."

I ran at her, pushed past her outstretched arms, and burst into the kitchen. "Daddy!" I screamed, falling down at his side. "Daddy wake up!" I forced myself to touch him—to prod his arm—and I screamed a genuine scream, piercing and high.

My mother grabbed me by the shoulders and began to pull me away backward, sliding me through the now-cold coffee. A piece of broken ceramic caught me in the back of my thigh, and I left a bright trail of blood in my wake. "Daddy!" I screamed again.

"Please," my mother begged. "Go back to your room. I've already called the ambulance. Please go back to your room. I can't—" She was sobbing now, and I placed a tentative hand on her arm.

"Mommy, what happened? Is he..." I forced tears to well up in my eyes. "Gone?"

"Just go."

I went to the bathroom instead and shed my coffee and blood-soaked pajamas. Surveying myself in the mirror, I twisted to see the small bite the broken coffee mug had taken out of my thigh, out of me. It'd be a scar, I reckoned. Something to remember today by.

I ran water over my face, rubbed until it felt raw, then examined my work: I looked red and new, like a baby just about to scream. It was the best I'd looked since Bethany had tried her hand at painting me.

I walked back to my room naked, pleased with what I'd done.

———

This is a story of extinction.

First there is noise, and then there is not. The birds chirping, the wind rustling through the leaves, it all abruptly stops and you stop too, glance up at the sky.

The scientist was driving with his sleeping children in the back. It was 1966, and this part of Louisiana was still rural, still only holding a small shack here and there in its sleepy folds. The scientist hummed a tune to pass the time and his wife patted his arm approvingly in time with the song. It was a pleasant evening, he thought, as he drove through the dark forest.

Then a city reared up on the horizon, sudden and misplaced. Or, rather, the lights of a city glowed on ahead of them, between the trees, and the children stirred, shielded their eyes from the brightness. He squinted through the mangled live oaks, and the thing grew brighter, brighter than his headlights, so bright it hurt.

And then it disappeared, plunged the world back into darkness.

The scientist, who had gone into his profession precisely because he was curious and picked apart the world with adept fingers, returned the next day. In a diner that served greasy pancakes and greasy mugs of coffee, he asked a hunter if he'd noticed anything strange.

"It's the damnedest thing," said the hunter. "All the animals are gone."

AT FIRST THE funeral kept her busy, and then there was the arduous task of picking through my daddy's unnecessarily complicated will, but when that was all over my mother sat down at the kitchen table, cigarette in hand, and didn't move.

She stared at the spot where he died. She stared out the window. She stared at the wall. She was so still she barely even blinked. I'd pass in front of her vision, and she'd twitch, but that was the most I got out of her. So, I microwaved my own food, took to cleaning the dishes myself, all the while my mother grew thinner and paler as if in a desperate attempt to simply fade from the world.

Sometimes I'd lay some food in front of her, a glass of water, but I was never sure if she ate it or not—they'd have simply disappeared, silverware and all, the next time I passed through.

The only time I saw her move was during her slow shuffle from the bedroom in the morning and back again at night. At least I knew she slept.

"Mommy," I said one afternoon. "We have to go grocery shopping. We're running low."

Her eyes rolled toward me in dim recognition.

"Won't you drive me to the grocery store?"

"Mm-mm," she mumbled. "I can't."

"Why not?"

"Can't afford it," she said and flicked her cigarette into the full ashtray, a movement so unexpectedly sudden that I flinched.

"Can we use your credit card or something?" I offered.

She sighed, laid down her cigarette. "There's no room on it. Not after the funeral."

My stomach twisted in hunger. "So, we're just not going to eat?" Her inactivity angered me. I had done something at last—moved and changed the world, brought down a great giant. But she was tainting it, dragging me down with corporal concerns. It had been a long time since I'd done a signing or a convention, but I didn't realize we were in that precarious of a situation. I thought the money I'd made them, made us, would go on forever.

She shrugged. "I'm going to get a job," she said.

"How?" I asked. I wondered how she'd manage that in her current immobile state.

She shrugged again.

"Maybe I can start doing talks again," I said. "Book signings too."

"Maybe. If anyone wants you anymore."

I blinked at her words, but held back the biting reply I so wanted to bark. I needed to take it slow, strategize. I couldn't imagine my mother accompanying me on the many trips we'd have to take if we wanted to earn enough money to get by. Mom rarely came to my events; Daddy was always the one in charge. I thought about Sylvia sitting there in the convention hall, poised and ready to hear the arcane stories and testimonials wrought by the alien enthusiasts.

She'd be the perfect chaperone. "I—" I faltered, unsure of how much my mother knew about my correspondence with Sylvia. I wasn't sure if Daddy had time to tell her. "I know someone from the conventions. They could help me, help us."

Mom studied my face. "Okay," she said. "Could they drive you? You'd have to do all the work of contacting venues, setting up gigs, but maybe they could help?"

"I think she'd be willing."

Mom's eyebrow rose. "Why?" she asked, then shrugged the thought away. "Talk to her, I guess. Tell her it will just be for a little while until I can get back on my feet. Driving to all those things. It's just so," she waved her hand in the air, let it fall to the table with a thud.

I nodded solemnly. "It is."

"I can't pay anyone," she said.

"I know. She wouldn't want money anyhow."

She huffed. "Who doesn't want money? Who is this woman, anyway?"

"Just a friend of mine and Daddy's," I lied, softening it. "Another abductee we met at a convention. She's an older lady. She's really nice."

"Hm," said Mom. "Ab.Duc.Tee." She broke the word apart, so each syllable sounded sharp.

"So can I ask her?" I was giddy with the idea. Not only would I get to return to the conventions where I could sit next to Sylvia, bask in her warm pink glow, but she'd be driving me too. I could spend entire weekends with her, away from this musty, dark house. Maybe she'd even start chauffeuring me to other events—replace Daddy completely. I shivered with the thrill.

"I guess so. Just don't be disappointed if she says no. It's a lot to take on."

"Yes!" I squealed and ran from the room. I headed straight for the computer.

"And I want to meet this person," Mom yelled from the kitchen. "I have to meet them first."

"Okay!" I yelled back. I had no doubt Mom would see Sylvia's kind genuineness immediately, I just wasn't sure what Sylvia would think of my mother, and our messy, stale-aired house.

The computer whirred to life, and I started typing.

————

Here's a story about a woman. Have you noticed yet how few of them there are?

Utsuro-bune came on a calm sea.

Drifting, the wooden vessel looked like a boat from a distance, but as it drew closer, the fishermen on the shore grew agitated, nervous. This was no normal boat—not like any seen before in Japan, 1803. It was shaped like an oblong incense burner—a saucer made of rosewood, crystal, and brass. It was beautiful, yes, but it did not belong, so they regarded it with suspicion.

At last, the thing floated near enough that they could wade out to meet it, peer into its crystalline windows. Inside, there was cake, meat, bed linens, and a small woman. They reared back, away from the vessel. But the woman came outside to meet them.

She was luminous and strange with her red and white hair and pale pink skin. She wore a glimmering gown and clutched a small box to her chest.

They reached for the box, her bizarre delivery, but she held it away from them and would not allow them to touch it.

She spoke, but her language was strange, garbled. No one could understand her tongue. Nor did she understand the fishermen. They stared at each other, disbelieving.

"Inside that box," said one of the fishermen. "Could be her lover's head. Perhaps she's being punished, this princess, for her infidelity and set to float."

"It has happened before," said another. And it had. This woman wasn't the first to wash ashore with strange offerings.

"Well, what do we do with her?"

"Return her to her destiny," said the oldest, wisest fisherman, the one who always knew the best times to fish, the best bait to carry.

So, they stuffed the bejeweled woman back inside her contraption and pushed her back to sea. They watched her float away, over the horizon, until she was gone. "It is her fate," they said.

Utsuro-bune means "empty boat"—but to the small, glowing woman with the box, it was her entire world.

CHAPTER 18
A REPRIEVE

DEAREST LAURA,

I am shocked to hear of your father's passing. I too lost my father young, and I want you to know it does get easier, believe it or not. Soon you'll be able to look at the good times not with grief, but with joy. I know you didn't always have a perfect relationship with your father, but you must cling to the good times, Laura. They will carry you through.

As for your question regarding traveling to conventions together: I don't see why not. Is your mother okay with this? Have you both considered the fact that we might have to stay overnight, depending on the distance? I am an early riser, Laura; are you sure you want to put up with an old lady like me?

I think it is a good idea to carry on with your normal routine, but don't rush things. I am happy to take you whenever you feel ready. Remember, conventions are overwhelming places and perhaps you need some time away to grieve. I am honored you thought of me and trust me with such an important job, but I don't want you to worry about things like that quite yet. There will be time.

I do wonder, though, if you'd allow me to sell a few of my books at your booth. It would be a great help financially, and having your endorsement would mean a lot to me. Think on it—absolutely no pressure.

In the meantime, please let me know if there's anything else I can do.

Yours, Sylvia

My heart leapt at her words. It was truly happening. I would get to spend more time with Sylvia and earn a little money to help Mom buy groceries and keep the roof over our head while doing it. It felt like the world was twisting around me, bending to meet me at last. I could hardly believe that just a week and a half ago I was grounded, wings clipped. Now I would fly.

I had no qualms at all about letting Sylvia bring her books along. Her book was good—riveting and vulnerable—and was proud to have her and her story on my table.

I looked up the soonest convention and was happy to find there would be one later in the month. Sylvia had said to wait, to let my emotions settle, but I hadn't felt much at all after my daddy's passing. I taught myself how to tear up when I looked at pictures of us from when I was a baby, and my heart fluttered when I stared into those eyes and remembered how they looked the last time I saw them, but in the end, I was faring well; I had a new goal, and it consumed my thoughts.

I sent an email to the convention organizers apologizing for the late notice and asking if I could please be considered one of the speaking guests and if they could place me at a booth to sell books. I explained The Incident, in the unlikely case they didn't already know the story inside out, and mentioned my book, a bestseller in the genre. Anything would be fine: reading from it, talking about abduction as a whole, leading a discussion group, taking tickets at the door; I didn't care. I just wanted in.

It felt strange to be using my tender story in this way. I was declaring my confidence in the story with every keystroke, using it to manipulate someone else instead of letting it eat me raw. It felt like Daddy. I felt like Daddy. But I would be better than him.

True, I had been complicit in every telling and retelling, but this was something new. By promoting myself, I was tacitly implying I knew the truth, had accepted every aspect of my parents' story verbatim and would now be repeating it, preaching it. I would have to work extra hard now to ensure the outside did not betray the longing inside—I had no one else to blame if it all came crumbling apart.

And I needed the money. I needed the fame to survive.

I thought about my Daddy's enemies, the doubters and non-believers. There was the folder he kept in his email labeled "Hate Mail." I had gone through it after he died—clicking through the over-punctuated, angry letters. Some insisted that the abduction never happened at all, while others believed in The Incident but decried the monetization of it. The monetization of me. A lot of people didn't think a child should be dragged across the country to work. A few people sent random Bible verses that made little sense.

It would be up to me to face them now, alone. I realized with a strange horror that in this moment I missed his safety. Even though he was ultimately defending himself when protecting me, my story, he had never left me to brave the wolves on my own. I thought about the reading I'd done so long ago—the one where the man had pointed and yelled and my daddy stood there, bewildered and frayed. While I had been the one to drive the accuser out with my voice, I sang because Daddy was there beside me. Though he'd tried to shush me, I only ever sang because of him. He'd created me, reinforced the lore of my song. He'd shown me what I could be, and it had ruined him. I had needed him, once. Did I need him still?

I considered writing to Sylvia, explaining this confusing web of revelation I had found myself tangled in, but I didn't want her to think I was grieving—she might not agree to go to a convention so soon if she knew my turmoil.

So instead, I wrote thanking her, told her I was considering speaking at the convention I had emailed, and that I was doing just fine. It was a bland, stiff letter, but I didn't dare write too much for the fear of exposing some objectionable weakness. I hoped she wouldn't mistake my restraint for rudeness.

After the email was sent, I found Mom still at her place in the kitchen.

"She said she'd do it," I said, unable to hide my smile.

Mom blinked in surprise. "That's great," she said. "I hope you can sell a few books. But I still want to meet this person."

"That's fine," I said even though the thought scared me to death. "Maybe before the next convention, when she comes to pick me up?"

Mom rubbed a hand along her arm as if she was cold. "That's cutting it awfully close. What if I disapprove?"

"Trust me, you won't."

Mom sighed and fumbled with her lighter. "If you say so," she said around a cigarette. "I'm a harsh critic."

———

Not every encounter is fraught and terrifying. Some are genuinely beautiful, filled with wonder and offerings. One such incident involves cookies, and I've yet to hear a story about cookies that fills me with dread.

Joe was just getting started with his day, finally rubbing the sleep out of his eyes, when there came a flapping, thudding noise from outside. He wondered if someone was there—an early visitor, perhaps. Maybe something had happened to his mother. His heart squeezed uncomfortably. He pulled the door open and stepped outside to check the driveway.

There on the yard, hovering inches from the ground, the blades of grass reaching up to touch the curved belly of the thing, was a flying saucer. It glowed silvery and bright—beautiful. Joe stumbled off the porch, agog. What was this thing?

He moved toward it with a slow tentativeness.

A hatch sprung open, and Joe recoiled. How badly he wanted to run back into the house, to slam the door between him and this strange ship. But he must see it through, this phenomenal occurrence. He would absorb it all.

A thin man climbed out of the ship, and Joe was relieved to find him rather plain in appearance. He had dark hair and skin and wore a turtleneck. He smiled at Joe and Joe smiled back.

In his hands he held a silver jug. He held it out to Joe, and he took it, felt the coolness in his hands. *Water*, thought Joe suddenly. *They want water.* He surprised himself with the knowledge, but went to the pump all the same.

When the jug was full, Joe returned to the smiling man and offered him the vessel. The man nodded in thanks and Joe was thrilled—he was doing the right thing, he knew.

He felt oddly relaxed, curious now. And he strode around the ship, squatting to examine the exhaust pipes erupting from the otherwise seamless hull. He even peeked his head through the hatch and saw the inside—a black cavern spangled with buttons and controls.

Three men gathered around a small, flameless grill, flipping brown patty-looking things with their tools. "What is that you're cooking?" asked Joe, unable to place the savory sweet smell.

The man who had offered Joe the jug cocked his head, scooped three of the morsels from the grill, and handed them to Joe. *Cookie*, Joe thought, studying the warmed brown discs. He pressed down on one with his thumb, and it crumbled in his hand.

The men waved their goodbyes, and Joe retreated to the house, cookies and crumbs in hand. The hatch closed, sealing the ship up tight. Then it was gone—blasting upwards with such force that the trees bent away, blown as if a bomb had gone off.

Joe took a bite of one of the strange, pock-marked cookies. It tasted horrible. *Oh well*, he thought and called the police.

CHAPTER 19
CHANGELING

WHEN AT LAST SYLVIA ARRIVED, my mother was not so brave. The "harsh critic" she had referred to was nothing more than a dog with its tail between its legs. At least she had gotten dressed for the occasion, choosing jeans and a t-shirt over her usual pajamas. In the end, my mother was quiet, nodded along to Sylvia's reassuring words and let me go.

The convention itself was unremarkable—they crammed me into a makeshift auditorium, nothing more than a meeting room with a podium at the front, and I read to fifteen or twenty people. I sold books, signed autographs, posed for a few awkward photos, and then it was over.

I spent the rest of the time following Sylvia around, not unlike a dog myself, nearly prancing with the joy and lightness I felt being in her presence.

She bought me lunch and sat across from me, eyes crinkled with a smile. "Thank you for letting me come along," she said, as if she needed me. "Are you enjoying yourself?"

"Definitely," I said. "I'm so glad we got to do this. My mom, she's not the type to come to these. Or anything, really."

"She's going through a tough time."

"She is," I agreed. "But I think she was always this way. I can't really remember." My heart pounded with the thought that perhaps The Incident wasn't the only thing wiped from my mind, but other more mundane things too. The way things were before my abduction, seemed farther and farther away all the time—and it was, but the past was hurtling away unnaturally fast, doubling the distance every time I reached for it. I wondered if it was simple aging, or a side-effect of the abduction itself, or just too much time spent with Daddy, always willing to reorder and scramble things to his liking.

"The meek shall inherit the earth," Sylvia said and dumped a packet of sugar into her drink. Sylvia had gotten tea, something so stereotypical old lady that I couldn't help but smile every time she sipped it.

"I guess," I said. "Do you think I'm meek?"

Sylvia's pale blue eyes ran me over. Then her eyebrows waggled. "No," she said. "I don't think you're meek at all."

"But isn't meek good? They're inheriting the earth and all that."

"Meekness is only valuable to the one in charge, I think," she said. She rubbed her chin. "I guess it only really works under the assumption that the one you're meek to is good, with good intentions."

In this moment, I missed Daddy, though I wouldn't care to admit it. I remembered our first trip to that radio station, the excitement we shared. And I thought about the first convention we had ever been to, when I was scared and shy and he held my hand, even when I spoke, my baby-ish voice quavering and stumbling. I was the youngest speaker they'd ever had, they told me, and it had terrified me. But now, I felt proud. I was the youngest abductee to come forward and write a book—even if I hadn't actually written it.

Sylvia reached out and patted my arm, sensing the emotions I was trying so hard to bury. "You'll be okay," she said. "You're the strongest person I know."

She was always doing that—reading me like a book and telling me exactly what I needed to hear. I wondered, at times, if she was a mind reader. Perhaps instead of poisoning her, like it had me, her abduction had gifted her with skills fantastic. I was supposed to have benefited too, become smarter, renewed, and angelic. But I didn't see that. I didn't feel that. Out of all the lies I told, that was the biggest of all.

———

Here's an old story about mothers.

In the olden days, you had to be careful. Especially if you were on the Isle, green and glittering. There were things there, old, mischievous things, that wanted you badly. They'd take you, even if you were a baby—*especially* if you were a baby, malleable and innocent—and make you their own.

They left one of their discarded in the place of the one they took —deformed, colicky, stunted. It was an efficient system, leaving the changelings. It solved so many problems, strengthened the stock. Their blood was so sweet, so nourishing.

Meanwhile, the changelings would cry and fight, recoil from their mother's touch. And the mothers grew tired and jaded, caring for these unknowable things, unlovable things. Sometimes the mothers would leave them to the wolves or to starve deep in the forest. They weren't really theirs, anyway—their children were taken, somewhere with the faeries. It was a public duty, killing off these foul things. They could only hope that their true babies would return.

But none ever did.

Worst of all were the sticks—loose, sloppy bundles of them clutched to a mother's chest. "My baby," she'd say, showing you the twigs. "She's not well." The villagers, the townfolk, the family never had the heart to tell them their baby was long gone, sucked dry by the fae. Maybe they'd come back for the mother—that would be a relief. It was so tiring, pretending this way.

I WALKED THROUGH THE DOOR, clutching the money in my fist. There was $117—all from book sales and autographs. Not wanting to take advantage of Sylvia's kindness, I had spent a little on snacks at the convention, so it was a weird, odd number, but I was proud when I laid it on the table in front of Mom.

She flicked the bills through her hands, straightening the bent and crumpled ones as she went. I admired how deftly she handled the money, like a card player shuffling the deck. At last, she folded the stack and placed it back on the table between us.

"Not bad," she said. "But not great either."

My stomach clenched. "What do you mean not great?"

"We're going to need a lot more than this." Her voice was deflated, affectless.

"Well yeah," I said, angry now. "This is just from one convention. I can do more."

Mom sighed. "You used to pull in a lot more money is all. What was this? Ten books? You used to sell hundreds."

I had never imagined my mother would be disappointed in me, I had done what she hadn't, gotten us some money. But she wasn't wrong—I was making more money, lots more, before Daddy died. How could I not with his big voice directing the crowd, preparing them to witness me, to admire me? Daddy was, if nothing else, a great promoter. At that point, I hadn't mastered the art of show business, and had simply walked up to the podium, did my reading, and backed away. Daddy always had said something before and after my shows, building the suspense, reminding them to buy my books to get the whole, unadulterated story. Daddy would have been prowling the crowds before the show, telling them I was there, and they couldn't miss it—it would have been a full room. Instead, I had simply trailed behind Sylvia all morning, breathing in her sweet perfume.

"Daddy's gone," I said. "I can't do it as well as he can."

Mom softened, her body going limp. "I know he was a big part of it, Laura. But maybe there's something else that has changed, too."

"What do you mean?"

"I just think it's the same crowd of these people everywhere you go. It's market saturation. Do you know what that is? You've reached everyone already—can't sell any books because they already have them, have already heard the story a thousand times. You need something new."

"But I don't want anything new." The thought filled me with dread. I already felt like I was giving so much of myself away whenever I took the stage, anything else might drain me dry.

"Then maybe it's time to think of throwing in the towel, retiring until you're old enough to get a real job. Stop going to the conventions, paying those fees."

"No!" I gasped. No conventions meant no Sylvia, and I couldn't bear it.

"Then you'll have to change up your act," Mom said, and I realized she had manipulated me. She had shown me two darknesses, and I would have to choose the lighter of the two.

"But how?" I asked. "There's nothing new to tell."

"I have an idea," she said. "You're going to sing."

I felt nauseous, the bile rising up my throat. "I thought you were going to get a job."

She brushed the thought aside with her hand. "I am. At the restaurant. I'll wait on people. But we need more than that—we need you."

I had never known my mother to be so direct, so involved with anything regarding The Incident beyond getting me ready for appearances, stuffing me into pretty dresses. In the early days she'd refused to participate entirely, leaving it all up to Daddy. But now she was running full keel into the heart of the story. It took three of us to replace Daddy, I realized and choked down a sob. Why did we want to replace him at all? I'd taken care of him and now, somehow, we weren't better. It was all so complicated. It was like we were slipping down the crater he'd left, drawn down without a choice.

"You've done it before," she said. "Sang in public, I mean."

"I know," I said. "But that was different. That was..." I struggled for words. I remembered the crowd I'd stilled with my singing, the telephone lights shining in the dark of Ray Trout's studio. I thought of Daddy lying dead on the floor.

"Genuine?" asked my mother.

"Yes," I said, relieved. Mom had a point—I could do it, I could open my mouth and sing, but I wasn't sure I could make anything occur if the desire wasn't from a place deep and yearning. What if I couldn't make anything happen?

What if I could?

Mom put a hand to my head, smoothed down my hair. "How about if it's only for a little while? Until we can see where we stand? Generate a little excitement? Then you can do it however you want."

"Okay," I agreed, unable to see the alternative and softened by my mother's understanding. "Just for a little while."

She cupped my cheek in her hand, my Mommy.

———

Here's one about never coming back.

The view, all hills and lush valleys, would have been pretty if not for the fighting. The Great War raged on the Gallipoli peninsula and Irvine was caught among them, perched up high on a mountain, surveying the wreckage below.

He watched regiments march through the valley, beneath the crystal-clear sky. Well, not exactly clear—there was a strange conglomeration of loaf-shaped clouds hovering about one hill, stuck to it as if by glue, for they did not shift or blow apart with the wind. Irvine eyed the clouds suspiciously, wondering if they were some new type of gas. His superior assured him they were just clouds, lacking the yellowy tint of poison gas. But why did they linger? Were they so heavy? Irvine didn't like them one bit.

One of the clouds was low—it rested in the valley, laden and thick. Irvine imagined it was touching the ground.

When a British regiment came around the bend and marched toward the cloud, Irvine perked and watched with great interest. Surely, they could see the thing—perhaps it appeared to them as dense fog, sudden but innocuous. They marched straight into the cloud without hesitation. Irvine's skin prickled.

He kept his eyes trained on the road leading out from the cloud, but the regiment never emerged. He watched and watched and recruited others to his cause, but the regiment was lost to the cloud. It had completely disappeared.

Then the cloud began to lift. It floated up until it joined the others higher up the hillside, and then they all departed, floating northward, moving for the very first time that morning. There was still no sign of the regiment, no trace of them left on the newly exposed ground.

When the war ended, the British inquired about their lost troops, demanding to know who had captured them so completely. But no account of the lost regiment ever surfaced—no one human encountered the First Fifth Norfolk again.

CHAPTER 21
A YEAR OF PLENTY

I AM NOT A PARTICULARLY good singer. I can hold a note, breathe in all the right spots, but I'm nothing special, nothing I do would stop you on the street. What made people listen was the provenance of my story, of the theatrics we implemented to distract from my nervous warbling. My mother, Sylvia, and I put together a show that was half decent, I had thought. With lights that shimmered and twisted around me, a few ominous words from Sylvia beforehand about a girl who summoned a star, and a black gown spangled with golden moons and stars, specially made at quite a price, I made a statement those voyeurs were unable to turn away from.

The dress was my favorite—it was so grown up and elegant, probably the first real adult piece of clothing I owned. It hugged my waist and flared away into a sparkling, poufy skirt that revealed delicate tulle when I spun. When I first saw myself in the dress, I suddenly understood the feeling brides get when they find the dress of their dreams—a resolute acceptance of the task to come, an acknowledgment of the body hereto unformed. *This is what I could look like*, I thought. *This is, somehow, me.*

I was nervous before the first show, felt close to vomiting. Sylvia offered me tea, lukewarm, and told me it'd help settle my stomach. But it didn't. It only filled it more, making it more likely to spill over. I hadn't sung since I'd killed Daddy.

"I can't do this," I said. We were in an unused conference room, and my words echoed off the hard table, empty surfaces.

"Of course you can," said Sylvia. "It's going to be much easier than what you've done before. No questions to answer, no reading to do. Just one song, that's it." Her own voice was sing-song sweet.

"But I'm not a good singer. They'll laugh at me. It's not the same as when I did it before," I said.

"Did what before, honey?" Sylvia had taken some knitting out of her bag and was fiddling with her needles.

"Sang," I said. "When I was, erm, abducted—they said it was good, that my voice was incredible. If I don't sing well now, it's like proof I didn't sing well then. It's like it never happened." I hadn't told Sylvia about the way my singing seemed to bend things, amplifying my wishes. So much hung upon those notes—the truth of my abduction, my power. To do it on command, to commercialize it, felt like a risk.

Sylvia placed the yarn and needles down on her lap. "Now that's not true."

"It is," I said, thinking back to the man who had stared down Daddy in a crowd so long ago, questioned him, my story. "There are so many people looking for cracks, for the untruths. They target the people like us."

"Maybe so," she said. "But these people are fans of yours. They've paid to be at a UFO convention, for one, and are paying extra to see you tonight. I doubt they're paying just to look for fault. These are dedicated people, I think. The true believers."

I jolted at her term—True Believer. Had I told her about Daddy's phrases, his categorization of the world? I wasn't so sure.

"Besides," she said. "You're a lovely singer. No one in their right mind is going to object to that."

I wasn't so sure but decided to keep quiet. I knew Sylvia wouldn't let me back down—the performance was already sold out—and as much as I loved her, I could only take so many of her platitudes when stressed.

Instead, I went to the mirror and tried my hand at applying the makeup my mother had given me. Waxy pencils, dark lipstick, a gray shimmery powder, all were mysteries to me. I thought of Bethany, trying to recall just how she had painted my face, and decided that perhaps she wasn't the best example to follow. I'd refer to it only as a cautionary tale. Lightly swiping the powder across my eyelids with a spongy brush, I was pleased to find I hadn't disfigured myself in the process. I traced the upper lid of my eye in black, doing my best not to press so hard. The effect was almost natural—a subtle thickening of the lashes. I decided to forgo the lipstick, fearing it would be the hardest of the cosmetics to control.

Stepping back from the little mirror we'd placed on the table, I admired myself in the gown, face newly done. I was proud of my work, my burgeoning body. At least I had that.

Sylvia clicked her tongue approvingly when I turned to face her. "Let's finish your hair. We don't have long to go."

I sat at her feet, and she wove my hair into an intricate braid.

"How did you learn to do hair so well?" I asked.

"When my girls were little, I used to do their hair all the time. They had such long hair, too. You have to get good with hair like that." She chuckled.

"Girls?" I said, my stomach tightening into a knot. "I thought you had a son."

"Oh?" Sylvia said. "No boys. Just two daughters, not unlike you."

I sat silent as she pulled and twisted at my hair. I could have sworn Sylvia had told me she had a son. But maybe I was wrong? But I could visualize the email, the words I read on the screen in the flickering darkness. Besides, the thought of other girls receiving her attention was almost unbearable. "How old are they?" I asked.

"Well let's see. I think thirty-six and forty now. Mothers of their own."

Grandchildren? I couldn't imagine sharing Sylvia with so many people. "Why haven't you mentioned them before?"

"Oh," she sighed. "They want nothing to do with me now."

"What? Why?" I refused to believe there were people who did not want to bask in Sylvia's warmth.

"It's a long story. But the gist of it is that they didn't like me coming to things like this, talking about my abduction. It scares them, I think."

My anger flared. "But it's important. We all have to tell our stories. Make sure the truth is heard."

Sylvia laughed. "It's an old issue now. No need to get upset. They'll come around someday."

"Don't you miss them?"

"Hmm," Sylvia said. "Of course I do. But I'm happy now. Aren't you happy, too?"

I realized I was. Despite everything, the doubt and the fear, losing Daddy, having to sing for money, I was the happiest I'd ever been. Sylvia gave me that. "I am," I said. "I'm ready now."

I walked into the convention room, head still buzzing with the conversation, and stood in front of the crowd. It was packed. Every chair was full, and those standing huddled together at the back. Someone snapped a picture, and the flash blinded me for a moment. Then the music came crackling over the speakers, and the lights we had built spun into action. I froze as the beam landed on me. I didn't realize I'd be so scared, immobilized. Yet somehow, though my body was rigid, and my arms pinned to my sides, my mouth still swung open, and I sang.

———

Afterward, they swarmed me. Their fingers grasped at the stray threads of my gown. They pushed and pulled me and cupped my face in their hands.

"Please," said a bent old lady who had forced her way to the front of the throng. "Tell them to come to me. Tell them to heal me, too."

I blinked. "What?" I asked.

"Cancer," she whispered.

Someone shoved her out of the way. "Is it true?" he asked. "That they gave you powers? Talents?"

"Of course she has powers," snapped a brunette. She lifted a bulky camera to her eye, and the flash blinded me.

I rubbed my eyes. How did they know? How could they know? I stood on my tiptoes, craning to see Sylvia over the mass. "Sylvia?" I called. But she was gone.

"I'm sorry," I said, elbowing my way through the crowd. "I need some air."

"But my baby," said a woman brandishing an infant.

I tried again to catch sight of Sylvia, of her white hair, but she wasn't in the room. My heart squeezed tight, and I wondered if she had missed my performance entirely.

A brochure was thrust into my hands along with a Sharpie marker. I wrote my name across the front—my own face and the words "The Girl who Sang Down a Star" obscured by my black scrawl.

"Here," I said, shoving the brochure into a man's chest.

"Wait," someone cried, but I was pushing my way out, stepping and tripping on toes.

"Sylvia!" I yelled. But she didn't come. The worshippers surrounded me.

Some want to be enveloped. Some want to be whisked away. The people in this story wanted neither.

The people came down from the sky, in groups of two or three, and shook the wonder from their bodies, stretched their limbs. "We have much to tell you," they said to the passerby. "Fantastic things."

Crowds formed; they did every time. It always went like this. First the people came down from the sky, then a crowd would form. The sky people would talk about such strange things—carts that move on their own, fires that came and went at the flip of a lever—and the townspeople had no choice but to kill them. The sky people were sorcerers, surely, sent to poison their crops and take their daughters. The townfolk would drown them and burn them alive, all the while the sky people screamed they were their own countrymen, having been taken and then returned. They simply wanted to tell them about the wondrous sights they'd seen, won't you listen? Won't you listen?

The townsfolk would snuff that talk right out.

But one morning a new batch of sky people came floating down, touched their feet upon the rutted road, and no sooner started talking of all the incredible sights they'd beheld when the crowd started forming, torches in hand.

"Shut up," scowled a woman. "We'll kill ye."

"Why!?" yelped one of the sky people. "I have just been taken on the most fantastic journey. The stars," he said. "They move. I've been among them and the people there are so—"

A gasp went up among the crowd. "That's wrong," said someone. "This man's crazed. Needs to be cut down."

A nod of ascent rippled across the group.

"It's true," said another. "And the things that make us sick—they're like tiny mites, breeding and eating and moving. It's not the smell at all that sickens us, but the—"

"That's not so," said a man in the crowd. "That's lies."

Three big men—one for each sky person—surrounded the dreaming trio and pulled their hands behind their backs. Someone passed them precisely cut ropes—they were always ready for more sky people.

They took them to the pyre—a place where the bones of those burned before still lay among the charred sticks and twigs. It smelled sweet, like a good hog roast. They bound the sky people to tall, scorched beams.

"It's all true," one shouted. "We were taken up and shown such things. Listen to us, please."

"And let you lot destroy our bounty? Starve us to death?" The bearers of torches inched nearer.

"Stop," cried the archbishop, having just exited the home of a sick child to see the crowd gathered round the charnel pit. "What's the meaning of this?"

"These sorcerers," said a woman. "Came down from the sky, started spreading filth about. Lies."

The archbishop prided himself on being not only a Godly man, but a most modern one at that. Sorcerers—that was talk from the olden days. Not the ones of God, but of a more feral, wild time. There was no place for that talk in Lyon today. "There are no sorcerers here," he said. "Or anywhere, for that matter."

"Yes, there are!" cried a man. "We just seen 'em come down from the sky. Explain that would you?"

"You did not see that," said the archbishop proudly. "That doesn't happen."

"Aye but it did."

"It did not," said the archbishop. "Such things do not happen under God's eye."

The people looked at each other uncomfortably, murmuring to themselves. They had seen it though, hadn't they? Hadn't they seen it?

"These are just men," said the archbishop. "Look at them." And he gestured at the trembling, bound trio. "There's nothing extraordinary about them at all."

So the townsfolk untied the sky people, set them free. And the sky people became just people, ripped clean of all that wonder. They shut their mouths, stopped telling their truth. They'd live, though disbelieved and whispered about for the rest of their days.

CHAPTER 22
HEALING

I REFUSED to learn any additional songs, refused to change my glorious dress, even when it got too short, but the show was successful all the same. People treated my miniature concerts like seances, eying the corners of the room as I sang, looking for apparitions, orbs of light. None ever came, but that didn't stop them from trying. It was said my voice had the power to heal, could bring down something from the sky. When my shows ended, they'd flock outside to stare up at the stars, to stare at me. I was no longer considered a shy little girl, but a mysterious, secret-laden fifteen-year-old.

A lady, holding both my hands in hers, had whispered, eyes shining, that I had a direct line to heaven. I wasn't sure about that, but I liked that she thought so.

I didn't deny their insistence upon my powers. I hadn't ever purged the cancer from someone's body, had never communed with God, but I had seen a red star moving across the sky. My Daddy lay dead in his grave. I began to enjoy it, to enjoy the throngs that gathered before and after every show. I became used to their persistent crush. The attention made me happy.

I also enjoyed the fights, I now admit. I'd pretend to act aghast; I'd scream and throw my hands into the fray in a hesitant attempt to push people apart, but really I wished it would never end. They were fighting over me. For the right to stand next to me, to lay their hands on mine and wish for something holy.

First, there would be the pushing, the shoving surge from the back of the crowd. And those in front would turn around, angered. And someone would shout and someone else would shout back, louder and crasser. It was the same every time.

But sometimes it went too far. Too far even for me, bloodthirsty as I was. There was the night in Cincinnati. Maybe you read about it in the paper.

I sang my song, changed out of my dress back into blue jeans and t-shirt, and stood near Sylvia's car, waiting for her to finish cleaning up the convention hall. As always, I was mobbed. I signed books and made vague promises to wish for the people's wellbeing. It was, at first, an extremely unremarkable crowd.

But then a woman, voice cutting through the murmuring adoration, called out, and I searched the crowd for her.

"I want my money back!" she yelled.

My face flushed, and the pen shook in my hand. "That's fine," I stammered. "I don't have the money on me. My manager, she has it. She's still inside." I titled my head toward the building, hoping the woman would wander off, become Sylvia's problem, but she just stared, unmoving. Her eyes, hard and glassy, were unblinking, boring into mine.

"I want my money back," she roared, pushing forward in the crowd. She stepped on toes and jabbed her sharp elbows into ribs.

A man held an arm up, barring her way. "Hey, now. Laura said you'd get your money inside."

Closer now, I could see the woman's lank blonde hair was unwashed, clumped together with grease. Spittle flecked her lips. I pressed my back against the car and tried the handle with my free hand. It was locked.

"Don't you touch me," she snapped. She pushed the man, and he stumbled backward, a look of surprise on his face. This woman was strong—stronger than her thin frame belied. And she was headed straight for me.

"I told you, I don't have it!" I squeaked. I was holding a book in my left hand, something I was meant to be signing, but now I wielded it as if it were a weapon. I'd smack her across the face with it if she got any closer. My body shook, my breath catching in my lungs.

The woman paused, looked me over. A smile played across her lips. "You're scared of me."

Someone in the crowd put a hand on her shoulder. "Come on. Leave her alone."

The smile dropped from the woman's face, and she spun about to confront whoever dared touch her. "No. I'm not going to leave. Not until I get my money."

"Lady, the money's inside," said someone.

"What's your problem, anyway?" asked another.

The woman's shoulders slumped and, for a moment, it looked like she might give in. "She's a sham," she said. "She scammed me out of my money."

"She did what you paid for. She sang, and now it's time to go," said the man who had tried to hold her back.

I scanned the crowd for an opening, a space I could run through.

"No!" the woman screeched. "Last time. Last show. In Dayton. I asked her to make a wish for me and—and it didn't come true!" Her voice, mangled with tears and accusation, was inhuman.

Last show—I tried to remember what I'd done then. It was two days prior, and nothing stood out to me. I had sat at a table, selling, and signing books and smiling for pictures. Then I sang to a sold-out room and, afterwards, held my usual court in the parking lot. I couldn't remember the woman and her straw-colored hair, but that didn't mean she hadn't come. I barely looked at the people who approached me, looked down on me with their tearful, hoping eyes. Shaking my head, I said, "I don't know what you're talking about."

"You liar! I asked you for a blessing and now my Gracie, she's dead. You lie! You promise what you can't do." She was crying openly now, and it took two men to hold her back.

An old woman stomped her foot and said, "That's not fair. That's not the way prayers work."

"How do they work, then?" spat the restrained woman. "You tell me how they work."

The mass was quiet. How did prayers work? I had never prayed to God, but I had wished for many things. I'd wished on shooting stars, I'd nursed dark secrets in my heart. I had sang—just a few faltering notes—and Daddy fell dead on the floor. Yet I had never wished for anything these people asked for. It simply wasn't worth my time. But maybe, I could do something now. I cleared my throat.

"Prayer," began the old lady. "Is a conversation, not a demand."

The madwoman shook her head. "And what are you going to wish for? Whatever it is, this little girl isn't going to save you." She was shouting again, her voice echoing in the otherwise empty lot.

I sang under my breath. I don't think anyone heard me. How could they, over the woman's ranting?

"I wasn't going to wish for a thing," said the old lady, oddly composed. "I was just going to tell her she did a great job, and be on my way. But you had to ruin our evening."

"It's idolatry, all of it," said another woman. Her face was thin and pock-marked. She was ugly.

"Then why are you here?" asked a man.

The madwoman laughed. "Do you think this little girl is God?"

"No one said that."

I sang a little louder, focused hard. I felt the wish deep in my chest, a squirming lump of a thing.

"I'll admit, I thought she was holy too," said the madwoman. "But then my Gracie died, and I realized this child is just playing at God. She's not God."

"Literally no one said she was God," said a teenaged girl.

"She's scamming you. She's nothing but a fake."

"Okay, it's time to go," said a man. He put his hands on the woman's shoulders, began steering her away.

"No," said the woman. She dug in her heels.

Please, I thought. I sang faster, willed the thing in my chest to burst.

"You're all fools. Blasphemous fools. When I die, if I die—"

"God wouldn't answer your prayers anyway," interrupted the old lady. Her voice was cold and steely, but her handbag was flying through the air, swung on a clean arc toward the madwoman's face.

It struck her square, and she raised her hands to her nose, shocked and slow. She opened her mouth to speak, but the old lady was swinging the bag again, this time with an awful scream.

At first, I smiled. At first, I couldn't believe my luck. I'd sung and now this lady would be swatted down, and I wouldn't have to lift a finger. But then the madwoman turned a horrid shade of crimson and, instead of rushing the old lady, set her sights on me.

"Why are you smiling?" she growled and lunged.

She caught the collar of my shirt and fell, pulled down by the crowd, dragging me down on top of her. I cried out, scared. I had dropped the book, my bludgeoning tool, and covered my face with my hands. The lady clawed at my fingers, tried to pry them apart. People screamed, shouted. Someone stepped on my foot.

"Come on," she said. "Let me see that pretty face."

She kneed me in the stomach, and I tried to scream, but there was no air in my lungs. I whimpered. I curled in on myself, protecting my soft core.

"Admit you're a liar," she hissed, so close to my ear I could feel her breath.

She grabbed my hair and pulled it hard. My hands left my face and reached up to untangle her fingers, but I instantly realized my mistake. She spat, a thick, mucusy gob, at my eye.

I was gagging when a man pried her away from me. He had his arms around her waist, and he lifted her. She reached down to me, hands desperately swinging.

I tried to wipe the spit away, but succeeded in only spreading it further.

Someone punched her in the head while she was still in the man's arms, and he let go, surprised. She fell to the floor like a dropped sheet, all folded and limp.

"Stop it!" screamed a girl.

The old lady kicked the madwoman in the ribs with the tip of her pointed shoe. She kicked again.

"I am NOT a blasphemer," she grunted as she kicked.

The old lady was pulled away, and I got a better view of the madwoman. She was unconscious, and a thin line of blood trickled from her nose.

"Come on," said a lady. She looped her arm through mine and pulled me to standing. I wobbled.

"I called the police," shouted a man. He was jogging from the convention hall, presumably having gone inside at the beginning of the fight to use the phone.

"Might need an ambulance," said another.

"Laura?" Sylvia's voice cut through the noise. She was coming as fast as she could, a slow-motion trot.

When at last she reached me, pulled my head to her chest, I began to cry.

"What in the world happened?" she asked.

I wondered that too. I had made a wish for the woman's destruction, and that had come to pass, but not before I was brought down as well. Hadn't I wished hard enough? Sang clear enough? Did gods stumble?

Sylvia ushered the people away, and they went quietly. When they were all gone, she tucked me gently into the car.

"It's alright now," she cooed. "You're alright."

When the shock wore off, I examined the scratches on my hands where the woman had tried to pry them away. They weren't so bad. My stomach didn't hurt anymore and my breath came easy. Sylvia was doting on me, treating me like a small child. She kept reaching over and petting my leg. "Poor thing," she sang. "Let's get you a special treat." And she pulled into a McDonalds. "An ice cream shake will fix you right up."

Maybe I had gotten exactly what I wanted.

Here's one about a miracle.

The doctor couldn't sleep. The aching in his leg was keeping him awake, and he hadn't slept well for a few nights now. He'd struck himself with the axe and now could feel his heartbeat there where he'd severed the vein.

He rolled over in bed, an awkward affair as he tried not to bump or jostle his injury or wake his wife.

There was a storm on the horizon. He could see the distant flashes through the gauzy curtains, could hear the low roll of thunder. It would be over the house soon, and he'd lose all chance of sleep then.

He sighed, pulling himself to sitting. Perhaps he'd go read in his office. At least then he could take his mind off the pain in his leg.

He'd no sooner placed his feet on the floor when the baby started screaming. "Shit," he whispered.

He hobbled down the hall. It was illuminated now by the flash of lightning. The storm had arrived much quicker than he thought. Maybe it'd depart just as fast.

In the nursery, the baby stood in its crib, screaming and red-faced.

"Hey, hey," the doctor soothed. "It's just a storm. See?"

He took the baby to the window, showed it the rain splattered against the pane.

After some time in his father's arms, the baby calmed and would allow the doctor to lay him back in the lonely crib.

"Atta boy," the doctor whispered. "See? Everything is okay."

When the baby shut its eyes again, the doctor limped back out into the hall. The rain had stopped, but the lightning remained, strange and rhythmic. He made his slow way to the front door, peered out the small window there.

There was something bright in the sky. A mass, shining and unmoving. His heart pounded in his chest, and his leg responded uncomfortably. He stumbled through the house, searching for the little notebook he carried whenever he left. He'd have ideas—bright streaks of insight that couldn't wait until he got back home. He needed his notebook now.

Finding it on an end table near the couch, he went as fast as he could back to the door—a strange gallop. When he flung open the door, he had to shield his eyes from what he saw there: two discs, high overhead, bound by a crackling ray of light.

He fumbled with the notebook, and the pen came sliding out of the spiral on top. It fell to the ground, and he felt for it in the damp grass.

He found the pen, straightened himself once more, and began sketching what hovered in the sky.

It was strange. The discs were identical and rotated, mirroring each other's slow turn. The charge between them pulsated, emitted great strobing flashes and a grinding, electrical sound.

They were dancing around each other, spinning up on their sides, glowing fiercely. They combined into one, a massive disc with a blinding beam underneath. It swung closer, sending the doctor faltering backward onto his bad leg. He screamed, and the notebook slipped between his hands.

He was scared, but not for himself. He thought of the baby in the crib and how it had cried out in the storm. Had there ever been a storm? He rattled with fear.

The disc tilted, aimed its white beam at the doctor. It washed over him, and he shielded his face, his eyes.

And then it was gone. He righted himself, and there was nothing in the sky, nothing crackling. The world was dark and quiet.

The doctor plucked the notebook from the ground and ran back through the house, pounded his way up the stairs. When he arrived at their room, his wife was sitting up in bed. "What is it?" she gasped.

"There were two discs," he said, pacing the floor. "They were bound together. Then they became one. I can't explain it. It was incredible."

"Wait," said the wife.

"It was horrible. It was so bright. I can't. I can't explain it." He waved the drawing in her face as he paced. "See?" he asked.

"Wait," she said again. "Stop."

The doctor stopped his parading.

"Can't you see? You're not limping," she said.

The color drained from his face. He stood on one leg, he kicked at the air. He put his leg up on the bed and pulled at his pants, exposing the bandage he'd wrapped around the wound. Fingers trembling, he unwound it. The skin there was unbroken, unscarred.

"What happened?" asked his wife.

"I—I don't know," he stammered. "It shined its light on me. I don't understand."

They both stared at his leg, unremarkable and pale.

"The healer has been healed," whispered his wife. She flopped over in bed, pulled the blanket up high over her head.

"You're going to sleep?" he asked, but she didn't respond.

He went back into the hall, down to the baby's room. He pulled the notebook from his pocket and began sketching the little form sleeping there.

CHAPTER 23
DECLASSIFY

THE NEW SHOW did well for another year. But as with the last iteration of my exhibitions, crowds began to dwindle. I sold fewer and fewer books. The lines for autographs got shorter and there were fewer people waiting for me behind the convention halls. There were fewer fights, fewer blessings. Everyone on Earth and beyond, it seemed, had already heard me sing and were satiated.

So, we had our few years of happiness—with Mom working and Sylvia taking me to shows, we did alright. There was always food on the table. But things faded, as they always seem to do in my life, until dinners grew scant, and my dress hung baggy on my frame.

Mom came home from work and returned to her seat in the kitchen where she smoked and fiddled with the skin on her hands, calloused now. Her eyes took on that faraway look; she was always somewhere else. Sometimes she cried, big silent tears that fell into her lap. I tried to stay in my room when she got this way—I hated how she looked when she cried.

"I think it's time you get a job," she said one evening as I picked through someone else's deflated cheeseburger. Mom had started bringing home leftovers from the restaurant, things left on people's plates, things left behind. I didn't like eating them and usually refused, but this time, the hunger won out.

"I have a job," I said, disliking where this conversation was heading. A job would take up so much of my time, would be inflexible to the demands of the road. And I was more dependent on Sylvia than ever—I couldn't let her go now.

"Do you?" she asked. "One that makes money?"

I shrugged. "I make more than I spend."

"But that's not enough."

I bristled. "Maybe you're not making enough. Maybe you need a better job," I said, immediately regretting it. I knew as well as anyone that there weren't any well-paying jobs in our neck of the woods; you could work at McDonald's, the gas station, the grocery store, the one bedraggled diner where my mother served and scraped at greasy tables twelve hours a day. There was nothing with any chance of promotion, of true sustainable income. It was a complaint I'd heard echoed by all the neighbors, most of whom had moved away to the next town over, one where there were factories and retail stores and people to frequent them. Our town was for the retired, the aimless, the burnt out.

Mom didn't respond right away. She rubbed a hand over her red-rimmed eyes. "You know I'm trying my hardest," she said at last.

"I know," I conceded.

"There's a man who's been calling here," she said.

"Oh?" I was curious despite my reluctance.

"He does a traveling show, a supernatural one. It sounds kind of neat."

"A supernatural show? What does that mean?"

"I'm not really sure," she said. "But he's very interested in your singing."

I blushed. "Did he come to a convention?"

Mom shook her head, then spoke fast. "He's coming next week with your contract to sign. You're going to work for him now. No more singing in half-empty conference rooms."

"Mom!" I shouted, my vision spinning into one black point. "I can't do this. I can't stop the conventions, I can't—"

She held up a hand. "You need to listen. There's one more thing."

I covered my ears, desperate not to hear whatever came next.

But I could still hear her sigh. "I knew this would go badly. There's one more thing, can you hear me? There's something else I need to tell you."

I growled, feral and low. I couldn't make my lips move.

"You are going to live with them, the performers, that is. They all travel together from city to city. It's the best way."

Now my stomach roiled with more than hunger, and I rushed from the room. I threw myself down on the floor in the hallway and pounded my fists until they were bashed and bruised. I screamed into the dusty carpet, screamed until my voice grew hoarse. Before I went away, I would ruin myself. I'd turn my song into a long, snarled croak.

I still get a tightness in my stomach, in the back of my throat, when I think about how I felt that night. I could feel the world ending. It was all crumbling beneath my feet.

———

This is less of a story than it is a demand.

There's a group of people in the United States fighting for something called Disclosure. They demand the government pull back the veil on its secret programs, declassify documents related to UFOs, and tell the American people the truth, whatever it may be.

Some say Disclosure will come in the form of a devastatingly large drop of documents and videos, while others believe it will occur more as a trickle: a few videos leaked here and there, a report or two, just enough to gauge reaction, deny if needed.

Disclosure may already be happening in the form of the latter scenario. In 2019, the United States government confirmed that three leaked videos taken from Navy cockpits in 2004 through 2015 do indeed feature "unidentified aerial phenomenon." You've probably seen them. They received special attention, played again and again across news segments and talk shows.

These videos, "GIMBAL" "FLIR," and "GOFAST" show angular, "Tic-Tac," and circular shapes performing strange maneuvers. They rotate in mid-air, fly against the wind, and dive into the sea. Debunkers insist the clips feature "space trash" and military technology, but when I watch them, hear the excitement in the pilots' voices, I know they are more than that.

We've already been given a spectacular gift in the form of these videos, but those seeking Disclosure want more. We want something definitive and real, something that will take the subject of UFOs from the realm of jokes and conspiracy theorists into something higher, more dignified. We want the truth. This has always been about the truth.

CHAPTER 24
VISITATION

I SPENT the week leading up to the strange man's visit sulking. I stayed in my room, refused to eat, wasting those meager scraps my mother had managed to pull together. I hated my mother for choosing this for me, for forcing me into it. I would have been happy doing conventions with Sylvia forever.

Sylvia—my heart ached with what I would be losing. She was my only friend, and those brief forays into the world together were the brightest moments of my life.

I sent her a long email, begging her, for the second time in our relationship, to please come get me, save me from this fate. As always, she was kind and sensible. She promised me she'd come see me when she could, wherever I may be, and that this was simply a new chapter in our friendship, and she always enjoyed starting a new chapter. I hurt all over.

It was spring, a promise of warmth in the air, and I considered running away again. I was older now and probably smarter, too. I would get farther this time. I would pack all the right things, dress properly. But the thought made me weary; I had so little energy from refusing to eat, and didn't even know where I would go. Every step I took exhausted me. Even pulling out a backpack made me want to take a nap. I was my own undoing in the end.

The man came on a Tuesday, a bright and sunny day that taunted me with its obliviousness. My mother had dressed in her finest work outfit, khakis and a polo, and frowned at me when I came into the kitchen that morning in my most tattered and faded pajamas.

"You're not wearing that," she said.

"I am," I snapped back.

She let her eyes roam my hole-strewn t-shirt, my stained and too-short plaid pants. The clothes hung billowing from my frame. "You can't," she said. "It's embarrassing."

I shrugged, poured myself a glass of water to keep the hunger at bay.

"Fine," she said. "Have it your way, but he knows what you're capable of. It doesn't matter." She busied herself with wiping down the table, the counters. Our house was the cleanest it had been in a long time. I hated that my mother was trying so hard to please this man, this greedy, tasteless man that would profit off a child.

I didn't brush my teeth or comb my hair and left the deodorant untouched on the bathroom counter. I wanted him to see what he was truly getting—an uncultivated mess. My truest self.

When the doorbell rang, I ran my tongue over my gritty teeth with something akin to pleasure.

My mother was already waiting by the door, eager to hand me away. "Mr. Robichek, welcome!" she chirped as the door swung open. A short, squat man with slicked back brown hair stood there, clutching a folder to his chest. He wore a crumpled suit and a tie. I laughed, he looked like he'd wanted so badly to look decent, and had failed. I couldn't wait to let him smell me.

"Mrs. Statley, hello," he said, extending a paw-like hand to my mother. "It's nice to meet you in person."

"It really is," she said, letting her own small hand disappear into his. "This is Laura," she said, gesturing toward my hunched form lurking just beyond the living room.

"Ah yes," he said, taking no notice of my appearance. "There's our star."

Mom stepped to the side, let the bearish man into the house. "She's, uh, having an off day. She's somewhat nervous."

"No need for that," he said. "This will be the most natural thing in the world for her. A simple extension of the show she's already doing."

Mom looked toward me expectantly, but I refused to meet her glance. "I'm sure she'll warm up," she said with a hint of uncertainty in her voice.

He shrugged. "Doesn't matter."

My skin prickled. What did he mean by that? How could it not matter? I went to my room and slammed the door, ashamed I'd even been in eyeshot of that man. I hated myself for being curious. I should have run, I thought. Should have carved into my skin with a knife, disfigured myself, cut out my vocal cords, punished them for selling me and profiting off my story.

"Laura?" Mom called from down the hall.

I curled onto my bed, pulling my knees to my chest. I wouldn't let that man look at me anymore.

I laid there fuming while they talked; bits and pieces of their conversation leaking through, and I bristled at the words I heard: "contract" "years" "expectation." They were selling me into servitude. I wished my mother had been the one bursting there on the kitchen floor, flailing in cold coffee, insides erupting into mush. I hated her. She would pay for this.

At last, I heard the front door swing open and allowed myself some optimism; I hadn't signed a thing. Perhaps my mother was displeased with the terms, had come around to my side at last and told the man to take his contract back to where he came from. My heart thundered.

But she came into my room smiling, waving a sheaf of papers. "It's all done," she said. "You have a job with the Twilight Revue."

"What? I didn't sign anything," I said, incredulous.

"Honey, you're a minor—your signature doesn't mean anything."

I thought of the thousands of autographs I'd signed over the years, all meaningless now, unable to do a thing to help me.

I groaned and rolled away from her, willing her to just let me be.

"You leave tomorrow," she snapped. "Start packing."

———

You've probably heard this one.

There's an area in the midst of the Appalachian Mountains called Flatwoods—it's called that because it's a flat wood, surrounded by the rolling hills of West Virginia. Compared to the small towns in the hills, it's an oasis of modernity. It's the site of one of the most notorious cryptid sightings in America.

It started with a light. Red and pulsing, the light streaked across the sky, startling Ed, Freddie, and Tommy as they played. They watched the thing rocket by and then crash on the hillside, light extinguished. "What was that?" asked Tommy.

"I don't know," said Ed, "But we'd better go get our mom."

The Mays boys—Ed and Freddie—ran home with Tommy Hyer trailing behind them, glancing occasionally up at the sky. Other boys joined them as they ran. They had seen the light too—they wanted to help. Someone's dog followed along, nipping at their heels and urging them on with short little barks.

After fetching the Mays boys' mother, the town trekked up the hillside, this ragtag band, some barefooted, some in their Sunday best. There was a National Guardsman among them, a seventeen-year-old named Gene, and he naturally took the lead. Tommy was glad. He didn't want to be first, not at all.

They climbed up the mountain, tripping on tree roots and slipping on dead leaves. Suddenly, Gene held out an arm, hushing them all. "See that?" he whispered. And they could—glowing eyes perched high in a tree.

But then Gene was screaming, falling backward into their troupe, scrambling desperately to get away from the thing that had taken a step toward them, revealing itself.

It was ten feet tall. Its body was blood-red while its face, moonlike and hissing, was emerald green and surrounded by an elaborate hood. It gleamed like enamel. The younger boys were screaming now too.

It glided toward them, hissing all the while, and Gene dropped his light. Now the only glow was from the creature's red eyes.

A mist enveloped them, pungent and toxic. They coughed and gagged as they ran, were nauseated for hours when they got home.

But now they celebrate the thing—there are museums and souvenirs to be had throughout the town. The Flatwoods Monster is commerce, a show, a novelty that "put them on the map," even though the townfolk said it was just the shadow of a barn owl, or the dying light of a meteor. They said the boys were lying, but gladly profited all the same.

FREAK

CHAPTER 25

A BURNING BUSH

MY HEAD BOUNCED against the window as we drove. The short man seemed to hit every pothole and imperfection in the road on purpose.

"God this road is bad," he said to no one.

It wasn't bad, I thought with offense. It was just that he didn't know how to drive the roads I'd grown up on, didn't know the right speed, the right angle to take on those bumps and curves.

Everything the man did was clumsy—from throwing my bag into the back and whacking his beige car in the process to his ham-fisted clutch on the steering wheel. I hated him almost as much as I hated my mother.

I had gone without much protest, much to my mother's surprise. In the end I just wanted to be away from her, away from the person who would sell another soul into slavery. She was worse than Daddy, I thought. Not only had she used me, she was weak. Daddy would have never caved into circumstance—he would have grabbed it and bent it and made it something new. I didn't shed a tear when the man's car rolled into the driveway. No hugs, no goodbyes. She was lucky I didn't sing her away like I had with Daddy. I wouldn't. Wouldn't waste my gift on her.

Mother had wept as I folded myself into the back of the man's car. I hadn't said a word to her since the day he came with the contract. I was glad she was crying. I wanted her to hurt. I vowed to never talk to her again.

I did not speak the entire drive. He tried, at first to make small talk. But he gave up when I did nothing but let my head flop against the window, ignoring his "So how long've you lived out here?"s and "I hear you like doing conventions."

Instead, I stared out the window and thought of ways to reach Sylvia. I tried telepathy at first, closing my eyes and thinking so hard my brain seemed to quake with the effort, but I didn't know if my message had been received or not. And it gave me a headache. I thought about stealing some money from this man, a little at a time, to buy a computer, but I didn't know if there'd be an internet connection where I was heading. I could try pay phones, but what if Sylvia wasn't home when I called? What then? My best bet was going to be letters, I figured, and had planned ahead, stashing a pad of paper, envelopes, and stamps into my bag. I was already composing a missive in my head: "Dear Sylvia, Please, get me out of this Hell."

At last, the man pulled into a Walmart parking lot and stopped the car. He swung around to look at me, one hairy arm on the passenger's side seat. "Okay, here's the bus. We're right on time. I have to give the car back at eight," he explained as if I cared.

I saw a field of semis, a giant, dilapidated RV, and a few camper vans speckling the blacktop. But nothing like the tour bus with bright lights, a banner along the side announcing the show, I'd envisioned.

The man had already climbed out of the car and was making his way toward the rusty RV.

I followed, but not before struggling with my bag and nearly falling to the pavement. I blushed, hoping the occupants of the RV, if there were any, hadn't seen me stumble.

The door of the RV swung open, and I climbed the mud-crusted stairs into the driver's cockpit. Two beaten brown chairs sagged before the controls; I inched past them and got a better view of the interior. It was a cavernous space—the biggest RV I'd ever seen. You could tell it had once been nice—it reminded me of something a country star would tour in—but now was a decaying mess. The entire vehicle smelled like stale cigarettes and corn chips. I wanted to gag.

"Here she is!" said the short man from the back of the bus.

I turned and found a group of people gawking at me, some with food still dangling from their mouths.

"Guys, this is Laura," he said. "Laura, I'd like you to meet Mike, Judith, and Warner. Everyone else must still be in the store."

A red-headed boy sat down his sub sandwich and offered me a mayonnaise-streaked hand. "I'm Warner," he said. "It's such a pleasure to finally meet you."

I reluctantly took his hand, wincing at the squidgy feel of the sauce.

He pulled back like he'd been burned and patted his pockets, leaving little streaks of mayonnaise there. A blank look spread across his face. "I lost my pen. I had a pen. For you to sign something with. If you would, I mean. I don't know," he said, growing quieter with every word.

"Uh, sure," I said.

A man with a lumpy, misshaped face flourished a pen and handed it to a grateful Warner. I assumed this was Mike. Drool trickled out of the corner of his mouth where it sagged, lopsided. His eyes were bloodshot and wet around the edges, as if he'd been crying. He was hard to look at, but I forced myself to make eye contact. "Hello," I said.

I signed the scrap of paper Warner gave me without glancing at it. There was someone else in the back. And, now that she'd allowed herself to be seen, I couldn't take my eyes off of her. She was stunning—long black hair, sharp cheekbones, and lips like a soft, damp heart, pursed around a cigarette. She didn't look up at me. She refused to meet my gaze.

"Err, that's Judith," said Warner. "And that's Mike," he said, gesturing at the drooling man. "Mike never talks much."

Okay, I thought. *But that doesn't explain Judith.* I turned toward the man who'd brought me to this place, looking for some sort of assistance in breaking the awkwardness that had fallen over the RV.

He coughed. "We love Walmart parking lots. You can stay overnight if you need to, and they don't make a fuss. And everyone can get out and get some grub."

Grub—the word put me in mind of fat, wriggling maggots. It made me sick.

"There are more of us inside," said Warner.

"Okay," I said, voice shaky. This wasn't the introduction I had imagined. But this wasn't the life I'd imagined either.

"I'm Robichek, by the way," the little man said. "Robert Robichek. But no one calls me that. I'm sure your mom told you that, though, and all about the show?"

"No," I said.

"Oh," said Robichek. He rubbed his face with a meaty hand. "Well, I'm the manager, as you probably guessed. Warner here handles fire." Warner waved and smiled. "Judith is our resident psychic, she's very good. And Mike, well he is an excellent musician. He plays all the accompanying music to everyone's acts." Mike brought his hands together in a silent clap punctuated with a small bow.

"Okay," I said.

"We can't wait to hear you sing. In person, I mean. I've heard recordings on the internet, of course, but in person? That must be something else," said Warner.

"I guess."

"She's phenomenal, guys. Really something else. Out of this world, as they say," Robichek laughed. I hated anyone who laughed at their own stupid jokes. "Well, I'm going to go take a leak. Oh yeah, that's another thing, Laura—try not to use the bus bathroom if you can help it. It really gets to stinking. And I hate emptying the damn thing."

I frowned, and Warner's face turned as red as his hair. "We stop a lot," he said. "Don't worry."

Judith strode past me, brushing my shoulder with her fragrant hair. I breathed her in, relishing the dark, earthy smell instead of the funk of the bus. She stomped down the RV steps and marched toward the store.

"Don't mind her," said Warner. "She's always like that."

"Mmm," said Mike.

"Okay," I said.

———

This is a story about disbelievers.

Lonnie was a cop. A damn good one too. He was chasing a speeding car up over the ridge when he saw the lights—bright white and scrambled in among the brush down in the arroyo. He called it in —"I think there's been a wreck. I'm going to check it out"—and gave up on his pursuit. The speeding car could get away for all he cared. If someone was hurt, that's what came first.

He had seen a fire in the sky shortly before, had heard a roar. He hoped the car hadn't exploded. His heart pounded as he approached.

At first, he thought it was an overturned white car, stranded like a shell-down turtle in the dry creek bed. But as he got closer, he found it was a completely round object, whitish aluminum, like an egg-shaped balloon. It hovered above the red dirt without making a sound. Two short people stood beside the craft. They wore white coveralls and Lonnie thought they might be kids, dressed alike and so small.

Lonnie was scared, he hated to admit it. But he'd never seen anything like it. Anything so—

And then it was burning, blasting an orange and blue flame out from the bottom. It rose with a roar.

Lonnie picked up his radio again. "Look out the window. At the sky," he said. "Can you see anything?"

But they couldn't. And Lonnie couldn't see anything anymore either. It was gone. "I still want someone out here," he said.

A bush burned bright against the mesa.

When his colleagues arrived, they kicked at the smoldering scrub grasses and didn't say much. What was there to say? They stood in silence for a long time, letting the smoke flow in lazy rivulets around their ankles.

Finally, Lonnie spoke. "There was writing on the craft. A symbol." He tried to describe it—an arrow housed in a bubble, a line below. He drew it in the dirt with the toe of his boot.

The men gathered round, looking down at the shape. "Could have been anything," said one.

"Something out of White Sands," said the other. "Some kind of test."

"The college is over yonder. Some kids messing with you," said the first.

Lonnie shook his head. He knew what he saw.

CHAPTER 26
LETTERS HOME

THE FIRST NIGHT was the hardest. It seemed like the entire world had climbed onto the RV, claimed stake to whatever chair, bed, inch of free space they could. After awkward introductions, more signings, and much crinkling of snack bags, people settled down into their spots and did not move.

The bus rocked into motion, and I felt a hollow feeling in my stomach—I was floating away from everything I'd ever known. Sylvia, my mother, Daddy's shiny granite headstone. I could feel it all receding, getting lost in the black haze that pressed against the bus windows. I wanted to cry, but nothing came.

Silence enveloped the RV, some people dozing off, and I wedged myself beneath the table with a pen and piece of paper. The first letter I wrote to Sylvia was messy from the darkness and bumps we hit. I read it so many times, lips silently forming each word. I wanted it to be perfect. I wanted it to work.

Dear Sylvia,

I am writing from beneath a table on a rundown RV packed with circus freaks. I guess it would sound funny if it wasn't so dire. Please do whatever you can to get me out of here. I don't care what it is; I'll even go back home to Mom. Please.

There are eight or nine other performers here. I can't tell for sure if everyone I've met is actually a performer or not—I can't imagine that all the people here have talents. Some can't even talk. I know for certain there's a psychic, a musician, a sword swallower, and a guy who thinks he's time traveled. I don't know why he's here. I don't think he knows.

Everyone here is so strange. They wanted autographs but now no one is even talking to me. It's like I was just thrust onto this bus, and we set off. I don't even know what city we're passing through—I can only see the lights reflecting off the chair legs. I don't know who to ask about the show, or what I'm expected to do, or even when the first one is. I guess the manager would be a good start, but I can't handle the smell of his breath when he talks. So I guess I will just sit here, staring at the floor, and wait for something to happen.

I hate feeling like this. Do you ever feel this way? Totally at mercy to something with no control at all? At the same time, I feel like a nuisance to these people, even though they're completely ignoring me. I'm the clueless new recruit, bumbling and getting in the way, sitting under the table when you're trying to eat your gas station sub. It's all so different from I thought it'd be. Everyone is either cramming food into their mouths or snoring, paying no regard to the scared girl beneath the table. Maybe they don't want me here? Maybe this is my real abduction story. If so, it's a lackluster one. Boring, beige, stinking.

I would give anything to be back with you at a convention, singing and signing books and drinking tea. I miss you so much.

Please try to find a way to write back. Don't go through Mom if you can help it—I'll never talk to her again if she doesn't take me back. She didn't even try to get me into a good show; she sold me to the first one that knocked on the door. I can tell they don't make much money—the RV is a total piece of crap, and everyone looks like they haven't showered in years. Please help me.

Yours, Laura.

I slid the letter back into my bag to await a chance at being mailed. I couldn't see to write much more, anyway. I tried to be quiet, unzipping the bag slowly and folding the note so it didn't crinkle as I tucked it between my underwear and shirts, but bodies stirred all around me as I fidgeted and moved.

Where was I supposed to sleep? I supposed the spot beneath the table was as good as any. There were people on the couches, chairs, three crammed into the little bed in the back and another that hung out over the driver's seat. Someone slept curled in the aisle, a lump to be tripped over.

Robichek was the only one not sleeping—he was driving now, tapping his fingers on the wheel, and grunting occasionally. The empty seat next to him looked awfully good, but I didn't want to be near him, especially in that vulnerable state of sleep. Besides, there had to be a reason no one else wanted the spot.

So, I wrapped myself around the pole of the table drilled into the floor and listened to the humming of wheels on pavement. I whispered Sylvia's address, her phone number, and full name in my mind. I would not let these things escape me. I said them again and again, these magic words. I said them until I fell asleep.

———

Here's one about a rock band.

Airmen in World War II were not immune from the

Phenomenon. Fiery balls flew above the battlefields, taunted the men's planes, almost seemed to play with them. You couldn't outmaneuver a foo fighter—everyone knew that.

Some twinkled like Christmas lights and others crackled like ball lightning. Some flew in formation, while others came alone. It was common to see them, and the Americans assumed they were secret German weapons. But the Germans and the Japanese were seeing them too—were being trailed by these strange lights. There would be many attempts at explanations—St. Elmo's Fire discharged by the planes, refractions from ice crystals, an actual secret weapon deployed by the Germans—but the pilots would insist what they saw was something more than that, something extraordinary.

Senator Ted Stevens was a U.S. Air Force fighter pilot during the war. While flying over Europe, he encountered one such foo fighter. He recounted his experience to Senator Harry Reid stating, "I was flying, and there was an object next to me. I couldn't get rid of it, I slowed up, it was there. I sped up, it was there. I would dive, it would be there. I called. Nothing on radar."

Harry Reid carried Stevens' statement with him for the rest of his life. He became one of the most enthusiastic proponents of UFO disclosure in Congress, creating a secret program allotted $22 million. The program was cancelled in 2012, but the head of the program, Luis Elizondo, is still fighting for disclosure. Strangely enough, Elizondo teamed up with Tom DeLonge of pop punk band Blink-182 to help spread the need for UFO transparency. Another band, Foo Fighters, took on the special term for their name. These rockstars are just like us, intrigued and wondering.

CHAPTER 27
LIGHT

WE DROVE for a whole day after that, stopping at increasingly rural Walmarts along the way. Mom had passed me a little spending money, but the thought of eating made me sick, so I just wandered through the store. I trailed my fingers along all the boring, domestic things normal people would buy—the irons, the bed sheets, the fake flowers—pretending I had a home to take them back to. Warner followed behind me, attempting to make small talk as I studied the rows of pillows and vacuum cleaners.

"So, are you excited to watch the show tomorrow night?" he asked.

"Mm-hmm," I said, hoping my nonchalant murmur wouldn't betray my cluelessness. I had hidden beneath the table for the majority of the trip so far, refusing to acknowledge the rare person who stooped down low to talk to me, to check if I was alright.

Robichek ignored me entirely. I had no idea when the first show would be, or anything of my role in it. But Warner had said "watch"—that meant I probably wouldn't have to perform right away. I was relieved, yet also a bit dismayed. The money in my pocket wasn't enough for the escape I planned to make.

"I handle fire," he said.

"That's nice." Robichek had already told me this the first night on the bus, but I didn't care enough to correct him.

His face turned red. "It's no big deal."

We walked in silence toward the cash registers.

"I'm really looking forward to seeing your act," he said.

"Thanks," I replied.

"I bet it's amazing in person. Hey, you don't say much, do you?"

Now it was my turn to blush. "I'm just a little..."

"Overwhelmed?" asked Warner.

"Yes," I said. "I guess. I just—I don't want to be here."

Warner's eyebrows raised. "Well, nobody really *wants* to be here. I certainly don't. But I need the money. I don't have much choice," he said.

"At least you have any choice at all," I snapped.

He stopped walking, held his snack cake up as if it were a shield between us. "Hey, now," he said, his voice calm and low. "Don't get mad at *me*."

I studied his pale face, the spattering of freckles across the bridge of his nose. It was the first time I'd really looked at him. He wasn't bad looking and couldn't have been much older than me. "Sorry," I said.

"All's forgiven," he said. "Can't hold grudges on the bus." He continued on toward the exit. "But what did you mean by all that?"

Now I was the one trailing behind. I shrugged even though he couldn't see me. I wasn't sure I wanted to give that part of myself away yet, especially to a stranger like Warner. Instead, I said, "So what's the deal with the toilet?"

"On the bus?" He laughed, a surprising sound, much higher

pitched than his voice. "Robichek's lazy, is all. He doesn't want to stop to clean it out. Don't worry though; we stop often enough and if, you know, really need to uh—"

I smiled for the first time in days. I enjoyed making him uncomfortable.

"Just say something, and he'll stop. At least I think he will. I don't know. I keep my distance from the guy myself."

"Why's that?" I asked. I wasn't a fan of him either, but I was interested to know what someone who had willingly gone along with the show might think of the man. It could be valuable information.

Warner sighed. "He just creeps me out. I don't know. He's just lazy. Lazy as hell. We mostly run the shows on our own. We set up, tear down, do it all. Robichek drives, takes tickets, advertises, things like that. But honestly I think we could do without him."

Then why do they have him, I wanted to ask, but we were interrupted.

"You two look like you're getting along," said a woman whose name I had already forgotten. She had short dirty blonde hair that fell shapelessly around her head. It was the kind of hairstyle that results from trying to grow out an even shorter cut. Her eyes were big and brown and sparkled in the fluorescent lighting.

The woman had been raised by wolves, I knew. Despite my predicament, I was curious to know how she'd work that into an act. But I was also wary of her—her sudden, barking laugh, the way she'd snuck up on us.

She'd come up behind us so silently I worried she had heard us talking about Robichek; I hoped she wouldn't tell him. That was all I needed—the manager upset with me. I already had so much to contend with, I didn't think I could handle much more.

Warner shrugged. "We were just talking about her act."

"Oh yeah," she said. "I can't wait to see that. I heard Mike practicing your music. No more recordings for you."

I blushed. "I don't even know what song I'm supposed to be singing."

"Hmm," she said. "Maybe you should talk to Mike about that."

"Mike?" I asked. "Does he—Does he talk?" I thought about the lumpy faced man I'd met on the bus the first night and the drool swinging from his lip. He hadn't said an actual word the whole time I'd been on the bus—only grunts and moans.

"Sometimes," said Warner. "Mostly he writes out what he needs to say."

"He's a real sweetheart. Don't let that face of his bother you," said the wolf woman.

I ran a hand over my sweating neck. The wolf woman talked so frankly—I was embarrassed to even be in her presence. "His face," I ventured. "What happened to it?"

"One of the world's first face transplants, Mike is," she said. "That's a dead man's face you're looking at."

"Oh," I said, mortified.

Warner coughed self-consciously. "A dog attacked him a long time ago. Almost died."

"They did a really good job," I lied.

"I think he was provoking them dogs, is what I think," she said.

"He's a talented pianist," said Warner, changing the subject.

"Hey," she began. "You know I play a little piano. I taught myself. I'm not as good as Mike, but I—"

"Susanna," Warner said. "We gotta get back to the bus. See you there?"

"Yeah sure," she said. "I just gotta buy something to drink—my mouth is dry as all get out."

"Wonder why," Warner said under his breath, his hand miming a talking mouth as she wandered away, muttering under her breath.

I laughed, surprising myself. That morning, it had felt like I'd never laugh again. Yet here I was. But I didn't deserve to feel anything but dread—not until I'd escaped. I thought of losing Sylvia, of the atrocities my mother had committed. I exhaled, letting the smile drop off my face.

"Do you know why I'm here?" I said, more of a statement than a question.

Warner frowned. "Uh, because you can sing? Because you were abducted? Because you can summon aliens and make things happen?"

I paused for a moment. What *things* had Warner heard about? I thought of the babies that had been shoved in my face, of the fights and the woman who spat in my eye. I thought of Daddy.

"No," I said. "I was sold."

He stared at me, unmoving.

"My mother, she couldn't afford me anymore, so she sold me to Robichek. She got rid of me. She hates me. She—"

"Hey, hey," Warner cooed. "It'll be alright."

"It won't," I spat.

"Okay," he said. "It won't."

I stared at him, unsure of what to say. I was embarrassed by my outburst, my honesty, and confused by his agreeance.

"Let's go back," he said and waved me on with his free hand.

I shuffled along beside him, lost in my thoughts.

———

It transforms. It keeps coming back. Roberto's story is subtle, but frightening in its implications.

There was something in the sky above Santa Anastasia church. The silver glare of it was almost blinding—Roberto shielded his eyes though it was night. "What is it?" he asked his mother.

"A disc," she said, matter of fact.

They watched it dip and dive about the spire. It was playful, Roberto thought. It looked like it was dancing.

They went home and went to bed, but it was hard for Roberto to sleep. Images of the dancing disc kept flashing through his mind. He had to know what it was. The room felt cold—colder than it had been a few minutes before, and Roberto pulled the covers up to his neck.

Then he saw the glow—a greenish light pulsating slowly near the door. An orb. Roberto shivered, turned away from the thing. He wouldn't look at it.

But now he was facing the window. There, he could see the big old tree that always scratched and scraped against the pane, the subtle sliver of the moon, and a body, big-headed and semi-transparent, staring in at him.

Roberto screamed.

His mother and sister burst into his room. "What is it?" they gasped. They had come so quickly Roberto knew they hadn't slept either.

"There," he said, and the body blinked out like a light.

Roberto didn't sleep for three nights. Every time he shut his eyes, he saw the silhouette in the window, vague yet imposing. When he at last collapsed from exhaustion, he had twisted, confused dreams.

MIKE WAS SITTING SIDEWAYS on a little couch that folded out into a bed. He stared out the window, drooling quietly. I was afraid to interrupt him, so intently he watched the landscape slip by. But I was beginning to feel anxious about the coming show and my place in it. I wasn't eager to perform, but I didn't want to be thrust upon the stage with no guidance. I don't like being made a fool.

"Mike?" I asked.

"Uh," he started.

"Um, I wanted to talk about my act."

He nodded, scooted to the side, and patted the spot. I reluctantly sat down beside him.

"Ughn," he said and shifted on his seat. He pulled a small paper pad out from his back pocket.

Up close, I could see the skin that hung from his face formed a type of mask. The flesh around his eyes was a different hue than the skin dangling from his buried cheekbones. His eyes themselves looked quick and sharp. They were comforting, amid all that looseness.

"I don't know what I'm singing," I said. "Or anything about it at all."

He nodded and flipped open his tiny book. A pen fell out from between the pages. "I was told we were doing 'Ave Maria.' Do you know that one?" he wrote.

"No," I said. "I only really ever performed one song. Don't even know the name of it. We had a CD." I spoke quietly, hoping no one could overhear that I was utterly clueless.

"Don't worry," he wrote, handwriting oddly neat for all the jostling of the bus. "We'll find you a recording."

"Thank you so much," I said. "I have no clue what I'm doing."

He drew a small smiley face in return.

"Everyone says you're a great musician," I offered.

He made the mouth on the smiley a little bit bigger.

His own mouth hung open, letting a drop of spit fall against the page. Mike didn't seem to pay it any mind. He shut the book and stuffed it back in his pocket. "Mmm," he said.

"Yes," I agreed.

"Why doesn't he talk much?" I whispered to Warner that night as everyone slept.

"Mike?" he asked. "I'm not totally sure but I think he doesn't have good control of his lips. It makes it hard for him. Sometimes he gets out a word or two, but mostly he writes what he has to say."

I thought about the drool dripping from his mouth. "Can't anyone help him? Surgery, or something?"

I felt Warner shrug in the dark. "I think he's done with all that," he whispered. "He told me once that his old life was of no interest to him. I think he's been really hurt."

"Huh," I said. I understood that feeling—that desire to slip away from all that weighed you down. Maybe I too needed a new face, one that wasn't on the back of books, front pages of newspapers, and plastered across the newest internet phenomenon, blogs.

"He was a good-looking guy," Warner said. "Susanna showed me his picture once."

"You talking about me?" Susanna snapped from some dark crevice within the RV.

"No, Suze," Warner said.

"Shh," someone hissed.

"She's got ears like a wolf, too," I said mid-thought.

"She does," said someone else within the darkness.

I wanted to write another letter to Sylvia, to curl beneath the table with a flashlight, and tell her all I had learned about the circus freaks. I had begun to find a strange comfort in that cramped space— it was where I communed with Sylvia, conjured up some small scrap of hope. But I could feel eyes on me, and what I wanted to do was private, secret. So I shut my eyes. I began the familiar litany: Sylvia's full name, her address, her phone number; I let it parade through my mind.

I drifted off to sleep sitting upright on a bench, Warner on one side of me and a Bigfoot researcher on the other.

———

There had been a sound—an awful thump and the screeching of tires. I awoke with a start. I pitched sideways and sprawled across the Bigfoot researcher's lap.

"What the hell?" someone gasped.

"Are you okay?" asked Warner, helping to pull me to my feet.

"What happened?" asked Susanna. "Why are we stopped?"

"Hit something," said Robichek, still staring out the bug-streaked windshield.

"What? What was it?"

"Dunno," said Robichek. The bus groaned and began to creep forward.

Susanna strode to the front where Robichek sat. "You're just going to drive off?" she said to the top of his greasy head. "Just leave whatever it is? What if it's someone's pet, someone's dog, and you're just going to leave it, suffering?"

Robichek said, "It was bigger than a dog."

A prickling spread across the back of my neck. The bus was quiet now, still.

"Someone has to go look," said a man at last.

I stared into the impenetrable dark outside the bus. It'd be easy to get lost out there, to disappear. "I'll go," I said.

"What?" Warner gasped.

In truth I was scared. Scared of the night, of the thing we'd hit, of the black, vacuous sky and whatever hovered there, waiting to take me. But I had to get to Sylvia. Nothing else mattered.

I felt all of their eyes on me, sizing me up. Judith scoffed from the back of the bus.

"You can't go," said Susanna. "It might be gory. It might be bad."

I pushed past Susanna and laid my hand on the door latch. Before I had the chance to pull it, someone grabbed my arm, and I wheeled around. "I'm coming too," said the Bigfoot guy, his sleep-mussed brown hair flopping into his eyes. "I hunt. I dress my own kills. You won't be able to handle it."

"No one's going out there," said Robichek.

"Let me go," I said, pulling out of his grasp. "I'm not a little girl."

"For Christ's sake," said Robichek. "Everybody just sit down!"

Ignoring him, disobeying him, I leaned against the door and spilled out into the night. I tumbled down the steps, landing hard on my knees.

I stood, and the smell hit me. I can still taste it. Thick and suffocating. Iron mixed with something earthy, something sour. Blood and shit.

I gagged.

"Told you," said the Bigfoot hunter. He descended the steps and stood next to me on the berm. "You should go back in."

"No," I said. I knew I wouldn't be able to run, not with the Bigfoot guy hovering over me, but I had to see this through. I had to prove to them, to myself, that I could do it. That I could do anything, no matter the gore, the smell. "I'm not afraid of death."

"Uhh," said the Bigfoot hunter. "Okay then." He walked away, to the front of the bus. Unceremonious, unafraid.

I tried to replicate his indifferent gait, but my legs trembled. I rounded the corner of the bus, and the glare of the headlights blinded me. The smell was unbearable here, overwhelming.

"It's a doe," he said.

I held a hand up to block the light of the high beams. A broken body lay before the bus, casting a long dark smudge of shadow on the road. The deer's neck was bent so that its head rested on its back, and its open eyes were dark, gleaming. Delicate eyelashes glowed in the headlights. "Is she dead?" I asked.

"Yep," said the Bigfoot man.

I blinked back sudden tears. "Are you sure?" I asked, kneeling next to the doe. Robichek had killed her, this beautiful, graceful thing. One minute she was running wild, and the next, a big, stinking RV driven by a big, stinking man had plowed into her. It incensed me, this intrusion into nature, this brutish violence. I hated Robichek with everything in me.

Up close, I could see the blood trickling from her nose, her mouth. Though bloodied and bent, I shut my eyes and wished for the doe to live. I felt for that place inside of me where my desires lived and sang under my breath. But this was a pleading song. *Please*, I thought. *Please don't die*. I repeated it in my head until my brain vibrated. It was working, I thought.

I reached out to touch her, to strengthen the wish, but the Bigfoot man interrupted. "I don't think that's such a good idea."

"Why not?" I drew my hand back. He had broken the spell.

"It could have fleas. And it's just weird," said the man. "If the buzzards and coyotes don't get her first, the state will move her off the road. Come on, now." His voice was gentle, plying.

"What's your name again?" I asked, prying my eyes away from the deer.

"Arnold," he said and stuck out his hand. Joined, in that moment, he pulled me back onto the bus.

———

Here's one about the cruelty of humans. Of children.

It was 1972 and Michio was walking home from school. He passed a rice paddy; the plants were knee high and a luscious green. He looked at the sky reflected on the water between the rows and felt happy—school was out and the sky was blue, is there anything better?

A bat darted to and fro above the field. How strange it was to see a bat this time of day—it was almost lucky. Michio squinted at the thing and caught a glint of silver. It was metallic! Coming closer, he saw it was no bat, but instead a small disc—the size and shape of a hat. It continued its frenzied dance above the paddy.

He waded out into the paddy, soaking his pants through. He'd catch the thing, he decided. His friends would be so surprised.

But as he approached, the disc tilted into the sun, shot a bright beam at his eyes, and blinded him for a moment. Michio stumbled backwards, pressed his fingers into his eyes until the brightness went away, and he could see.

Then he ran. He ran all the way to the old meetup spot, and there he found his friends sharing a stolen cigarette. "There's something in the field," he told them.

"Yeah, rice," said one.

A mean-spirited chuckle rose among the boys.

"No, a flying saucer. I swear it," said Michio.

"Let's see then," they said, and pulled themselves to standing.

When they got back to the field, Michio felt a dipping sensation in his stomach—the thing was gone.

"Told you so," said one of the boys.

"You're full of shit, Michio."

"Look!" cried Michio, and the boys' mouths hung open.

The disc had returned, swooping up over the horizon and beginning its chaotic survey of the field once more.

They watched it dance for what felt like hours—the sun slunk down, and the world turned dark. The silver glow of the thing was gone, but now it pulsated with a rainbow of colors. Michio was glad they had stayed.

"Yuji, go touch it," said someone.

"No way, you go touch it. I'm not getting near the thing," he said.

"Michio should touch it. He's the one who brought us here."

"Michio's pants are already wet. He should go."

Michio couldn't argue with this logic. He rolled up his shirt sleeves and waded back out into the paddy.

Once again, he approached the disc, this time unafraid of the bright glare. After all, there was no sun now to blind him.

When he got within a few feet, it stopped. Michio stopped too. The thing hovered there in silence, rotating slowly. Then it turned a fierce blue. It lit up the countryside with its glow.

CLICK—a sudden sound like breaking, or a revolver being cocked echoed through the valley.

"Run, Michio!"

And so, they ran together, all the way back home.

But they couldn't stay away. Every night they'd visit the field, looking for the small disc. Some nights it was there, spinning and dancing above the paddy, and some nights the sky above the field stayed dark.

Once they came with a camera stolen from one of their parents. This would be the night, they decided. They'd get proof.

But before they could even get to the rice paddy, they found the thing laying on the ground in the middle of the lane.

"What's wrong with it?" whispered one.

"Maybe it's broken," said another.

Yuji raised the camera to his eye, took a picture of the disc laying there in the dirt. The flash sparked the thing back to life, and it began to whirr and spin and lifted off the ground.

It flashed, even brighter than the camera, then fell back to the earth. It spun sadly, digging into the ground with every rotation.

"I think it's dying," said one.

One of the boys pulled a plastic bag from his sack. "Put it in here," he said.

"Are you crazy?" asked another.

"What's better than a photograph than the actual thing?" he asked.

So, Hiroshi stepped forward, grabbed the thing with his bare hands.

"There's something moving inside!" he squealed.

"Quick, put it in the bag!"

They wrapped it carefully and took it home.

They studied it together—31 small holes poked in the bottom, a strange pictograph drawn on it, of a bird or a cloud or something flying, and a lid that wouldn't open. It was heavy—heavier than it looked. They took turns passing it around, each boy swinging it up and down. "We should take this to my father," said one of the boys.

His father was director of the Center for Scientific Education in Kōchi City—he was the perfect man for the job, they thought.

But when they presented the disc to the old man, he simply turned it over in his hands a few times. "It looks like an ashtray," he said.

"But it flew!" they cried.

"I'm sure it did," said the father, handing the object back to one of the boys.

It went back into the sack, back to one of the boy's bedrooms to await further analyzation. But the next morning when he went to check on it, it was gone.

They returned to the field once more, this time with hammers and buckets and wires and rope. They wouldn't let it get away.

"Have you noticed it never comes when it rains?" asked one.

"It's afraid of water," said another.

They eyed the bucket.

Sure enough, it came flitting over the horizon to meet them.

"Now," said one.

And they flung a towel over the thing, dumped water on it until it stopped spinning. They beat it with hammers, poked wires in its many holes, and pried at the thing until the top opened slightly. Inside were wires, cryptic drawings, and a strange liquid.

"Let's take it home and put it in the oven," said one.

So, they kept the thing a few more days, subjecting it to all kinds of horrors only little boys are capable of, until one night, just as before, it went away.

They returned to the rice paddy often, but they never saw it again.

CHAPTER 29
A SHOW

THE FIRST SHOW came in an anticlimactic jumble of boxes and wires. We arrived at the theater in the early afternoon and immediately started unloading. I stood on the outskirts of the activity, not wanting to help and also not wanting to get in the way, but every once in a while, someone would hand me a small box or bag, and I'd heave it into the pile with all the others.

I watched as the performers built the scaffolding for the lights, arranged the smoke machines, set up Mike's keyboard on a small pedestal in the mid-back of the stage. I tried to study where everything went in case someone tasked me with helping next time, but it was all so intricate; I would probably just get in the way.

At last, the sky darkened, and people began lining up beneath the old marquee, *Twilight Revue* spelled out there in faded plastic letters.

I was alone, wandering down the sidewalk. I could have just kept on walking, gotten lost in the city, but something held me back. There was fear—I'd never been alone in a city this big before—but also a nagging question. I had to know what my mother had sold me to. I had to see the show.

I would wait until I had more money to run, I decided.

I watched the people waiting to get into the theater—wrapped around the block in a line so long it nearly doubled back on itself—trying to figure out what type of being would come to a show like this. They seemed normal, whatever normal means, with their shiny shoes and economical handbags. They were the type of people who, if asked to describe them later, you'd just draw some generic approximation of a smiling face, blank and staring. There were few children, but those that I saw seemed quiet, well-behaved.

Beneath the ruse of curiosity, I scanned the crowd for Sylvia, hoping beyond hope she had traveled all this way to rescue me. It could all be over before it truly began. I'd never have to sing again. But she wasn't there, wasn't waiting for me.

When I tired of disappointment and people watching, I slipped through the theater's back door and found most of the performers gathered together in a huddle, Robichek in the middle.

"Everything as usual tonight, folks," he said. "Laura's not going on until next show, so same order, same calls. Any questions?"

The group stayed quiet but for the click of Judith's lighter.

"Okay, great," Robichek said and turned away from the group, unceremoniously waddled down some dimly lit hallway.

"You better go grab a seat," Warner said, suddenly beside me. "I think this one is going to fill up fast."

"Good idea," I said. "Thanks."

Warner pushed a hand through his auburn hair.

"Uh, break a leg?" I said.

"Thank you, I will," he smiled.

I could feel my face burning; I was always so unsure of what to say. It all sounded stupid coming out of my mouth. Everything I did betrayed how inadequate, how sheltered I was, and it didn't help to be surrounded by all these adults. Did people really say "break a leg?" I hadn't a clue. I missed Sylvia. I never felt awkward around her.

Pushing through layer after layer of swinging doors, I found myself in the empty theater, cavernous and velvet. I sat down in the middle of the front row and waited for the show to begin.

The seats filled around me and a muffled din rose to meet the chandelier with coughs and whispers and squeaking shoes. My stomach pitched—next time it would be me commanding all those voices to be silent. I wasn't sure if I could do it. I turned and squinted into the dark rows of seats; there had to be at least triple the people there than ever came to my convention shows.

The lights darkened, and a single beam shone down on the stage, revealing the time traveling man wearing a satiny suit that shone in the light. I hadn't seen him walk onstage—I wondered if he'd materialized there or had been lurking in the artificial smoke. I tried desperately to remember his name—Mark? Marvin? Something with an M, I was sure.

"Ladies and gentleman," he said, voice thundering over the valley of people. "I am from the future."

A giggle erupted from the back, and my face flushed.

"I have seen wars, plagues, cities washed away by the sea—nightmares unimaginable. But I also have seen joys, triumphs of the human spirit. And tonight, you shall witness one such triumph. It will astound you, confound you. I should know—I've already seen it."

Polite laughter sparked about the hall.

"I present to you the Twilight Revue."

Muffled applause ushered him off stage, and now I could see Mike dimly lit, seated at his keyboard. A small gasp echoed through the crowd when the light hit his face, and I squeezed my hands together in anxiety; could they see his misshapen face so clearly all the way in the back? It wasn't fair, I thought, all these people staring and pointing at something he had no control over. He played a baleful chord.

First came Susanna, the wolf woman. She stalked around the stage on all fours to sparse laughter. She snarled and snapped at the crowd, teeth rattling together with every bite. The laughter faded into something more nervous—some coughing, the sound of clothing being adjusted. At last, when the awkwardness seemed like too much to bear, she pulled herself upright and took to the microphone. "I was raised by wolves," she said. "They treated me like one of their own."

She howled, and Mike played a few notes to match. "The instincts never left me," she said. "I have razor sharp vision, a sense of smell so keen I can tell you, there," she gestured toward a man to my left, "You had pastrami for lunch. I smell it on your teeth."

"Is it true?" squawked a woman somewhere behind me.

The man nodded, face red.

"Stand up and tell them," said Susanna.

And the man stood, still nodding. The crowd murmured their approval, clapped.

Susanna went back to prowling on her hands, occasionally sniffing and snapping at the people closest to the stage. Then she leapt down, was among the crowd, and someone screamed.

Mike played a loping, slow tune as she inspected the horde. Everywhere she went, people drew back, afraid of her white, gnashing teeth. Some people laughed, but when she sniffed at them, they grew quiet, disgusted with their own scents, their humanity, and what it might betray.

At last, she disappeared into the lobby through the back of the theater with a final howl. The crowd released, breathed together, whispered wondering words to each other. Mike silenced them with a bright riff.

Then the sword swallower was onstage. His name was Richard, Rich. I never learned much about him because he kept to himself, always reading on the bus, or listening to music with his headphones on. I had borrowed his CD player to listen to the recording of "Ave Maria" that Mike had found for me, and he seemed nice enough, though quiet.

He didn't speak when he took the stage, simply showed the crowd his long, gleaming sword and then shoved it down his throat. No fanfare, no music. The mass squirmed, looked away. Mike played for a while, an oddly bubbly tune, and then Rich twisted the sword in his throat. Rich's eyes were wide, as if surprised by the pain he'd swallowed. Someone moaned.

He slowly slid the sword back out, waved it in front of our faces so we could see the spittle speckling its edge, and smiled a shy smile. Then he tossed it in the air, caught it by the blade. There came scattered applause.

Rich simply turned and walked offstage, having done what he'd come there to do.

The crowd squirmed.

Then it was Judith's turn. I was so keen to hear her speak that I sat on the edge of my seat. She hadn't said one word in my presence since I'd arrived, and for some reason I didn't quite understand, I longed to hear what she sounded like.

She wore a long, dark blue velvet dress that made her skin glow. Her dark hair hung long and wavy about her face. She was gorgeous, imposing. The light danced around her like fireflies.

"Ladies and gentlemen," she said, voice deep and soothing. "I sense a spirit in the house tonight."

People looked at one another, at the ceiling, the floor.

"Someone who's recently passed. A man," she said.

I heard a few whispers from the back of the room.

"Tony? I am getting the name Tony," she said. "Does anyone here have a Tony that's passed in the last, say, three or four months?" Judith's hungry eyes roamed the crowd. I got the sense she was even more of a predator than Susanna.

The crowd twisted around, looking to see if anyone would answer the psychic. At last, a tentative hand rose in the middle of the auditorium. A gasp flared and fell away.

"Please stand," said Judith.

An older lady with a handbag clutched to her chest rose above the crowd.

"Margaret?" Judith asked.

The woman grew pale, nodded. Robichek was there, passing a microphone over the heads of ducking listeners. "That's me," she whispered into the microphone when it met her lips.

The crowd applauded. The woman grew even paler, somehow.

"Excellent," purred Judith, pleased with herself. "Your husband, Tony. He wants you to know he's okay, he's alright."

"Oh," whispered Margaret. She swayed on her feet.

"He wants you to tell Mary he's fine, and to live her life. May I ask, who's Mary?"

"Our daughter," she croaked.

The crowd erupted. The old woman tried to sit back down, but someone hoisted her back up.

Judith smiled, narrowed her eyes at the woman. "He misses Snuffles," she said.

This time the woman squeaked and pushed her way out of the row, down the aisle and out the back. The crowd stood, roared for Judith.

"Thank you," she said. "Thank you. That's all from me tonight, I'm afraid. Make sure you drive safely when you leave—I see an accident. A beige car. Thank you!"

She disappeared from the stage in a cloud of smoke. The audience coughed and clapped, whooped and talked excitedly. They'd scan the parking lot when they left, desperate to see the doomed car.

A square of light shone on the dark velvet at the back of the stage, and the people hushed. The light flickered, bounced.

"My name is Arnold," came a voice.

The square transformed, revealed itself to be a projection from somewhere on high. The famous video of Bigfoot, which I'd later learn through Arnold's excited prattle was called the Patterson-Gimlin film, played again and again. Bigfoot strode across the screen, long limbs swinging, head turning slightly, and then started all over again.

Then Arnold's shadow flitted across the screen, and he stood before us, projection skimming the top of his head. "I'm what you would call a Bigfoot enthusiast. I've encountered the beast three times."

Arnold's performance, if you could call it that, was more of a lecture. He described various myths regarding the cryptid, brought out plaster casts of lumpy feet. While some in the crowd were riveted, some slipped out to use the restroom, others began to whisper. I was sorry for Arnold, who continued oblivious to the growing restlessness in the theater. I hoped my own show wouldn't elicit such a response.

At last, the projector flicked off, the light extinguished, and Arnold collected his memorabilia to relieved applause.

There were a few minutes of silence, then Warner scrambled onstage to imposing, dramatic music that did not at all match his fumbling approach. The spotlight, once a brilliant white, burned red and ominous. Warner dumped an armful of hoops, torches, and other strange equipment at his feet.

"My grandmother caught fire," he said, his mouth too close to the microphone. He breathed. "Spontaneous combustion."

Someone behind me kicked my seat.

"When the neighbors smelled smoke, they knocked her door down to find nothing but her slippered feet, pristine and untouched by the greasy ash that befouled the bed."

Mike played and Warner pulled a long lighter from his pocket. "Don't try this at home," he said. "Or else you might end up like Grammy."

With a swoop, he lit one of the torches at his feet. He picked it up and swung it above his head in a crimson arc. We in the front row grimaced, flinched away from the heat, but Warner stepped forward, swiped at us with his glowing hand.

He tossed the thing, swung it wildly. For the next ten minutes he juggled and whipped the flames around his head, his thin body. He tossed hoops, ribbons, and burning sticks into the air and caught them behind his back. I was close enough to see the sweat dripping down his forehead, and I wondered if it was from the heat or nervousness. The sweat ran into his eyes—blinding him, yet he juggled.

Finally, he threw down his smoldering props and bowed. The crowd stood for Warner, clapped their hands. "Damn, I would have come just for this," said someone to my right.

Mike played a mournful song, bringing the time traveler back on stage. "So here we are again," said the traveler. "Back where we started. Yet we've traveled forward, into the future, carried by these talented friends who touch the edges of reality. We hope you enjoyed your time here. Thank you."

The house lights brightened, bleaching the stage, diminishing it to nothing more than a raised area strewn with wires and smoldering sticks and a lonesome keyboard. The show was over—the performers gone.

I wasn't quite sure what I'd just witnessed; some strange hybrid of talent show, lecture, and circus. I wasn't quite sure if what I'd witnessed was any good.

I went to bed that night, curled beneath the RV table, replaying the show in my head, trying desperately to unravel it, to suss out the larger theme. Was it truly a show, or just a smattering of people Robichek had pulled together from desperate and disparate places? I could see how I'd fit in, but what did it mean that I belonged? Reality, said the time traveler. The edges of it. That was the key. I pulled my knees up to my chin, unsure if I understood the center, let alone the edges.

———

This one's about spotlights, about illumination.

There were lights on the road, bright, like headlights, and Eugenio slowed down. It looked like someone was approaching on the wrong side of the road, barreling down on him and his loaded coal truck. It would be a hell of an accident, he thought. All that black coal tumbling forward, burying him in the cabin, crushing him in darkness even if the oncoming vehicle did not. Eugenio pulled to the side.

The light intensified, grew so bright and hot that Eugenio had to pull down the visor and shield his eyes. He'd spent a lot of time on the road, too much time, perhaps, and he'd never seen headlights like these before.

And then, just before it grew too bright to comprehend, the light faded, leaving brown, pulsating imprints in Eugenio's vision. He shook his head, rubbed his eyes. He felt as if he had stared at the sun.

When his sight cleared, he squinted into the darkness of the road ahead, desperate to see what sort of machine could make all that light. If it was another truck, well, he'd have a word with him. He fingered the revolver he kept on the center console.

Then he saw it—a metallic circle, thirty feet high. It blocked the entire road. Sweat beaded on Eugenio's forehead. The circle opened, and that blinding light poured out. Three figures broke that violent brightness, silhouetted against the glow of the ship. They were big— twelve feet tall. Eugenio gripped the weapon, hand moist and trembling, and climbed out of his truck.

"Hey," Eugenio yelled. "Get out of the road." He couldn't think of anything better to say and instantly felt small, dwarfed by the giant beings. He was shaking hard now.

They turned, and a ray of red light washed over him, burning every inch of his body, making it tingle all over.

He fired at the beings. Three shots—one for each, but they did not move.

Eugenio, still basked in that red, fiery light, dove back into his truck. He drove in reverse, begging God to not let another car come, until he could find a place to swing the big truck around. The engine roared as he thundered home.

The light followed, danced around the truck, making him itch and sweat. He passed streetlights that dimmed, that turned violet and green. He drove faster.

It stank now. He wondered if it was his own flesh burning or his truck giving up. He realized he wasn't going to make it home and pulled over at the next house, falling out of the vehicle in his haste.

Inside, a family gathered around a corpse. They were in mourning, surrounded by pale flowers and candles and shadow.

"Help me!" Eugenio screamed at their door. "Help me, please."

The warm candlelight flickered, turned a lurid shade of green. The shadows danced and spun around the room, and the corpse was bathed in strange, fluorescent light.

The family ran to the door, either desperate to be free of the changing room or to see what the man crying outside wanted, and found Eugenio collapsed on their stoop, clutching a gun to his chest.

"What is it?" asked the grandfather. He tore his eyes away from the sad man and saw the streetlights were flickering, glowing purple. "What the hell is going on?"

"A craft," gasped Eugenio. "It burned me. For the love of God, help me."

They took Eugenio to the police station. They had heard about the lights—they'd been fielding calls about those for the last half hour —but they hadn't seen a craft.

"I'll go take a look," said a young deputy who believed he was afraid of nothing, of no one. Meanwhile, Eugenio was transported to a doctor. He was found to have been exposed to radiation, his entire body burned and sore.

Back on the road, dark and empty, the police and a few gawking villagers stared into the space where the craft had been. "Nothing here," said the deputy. "Guy's crazy."

"Look!" someone cried, gesturing frantically at the ground. "Look here!"

"Well, I'll be damned," said another. "It's a footprint."

Twenty inches long, sunk deep into the earth, the footprint faded in the rain.

CHAPTER 30
CONSPIRACY

THE BUS DROVE ON, lulling us all to sleep with its gentle rocking. I dreamed of fire, of dogs, of black skies, of lights extinguished. Despite the contents, it wasn't a bad dream. Just a new one. I registered with some relief I wasn't dreaming of aliens and ships. Though it was a stinking, ancient vessel, I felt safe on the bus—constantly on the move, a hard target to hit. I knew so many encounters, so many incidents, began in cars, lights shone through windshields on desolate, tree-lined roads, but I had never heard of any stories about whole buses of people accosted. And if it did somehow happen, well, I would not be alone this time.

When I awoke it was dawn, a pale rosy light licking at the windows, and I felt a strange surge of fondness for the hunched forms huddled against the seats, laying spread across the floor. It surprised me. I was so determined to feel nothing but contempt for my situation, it was a kind of betrayal to feel anything beyond hate. But the show had endeared me to this motley bunch. Forced to perform, to exhibit their strange talents thrust upon them in myriad, perverse ways, we were not so unalike. Perhaps this was the place for me, after all.

I composed another letter to Sylvia, willing my pen's scratchings to quiet, to not wake the others. While I still urged her to rescue me, to intercept us somewhere on the road, I also wrote at length about the show, its strange magnetism. For it was truly magnetic, pulling you closer and closer to its molten, confusing core. It was something that invited you in despite its bizarre composition. You could be one of us, the show seemed to say—drawn upward, inward—by no choice of your own.

Twilight Revue—I thought the name corny at first, assuming the reference to crepuscular hours a mere allusion to the time the show took place, but I recognized now that twilight, like dawn, is a between time full of strange happenstance, of feelings hereto unanticipated. It was a good name.

Before sealing it up in its envelope, I read the letter again and immediately wanted to rip it to shreds. I was too kind to the show, to its performers. I was embarrassed that I'd let it affect me this way. I wanted to hate it forever, but it was a strange, alien show, and I couldn't help but see something of myself in it. So I didn't rip the letter up, but I didn't send it, either. I still have it kept in a box somewhere.

Someone stirred—Judith lighting her first cigarette of the morning, and the smell roused the others.

Mike dabbed at the drool accumulated on his shirt during the night, and Rich cleared his throat, a craggy, coughing sound. Robichek's eyes glinted in the rearview mirror. "We'll stop at the next place," he said. "Now that everyone's up."

"I could use some coffee," said Warner, plopping himself down next to me.

"Could we make some? On the stove?" I asked.

Warner glanced over at the little stovetop, covered with books and papers topped with someone's bra. "I don't know," he said. "We've never used that the whole time I've been here. Robichek probably doesn't keep gas in this thing. I'll just wait until we get somewhere."

"How long have you been here?"

"Oh, a few years now. Three or four."

"God, that's forever," I said.

"Tell me about it," he said. "I started when I was about your age. You know, my grandmother, she raised me. So, when she died..."

I nodded. No need to tell me about how death changes things.

"It feels kind of sick, sometimes, profiting off her death. But I had nowhere else to go. We didn't have much money," he said.

"I understand that," I said. "It wasn't my choice to profit off what happened to me, either. I was so young. It makes me feel dirty, sometimes."

"But what happened to you," he said. "It happened directly to you. It's yours to use."

Something cracked inside me like an egg, yolk spilling out warm and yellow. "Can I tell you a secret?" My voice was low, nearly imperceptible above the hum of the bus.

"Of course," he said.

"I don't remember it, the abduction. Sometimes I'm not sure if it ever happened at all. My dad, he made so much money off the thing... I just don't know if it's real or not." I raised my hands to my mouth as if to stop the words from tumbling out. I had never told anyone but Sylvia about my doubting, the cloudy murk surrounding the whole Incident. There was the familiar pricking of unease spread across my skin. Warner would hate me now, hate me for lying, for conning the people who came to see something close to magic. I wasn't sure why I'd said it. "Please don't tell anyone," I said.

"Laura," he said, voice even-toned and flat. "Do you think my grandmother really spontaneously combusted? That Susanna was really raised by wolves? And Marvin is from the future?"

"She didn't?" I asked. "Your grandmother?"

"Hell no," he said. "She was smoking in bed and fell asleep. Burned the whole apartment complex down, that one did."

"Oh," I said.

"And Susanna? She's a freak, surely, but just grew up with dog breeding parents. A puppy mill. She just likes dogs."

I looked out the window, at the passing fields all kissed with dawn's light. "And Marvin?" I asked. The time travelling man and his satin suit intrigued me.

"Mentally ill," he said under his breath.

"It's kind of cruel," I said. "Playing these tricks, making people do this when they're unwell."

"Do you think a man who'd take a child from her home would give a shit? He's a collector, is all. He collects misery, abomination."

I felt faint. I thought of Mike's lumpy face, of the dog ripping him apart. "What about Judith?" I asked.

"Eh, I think her family situation wasn't the greatest. She wanted out any way she could. At least, that's what Rich told me. I don't know. She may be what she seems," he said. "It's hard to say. But she is miserable. That I know. I mean, look at her."

I turned and found Judith at the back of the RV, curled up on the bed, knees nearly touching her chin, her eyes wide and staring at nothing. Warner was right about us being a collection, but instead of being bound together by talent, it was desperation that marked us. Though that was no excuse for Judith's sour behavior toward me. "Why's she like that?" I asked. "She's always so..."

"Rude?" asked Warner. "She thinks she's better than the rest of us. I mean, if she's truly that talented, she has the right, I guess. Maybe she can read our puny little minds. But she's been a lot worse since you got here."

I crinkled my forehead. It was hard to imagine Judith any other way. "Me? What did I do?"

"Well let's see. You've been on national TV, have a very

successful book, can sing people's socks off. I could go on and on. She's jealous, Laura."

"But she's so talented. I would love to see the future," I said. Perhaps, with the gift of foresight, I could have protected myself, could have avoided the abduction altogether. And if that was something immutable, well, then I would have known to dispose of my mother before I ended up in Robichek's band.

"It wouldn't be fair for you to have everything."

"Well, she can have my fame," I said. The power—what had it gotten me? I had managed a few feats, had felt the warmth of adoration, but I ended up in Robichek's show all the same. "Has she ever given you a reading, or whatever it's called?"

"Yeah. Sure. She spouts off every now and then, something she can't keep to herself. It's always true, always comes to pass. But you can't be sure if she's just lucky, or if someone tipped her off."

Luck was a preternatural blessing too, I thought. It was no more bogus than Susanna's dog woman act, or Marvin's rambling. Luck stood to be possibly the greatest, truest gift amongst us. "Do you think it happened to me?" I asked. "The abduction?"

Warner eyed me up and down, sighed. "You know what? I do."

"Why?" I asked, somewhat surprised. "Why?"

"You've lost too much to it. There's got to be something there."

He was right, I knew. It was horrifying to have been taken, to not remember, for my parents to have violated and pulled me apart and put me back together. But for it all to have been for nothing? That was an abyss darker than night. "My family," I added, another loss.

"You should ask your parents," he said. "Be vulnerable and upfront."

"There's just my mom now. Daddy passed away a few years ago. He —"I cut myself off. There was something about Warner that just made the words fall out of me. I imagined myself telling him I watched my father die, wished him dead, killed him. I doubted he'd be so generous then.

"I'm sorry," he said.

"And it's not that easy," I explained. "I can't just ask. My mother —we're not speaking. I don't want to talk to her ever again, not after getting rid of me."

"But it'd be worth it, right? To speak again, just to ask? If you got the truth wouldn't that make it all worth it?"

The truth—that's what I wanted more than anything. To know if I had been swept up, if I had been changed, if I could do what I thought I could, if I had been conning everyone all along. I wanted to know if my house had been built on lies, even though there was not much to be done about it. Not this far along. But I saw the value in knowing how the house was constructed in case anything went wrong. Maybe I could fix it.

I shrugged. "I don't know," I said. It seemed the only things my parents ever divulged were meant to bolster the business. Nothing satisfying, nothing to hold on to. Things were only told to me if it would make the money come in faster, make me perform better. I realize now that their withholding wasn't always some nefarious plot to keep me in the dark, but was rather a marketing move. Anything to keep the money from running out.

"I don't know if I can trust her. It's so hard," I said. "Knowing who to trust."

"Well, you can trust me," said Warner.

"I do," I said. And I did. Something about his candidness, his big green eyes, anesthetized me. His kindness, never asking anything in return, reminded me of Sylvia, and I felt safe.

He smiled.

I smiled.

The RV's brakes screamed.

———

You've heard of this place. It's familiar, almost prosaic.

Area 51 has long stood as the pinnacle of American conspiracy theories. Its vague name and desolate location—tucked into the

Nevadan desert—make it ripe for speculation. Some believe this location serves as a place to study downed UFO, while others insist it's a facility used for weather control experiments. The government, for sixty years, claimed it didn't exist at all.

The name, Area 51, isn't even an official government one. No one quite knows where the random number came from. Perhaps an electrical company grid with squares laid out and numbered, some guess. Its real name is Homey Airport, or the Groom Lake facility. But those names lack the snappiness of "Area 51," the mystique. Who is Homey, anyway?

Finally, in 2013 thanks to a Freedom of Information Act request, the government admitted the secret base existed. They said its sole purpose was the experimentation of new aircraft, thus explaining away the strange lights in the sky seen over Groom Lake. But that didn't satisfy—the government rarely does.

CHAPTER 31
POISONED

WE STOPPED at a gas station one morning—a rural one with a sea of corn swaying all around it—and I nearly ran to the phone booth. It was a sad blue box with grimy windows etched with names and hearts and "fuck-yous" by lonely callers, but in my eyes, it was the most beautiful thing in the world.

I pulled some change out of my pockets and dropped them into the slot, fingers trembling. I dialed Sylvia's number; though we had rarely talked on the phone while I lived at home, I knew her number by heart. I'd been whispering it to myself at night, a comforting mantra, my chance at salvation.

I watched the performers flit in and out of the gas station as the phone rang, coffees and packaged muffins and last night's overcooked hot dogs in hand. At last, the ringing stopped, and I heard a familiar intake of breath.

"Hello?" asked Sylvia.

"Sylvia!" I cried. "It's me, Laura. I'm at a gas station in… I don't know where."

"Laura!" she cooed. "I've been hoping to hear from you."

I fidgeted, adjusted my shirt. "Did you get my letters?"

"No, not yet, sweetie, but these things take time. I'm sure they will arrive soon."

Warner had shown me the big metal boxes that sprouted up occasionally at intersections near our stops. I had never mailed anything on my own before and letting the letter fall through the slotted box was strangely exciting. But I was running out of stamps. I wondered if Warner knew how to get those, too. "I haven't been able to write much. Or call. We're stuck on the bus most of the time. Oh god, the bus, Sylvia. It's rancid."

She laughed. "Is it all that bad, honey?"

I considered the half-sleep I'd had the past few nights, the pungent smell of bodies and gas station food, Judith's haughty behavior, greasy, greedy Robichek, and his troupe of odd talents, the pain of my arrival, my mother. But I also thought of Warner's kind smile, his near clairvoyance, and the strange, glimmering show—the way they both made me feel somewhat scared, uncomfortable but intrigued. I liked that feeling, I realized. It was a familiar one. "There are some nice people here," I conceded. "And the show's weird, but in a good way."

"That's great to hear," she said. "Have you performed yet?"

"No," I said, "My first one's tonight."

"Oh, wonderful. You'll do great, I know it."

"I wish you could come."

"Me too, honey. I've been keeping an eye on the tour bill. I'll try to get to one when you're closer to home."

My eyes filled with tears. I knew it made sense for Sylvia to wait for the show to come back around, but I wasn't sure how long that would take. I needed her now. She needed to make the sacrifice to see me. "I hope it's soon," I said. "When you come, could you take me home? Before the show, I could sneak out, meet you?"

She sighed. "I'm not sure if that's such a good idea, Laura. I talked to your mother and—"

"You didn't!" I cried. "I begged you not to. I hate her. I hate her." My breathing was fast and uneven.

"Laura, listen. I know. I know you're upset with her. But she feels like she had no other option. In her mind it was either watch you suffer at home or send you away. Do you understand? That she did this to help you?"

"No," I stammered. "No. She wanted to get rid of me. She hates me."

"Laura, stop it right this instant and listen to me. Please."

The phone beeped a warning, a plea for more quarters. I shut my eyes, willed myself to calm down.

"She's struggling, Laura. More than you know. She's sick, honey. She misses you so much. But she couldn't do it on her own. You have to understand. You—"

With a click, Sylvia's voice died, and I was left listening to the long wail of the dial tone. I placed the phone back on the hook and pressed my forehead to the smudged metal of the machine. Sick? I thought of my daddy on the kitchen floor, floundering and panicked, a fish struggling for breath. Sick. My mother had been losing weight, but I assumed that was from the lack of food in the house, her refusal to eat. I hadn't thought that there was anything wrong with her that wasn't by choice.

Or maybe Sylvia had meant a mental sickness—that my mother was depressed and falling deeper every day. That seemed more plausible to me but hurt more—that she couldn't see me through all that haze.

I left the phone booth feeling heavy and sluggish. I knew I should have felt bad for the call ending that way, but I didn't. Sylvia had gone behind my back and talked to my mother. The call was supposed to have buoyed me, brought good news, but it seemed like every time I reached back into my old life I came away with soiled hands.

I climbed back onto the bus without entering the gas station, with nothing to eat or drink. I'd spent the last of my money on the phone call.

———————

Here's one about becoming tainted, irreparable.

The agriculture program at State was supposed to be one of the best in the country, but at times like this, when Harry was scooping pig shit out of a sloppy pen, he wasn't so sure if he'd have been better off majoring in something else. Something clean and tidy, like accounting. He'd have made a poor accountant, but it beat the stink he was breathing in day after day.

It was lunchtime by the time he took a break, and he changed his clothing behind the barn. He didn't care if anyone saw him; he'd left his dignity in the pig pen. He strolled up to the house, a pretty white gabled thing on top of a picturesque hill overlooking the fields and barn and pastures and saw Jem already sitting at the little kitchen table, eating his sandwich and listening to the fuzzy music streaming out of the radio.

"Boy you stink," said Jem. Harry plopped down beside him. "Smell like pig."

"You're a genius, Jem," Harry said. "Don't know how you figured that one out."

Jem snickered, bit into his bacon sandwich.

"Don't laugh, Jem, you're on pig duty tomorrow."

Jem moaned, then changed the subject. "Say isn't this that new band?" He pointed at the radio. "The one with the guitars?"

"What the hell are you talking about?" asked Harry. "All bands got guitars."

"You know what I mean," said Jem.

The radio sitting on the counter played low, and Harry couldn't hear whatever band it was, anyway. And it didn't really matter. Not really. "I have to turn in my final tonight," he said.

"You're lucky Miller gave you an extra day," said Jem.

"I know it," Harry said. "Don't I know it."

Then came a wail from the radio, loud and piercing. Both boys started.

"What the hell?" asked Harry.

Jem jumped up, turned the dial to another station. That one squealed too. "Damn thing's on the blink, it is." He pounded at it with the palm of his hand.

"Turn it off, for Christ's sake," said Harry.

Jem turned the dial all the way down. "Have to tell old Mick about that. Have to tell him his radio went and blew."

Then the radio—the supposedly turned off radio—began beeping. It was an erratic, annoying beep.

"I thought you turned that thing off!" yelled Harry, slamming his sandwich down on the table, squashing the bread.

"I did!" Jem was back at it, screwing with the dials and smacking it hard. "Damn thing won't shut up."

"What the hell is that?" asked Harry, now looking out the arched windows in the front of the house.

The other boy turned, saw what he saw. Two saucers stuck to one another hovered low in the field.

"What the—" came Jem.

They rushed out the door, pushing into one another as they spilled out onto the front lawn. The thing was silent as it flew, leaving the scent of burned gasoline in its wake—a smell even stronger than Harry's pig stink.

"It's going up!" cried Jem. "Look, it's rising!"

They watched the thing go straight into the sky, into some green-tinged clouds and fade away.

"What the hell was that?" asked Jem.

Harry shook his head, but went back to work. Pig shit didn't scoop itself.

The next day, on milking duty now, Harry struggled to get any milk out of the cows. He and Jem hadn't told the farm owner, Mick, what they'd seen the day before, but he'd have to tell him about his cow. He didn't want it to reflect poorly on his grades. Patting the cow's side, he felt her tremble slightly. Maybe she was just getting old.

Harry moved around her, looked down into her big glassy eyes. "What's wrong, huh?" he asked. This didn't look like an old cow. In fact, she'd always been one of the highest producers. It didn't make sense. *Ruined*, he thought. *Poisoned*.

The cow swung her head away, stared out at the sky.

I WAS STILL FEELING low from the phone call with Sylvia when we pulled into our stop for the night—a theater even smaller than the last in a town with only two stoplights. There was only one dressing room, and everyone was pulling on their costumes with no apparent concern. So, I stripped next to the wolf lady.

"Is that a tattoo?" she asked.

"What?" I wasn't old enough for those, and I couldn't imagine what design I'd get—a UFO? A star? The question was so absurd, it was like my brain short-circuited, blank.

"That little heart on your leg. It's cute."

"Oh," I said, fingers trailing over the pink scar on my thigh.

"I have a tattoo," she said. "Wanna see?"

But I was lost in myself, fingers still pressing the little imperfection where I'd gotten cut so long ago, dragged across the kitchen floor while Daddy lay cold in a puddle of brown. No one had ever noticed this reminder, this souvenir. I scrambled for some explanation, for some lie I could tell, but nothing came. The truth came so close to the surface I could see it, gently warped beneath the waves. Daddy's eyes bugging out of his head. I opened my mouth.

"Hello?" Susanna waved a hand across my face. "You in there?"

"Sorry," I said. I slipped on my old velvet gown, momentarily hiding my face in its folds.

"Ooh, that's pretty," said the wolf lady. "I like the little stars."

"Thank you," I said, knowing the dress was smaller than ever and probably didn't look as good as Susanna was making out. I was thankful that the scar was concealed now, secreted away. "I've had it for a long time."

"Looks brand new!" she barked. "Beats my old slacks and shirt any day." Susanna's costume was a simple pair of gray pants and a brownish roan shirt. Wolfish colors, I thought. Like a pelt.

"Can you do makeup?" I asked her. My hands were shaking, and I was unsure if I could hold a brush.

"No," she said. "You'll want to ask Judith for that sort of thing. She's a pro."

I looked over at Judith combing her hair in the mirror, staring into her own eyes. She wore a different gown tonight—something gauzy and black like dusted spiderwebs. She looked amazing.

"I'll do it myself," I said. I balled my fists up tight, squeezed my fingers together.

Susanna laughed. "Don't let her think she's alpha dog," she said. "She's here, is she not? In this shitty little show?"

She had a point. I wondered why Judith would allow herself to be affiliated with a ragtag group like this. She deserved a headlining role, an entire show dedicated to her. I knew men would pay just to stare at her, for heaven's sake. "What's her story?" I whispered.

Susanna shrugged. "Doesn't have one. She's been here as long as the show has been around, never said anything to anyone about her past."

I was thinking of Judith as I pulled the little satchel of makeup out of my bag and began working on my face. My hands were steady now, my mind preoccupied.

"Looks like you don't need her anyway," she said.

Warner was staring at me in the mirror, eyebrow raised.

"Shh," I hissed at Susanna. "She can probably hear us. Warner can. Look."

Susanna turned and waggled her eyebrows at Warner. "Oh, trust me, she's lost in her head, anyway. I'm more concerned with why that boy keeps staring."

Warner flushed, turned back to arranging his sticks and wands.

"You watch out for him," Susanna whispered, leaning into my ear.

I started—I'd never heard her lower her voice. It was an ominous sound. "Why?" I whispered back.

"He's crazy," she growled.

"What?" I asked, but she was already stalking away, heading for the dressing room door.

"Wait!" I called out, abandoning my face half done. I ran after her out into the dry dark of the backstage. "Susanna, wait. What do you mean?"

She turned, a smooth, fluid motion, and scowled. I shrank down beneath her intense glare. "Stop following me, okay?"

"I don't understand," I said. "About Warner."

"Are you that stupid?" she sneered.

My mouth fell open. I couldn't comprehend the words Susanna was saying. They were so unlike her, so unlike the conversation we were just having in the dressing room about makeup and Judith. "Stupid?"

She took a step toward me, and I took three back.

"I know what's going on here. I have you all figured out," said Susanna.

My skin prickled and a sickening wave of cold washed over me. What did Susanna know? She'd seen my scar, seen the proof etched right across my skin. What else had she seen?

"You think you're better than everyone else," she said. "Well guess what? You're just some singing brat. All that nonsense about summoning aliens, making things happen? That's all it is—nonsense. The show doesn't need you."

"Okay," I whispered.

"All buddy-buddy with Warner. It's disgusting. You can't trust him," she spat. "He's a liar."

We stared at one another in silence. I hugged my arms against myself to try to still my shaking. Susanna gave me one last look of contempt before spinning around and disappearing into the shadows.

My face was red, burning hot, and my heart pounded. My breath came out hitched and shallow. I didn't understand what was happening to my body, why it was responding like this. Now I realize it was the way she'd made herself seem so big, towering over me, dominating me. It reminded me of Daddy.

I retreated to a dark alcove near an emergency exit. When I felt less shaky, a little more calm, I cautiously ran through the interaction in my mind. What had I done to make her so mad? What had *Warner* done? The only thing I could think of was the conversation I'd had with Warner on the bus. Susanna, with her impeccable hearing, must have heard us talking about her—about her puppy-raising parents. It was stupid to think we wouldn't be heard in those close quarters, especially by Susanna.

Susanna was the crazy one, that was clear. And she had just fed me a lie—yet another to stuff in my pocket, hold close to my heart. People respected me the way they respected a child—dull annoyance, careless, empty replies meant to, at best placate, and at worst, provoke like a dog in a ring.

Performers began trickling out of the dressing room, sparkling now in their costumes. I hoped no one could see my anger.

When the show began, I huddled just off stage, awaiting my cue.

I was near the middle of the show, a place in which I wouldn't stick in anyone's minds for long. I was grateful for that—it'd have been too much pressure to begin or end.

Then I was being pushed on stage, out from the dark of the wings into a great beam of light. It was hot and bright, yet I shivered in my gown; was there a familiarity there? A remembrance of rays and beams from above? Or was the sensation of slipping back into something known simply a result of returning to performing? I'd been doing it for so long, acting my entire life.

I thought about running, sprinting back to the blackness off stage. The microphone before me had been set to exactly the right height. I could simply lean into it, tell them all how Robichek had stolen me, my mother an accomplice. I could tell them about the cramped, stinking bus, the way we were all forced together through spite and luck. I could bring this show to a screeching halt. But I needed the money. Needed to get back to Sylvia.

The crowd was nothing more than a writhing mass of black. I spoke to it, explained that I was abducted, swept away singing, and it stilled.

Mike played the beginning notes of "Ave Maria," a song whose words I now knew by heart but did not understand, and I sang. I lulled the squirming black into a gentle swaying ocean. When I slowed, Mike did too, sensing my tempo with a musician's foresight. I wondered if Judith was listening, if Warner and Susanna and Robichek were backstage, listening too. Maybe now that I was pulling my weight, Judith would accept me. I thought of her silence as I sang, imagined my voice burrowing into her brain. Into everyone's brains. They'd seen me now, truly.

The crowd applauded as the closing note faded into the dark, and I took a little bow, an action that surprised me. I was becoming more of a showman all the time, it seemed.

Later the freaks tore down the set, packing it all back up into beaten cardboard boxes and dirty bags. The teardown went much faster than the setup. I picked up a box and followed the crew through the back of the theater. I didn't mind helping—it felt good to be doing something, thinking about something unrelated to my plight.

A crowd waited outside, and we pushed through them with our boxes and bags.

"Psychic! Hey!" someone shouted. "I have a question."

Judith didn't look up at the man.

People held out their tickets to be signed, but no one had a free hand or cared to sign them.

"Laura!"

I stopped, swiveling about on my heels. Someone here knew my name, and it startled me. I hadn't been introduced by name—only as an abductee, a random person held captive and singing in an alien ship's beam. This had to be someone who knew me from the convention circuit, from my old life. Maybe they knew Sylvia. Maybe they knew Daddy. I searched the crowd for whoever had spoken.

A woman rushed forward holding a disposable camera above her head. "A picture, please!"

Judith hadn't paused when someone called out for her, but she was still now, an immovable rock in the stream of people that parted around her, around me. We both stared at the lady.

"Can you take our picture?" she asked Judith. "Please?"

Judith frowned, shook her head. "Can't," she said.

"If not a picture, then could you say a prayer for my mother, please?"

"A prayer?" Now I was the one frowning.

"Was that really the song you were singing? When you were abducted?" asked a man.

I turned away from him, unsure how to answer. My parents hadn't known the song I was singing, full of dissonant notes, strange chords. Everyone knew that. It was mentioned in the earliest articles —commentators obsessed over it. If this man didn't know this simple detail, he wasn't worth my time.

"She's sick," the woman with the camera explained.

"Sure," I said, hoping she would let me by.

"I could send you her picture if that would help," said the woman. "Maybe you could channel something, an angel."

I wasn't sure I believed in angels. The few times I'd been to church, they were always discussed in the abstract—peripheral creatures that existed in the liminal space between Earth and Heaven. Ineffectual. The only angels I was interested in were the fallen ones —Lucifer, Belial. The ones cast out, returned changed and fearsome. "What angels?" I asked.

"They were angels," she said. "What you call aliens."

"I'll take your picture," said the man. "Give me the camera."

The woman leaned into me and smiled. The flash was blinding, a burst that left bright imprints in my vision.

I slept well that night, exhausted and drained. I dreamed of Warner's grandmother, smoking in bed, dozing while the ember ate its way down the cigarette toward her fingers. The ash falling on the floor. Fire spinning and dancing in a young man's hands, a reinterpretation, a dream of a dream. If he could do it, so could I.

————

1897 is a year you'll come to remember. I find it again and again in these stories, a shining lodestar in the history books.

Lake Erie was still cold in April. You wouldn't want to fall in. The waves bounced Captain Singler's ship that morning in 1897, and the men struggled to cast their fishing nets. It'd be a good for nothing day, Singler thought. He tightened his coat against the cold.

They hadn't seen another ship for hours—no one else was dumb enough to go out on a morning like this—and Singler's men were growing impatient.

"There's nothing out here today," said one. "I could be drinking. By the fire."

The others hummed in agreement, soaked to the bone.

"It is our duty," said Singler. "To bring in these fish. We've got to meet our quota, even if hell stands in our way." Singler was given to grandiose turns of phrase—it was one of the things the men hated most about him. But he could see it, even now, the quotes emblazoned in brass, in books, his words turned to stone. He wanted everything he said to be just right.

The men grumbled, turned back to their tasks.

A ship loomed on the horizon now, a dark thing with a canopy. *Smart*, thought Singler. He could use one of those.

"We'll move toward that vessel," he cried to his crew. "We will see what the lake's given her today. Perhaps she's had better luck."

They approached the ship slowly. It grew bigger and stranger as they approached. A family could be seen on board—a young man in a hunting jacket, casting a line out into the water, a woman, and young boy at his side.

It was rare to see women out on the water on a working ship. Especially in this cold. Singler frowned.

"Hello there," cried Singler. "It's the *Sea Wing*, here."

The man looked up from his fishing, studied Singler standing there on the prow. Behind him, a balloon began to rise from the middle of the ship.

"Hello there," cried Singler again. "What use is that balloon to you? A signaling device?"

But the balloon kept rising, up through the clouds, and the strange man's boat began to lift up from the water.

"I'll say, your boat is truly floating now," said Singler. "What is the meaning of this?"

The boat flew above them now, circling like a bird of prey. Singler shielded his eyes against the stark white of the sky. "What is the meaning of this?" he repeated.

He and his men watched the boat fade into the clouds.

The boat was silent. No one said a word, not even Captain Singler. It was a rare day when the captain was left speechless.

When they finally put feet on land, the men dispersed back to their homes, hearths and whiskey awaiting them. But one man hesitated, waited for Singler to disembark. "Do you think we'll see it again?" asked the man. "The ship with the balloon?"

Singler shook his head. "God willing, we won't."

CHAPTER 33
MALICE

THE NEXT MORNING was cold and clear, the kind of morning that makes you breathe in deep and hold it there for a moment, appreciating the taste of it.

I sat with my head next to the open window, waiting for the bus to begin moving again. We had stopped at a mall, and I'd found a blue box for my latest letter. I was feeling hopeful, almost happy.

Sylvia would come and get me soon. I could feel it in the air—an electric current that barbed me awake. Something was going to happen—something had to happen. I watched two birds pick at a discarded chicken nugget container.

Robichek climbed on board brandishing a greasy bag of soft pretzels. "Almost time," he said. "Looks like almost everyone is here."

Mike tapped a rhythm out on the table with his pencil and Judith murmured something unintelligible to Rich, the sword swallower. It seemed even she was in a good mood.

I got up. I'd ask Robichek where we were going next, see if we were heading toward home.

"Oh," he said as I approached. "Here, hold on." He sat the pretzels down on his seat and shoved a hand into his pocket.

Robichek handed me a fifty-dollar bill. "I'll send the rest to your old ladies," he said.

I clutched the money with wonder—I didn't know I'd get such a big cut. With enough shows, I'd have the money for a bus ticket back to Sylvia, or maybe even a flight. The faster I got there, the better. "Lady," I said. "Just one old lady."

Robichek frowned. "Your mom and the white-haired gal, what's her name?"

My head grew light, and I bit down hard on my tongue. "What?"

"You know, nice old woman. Smells like peppermint."

"Sylvia." The word was putty in my mouth.

"That's it! Yeah!" Robichek was turning away, climbing back into his seat at the wheel.

I grabbed him by the shoulder, dug my nails into his skin. "How do you know Sylvia?"

The bus was silent now, everyone watching me lay my hands on this elephantine man. "Hey," said Robichek. He looked a little scared. "Calm down."

"Tell me!" I yelled, pushing my nails in deeper. "Tell me how you know her."

"Laura." Warner's voice was soft, far away.

"You're hurting me." Robichek swatted at my hand. I let it fall.

"I don't understand," I said. My vision swam, blurring. I laid a hand on the dashboard, afraid I might pass out.

Robichek rubbed his shoulder. "Sylvia called me and put me in contact with your mother. She's how I learned about you and your, uh, gift. She must have seen the show and looked me up. I don't know!"

I felt bile rising in my throat, burning my chest, my esophagus. I choked it down. "She's making money here? Off of me?"

"Well yeah," said Robichek. "Finder's fee and all that. Splits their half fifty-fifty with your mom. I'll send it to her, don't you worry."

I felt a hand around my wrist, Warner tugging gently. "Come on," he said. "Let's go sit down."

I pulled my arm from his grasp. "Don't touch me," I said.

"Go, Laura," said Robichek. "We're gonna leave soon."

"Why didn't you tell me?" I cried.

Robichek raised an eyebrow. "It was all in the contract. I don't understand why you're so upset. Didn't you read the contract?"

I hadn't read it. I hadn't signed it. Everything that happened, happened without my consent. "Don't send her any," I yelled. "Don't send her anything."

"Listen," said Robichek, turning at last to fully face me. "I don't know what's going on here. Whatever it is, it's between you and the old lady. I'm just going by the contract, okay? You should be happy; you're getting the biggest cut!"

"I don't care about the cut!"

"Please, Laura. Can't you see I'm confused? Please just go sit down." Robichek's eyes were wide.

Warner grabbed me by the shoulders, steered me back toward my seat. My feet were leaden, and I stumbled along the way. "We'll talk about this later," Warner said. "For now, try to relax, okay?"

I couldn't speak. I couldn't move. It felt like my body was exploding, breaking apart from the inside. I was dimly aware of Warner sitting next to me, of the bus rocking into motion. I thought of my letter sitting in the blue box. I wished I could have plucked it up through the slot and shredded it to pieces. Sylvia didn't deserve my words, my time. She deserved nothing but pain.

Sylvia was worse than my mother. Than even Daddy.

———

Here's a song of sadness.

Raul had been drinking. There was no denying that. He stumbled as he walked through the streets of Ricardone, tripping over every bump in the road, tripping over his own feet.

"Focus," he said aloud. And for a moment, it worked. For a moment, his vision cleared, and he walked a straight line. But then he forgot he was focusing, and the blur descended upon him once more.

Ricardone, Argentina was a small town in 1968, and the streets were deserted. It was four in the morning. There were no cars, no pedestrians, just Raul careening from one side of the road to the other like an errant pinball.

He was almost home. He may have been drunk, but he recognized the dusty buildings, the subtle curve in the road. He closed his eyes. He'd have a leftover empanada when he got there. His stomach growled in response to the fantasy.

He opened his eyes and paused. There was the silhouette of a tree in the middle of the road. Limbless, leafless, just a tall dark trunk sprouting out of the car-hardened earth. It hadn't been there when he'd left five hours before. This was something new, and Raul approached it with suspicion.

He crept closer to the tree, suddenly able to concentrate, to walk without lurching. He was five feet from it when it twisted about, revealed its face.

Raul screamed. The tree wasn't a tree—it was a man, ten feet tall. His skin was waxen and yellow.

The man raised a massive hand and pointed a thick finger at Raul. "Stay," said a voice in Raul's mind, deep and thunderous. The giant's lips hadn't moved yet Raul had heard the man.

Raul tried to turn, to put one foot over the other, but something pinned him to the spot. A tear slipped down his cheek.

"Stay," came the voice again.

He felt something pulling him, drawing his body toward the giant. He took a halting step forward.

"No," whispered Raul. The giant's face fell into a look of deep sadness, cheeks sagging and eyes downcast. There wasn't any malice in that look, but it was grotesque all the same.

And then Raul was running, sprinting away from the giant and his strange magnetism. He cut one street over, glancing behind him all the way home.

He fell through the door and lay sprawled on the floor. His chest hurt, on the verge of bursting. He sobbed into his hands until the sun came up.

CHAPTER 34
OUT OF TIME

IT WAS as if I had lost all feeling in my body, my hands and feet, my heart. I knew I was on the bus, but only faintly, as if the seats and hunched bodies in them were viewed through a dense fog. Warner said things in my ear, patted my arm, but I couldn't understand. He was speaking a different language—a tongue taken up among the living, the unwounded. Mine was the language of grief.

Someone sat a bottle of water in front of me, and I took little sips, but the water only served to replenish my tears, it seemed. I cried for a long, long time. I cried until my stomach spasmed with cramps, until my nose was raw with having rubbed at it so many times. I felt the physical pain distantly, aware that it was there, but something greater triumphed it—a deep, furrowed hurt.

I could feel everyone staring at me, gawking. Let them stare, I thought. Let them wonder. I imagined my anger radiating off of me like some dark pulse. I hoped it touched them, seeped into their skin.

A weight settled next to me on to the bench seat. I looked up and found Marvin, the time traveler, perched alongside me. We'd never really spoken beyond some platitudes, but I knew a little about him from Warner. He'd told me Marvin was crazy. I looked at the man through puffy eyes. He looked well enough with his neat black hair and clear skin. I wondered how he'd ended up here among the freaks.

"Hi," he said.

"Uh, hi," I said, wiping my nose on my sleeve.

"I'm sorry you're upset," he said.

I shrugged. There was nothing anyone could say to blunt the pain.

Marvin scratched at his temple with neatly manicured nails. "What would you say if I told you, you could go back?"

I wished he'd leave me alone. "I don't know what you're talking about," I said, turning away from him.

"Go back to a time before the hurt, prevent it somehow," he said.

I sighed. Warner was right; Marvin was crazy. "I can't," I said. "None of that is real." I knew what I was saying to him was cruel. I thought of all the deniers I'd encountered over the years, remembered the sting of their voices. Being told your quest for truth, your life's work was a folly hurt. But in that moment, I didn't care what I said.

"But it is real," he insisted. "You can go back."

"How?" I asked snidely. Even if I could go back, I wasn't sure where to begin. Before I met Sylvia? Before the abduction? I wondered if my younger self would even listen. I had been under Sylvia's spell, had bent so easily beneath Daddy's will. There wasn't room for anyone else. If it didn't work, I'd be forced to watch my whole life over. I shook my head.

Marvin blinked twice. "It's possible. I went back in time. I'm here, aren't I?"

I could feel Warner watching me from the back of the bus. A hot, unpleasant feeling. "Listen," I said. "I appreciate you trying to cheer me up, or whatever you're doing, but I am unfortunately stuck in the present."

"That's your choice," said Marvin. He leaned back, stretched out his legs.

Marvin made me nervous. His certainty, his dedication—it was embarrassing and intense. "What did you do?" I finally asked when the silence stretched. "Before the show?" Maybe if I asked the right question, I'd be able to catch him up, make him fumble, prove it wasn't real.

"Oh," said Marvin. "Well, that's complicated. There's both before and after the show, you know."

I frowned. It seemed his madness went all the way down to his core. I'd been around plenty of UFO fanatics, people who believed they were impregnated by aliens, were descended from star seeds, but I'd never met anyone who embodied their belief as much as Marvin.

"Before the show, I was homeless," he explained. "I'd stumbled into time, you know, and ended up thrown back here, in the past. I couldn't get a job; I don't have any of my papers or proof that I am who I say I am. See, I don't exist yet. So, I slept on the streets, eating trash out of dumpsters and begging for a few quarters here and there until I saw an advertisement for the show. I waited out back, and the rest is history. Literal history."

I shook my head. I was beginning to feel bad for him. Why didn't anyone here get him some help? The way Robichek used him, propped him up on stage, was wrong. It didn't surprise me that Robichek would stoop so low, but it was startling to see just how vulnerable Marvin was—possibly more than I was when my mother signed me away. "So, you feel like the show is helping you?" I asked.

"Oh yes," he said. "Every show, I hope there's someone out there like me, who can help me. Every time I get up on stage and tell them I'm a traveler, I'm that much closer to returning. I need to get back to my own time."

"Why's that?" I asked.

"I have a family, you know," he said. "A wife and daughter."

"Oh." I wasn't sure what to say. I wondered if he really had a family somewhere, if he'd gotten married before he went mad. He was so confused. Maybe he'd always been this way.

"I don't have them yet, is all."

"I see," I said. "And when, exactly, are you from?"

"I was born in 2035." He looked down at his hands. "Well, I'll be born then."

"What did you, uh, will you do in the future? Like for a career?"

"I'm a bookseller," he said sadly. "I have a little shop in Minneapolis."

"How did you get back here, anyway?" I asked.

Marvin sighed, rubbed his hands together. "To make a long story short, I walked through the wrong door. I was messing with things I shouldn't have, reading the wrong books. You get a lot of strange stuff coming through the door when you deal in used books."

I nodded. "I bet."

"I got invested in the paranormal. You know, poltergeist activity has been found to occur after UFO sightings—did you know that?" His voice was quick now, excited.

I'd heard of the theory but hadn't given it much thought; I'd never experienced anything out of the ordinary beyond my own psychic suffering. If anyone should be encountering post-alien poltergeists, it'd be me. Or would it? Maybe the lack of shattered windows, flying utensils, chairs arranged in cryptic circles in my presence indicated it hadn't happened after all. I frowned. Everything felt like a trap these days. "I've heard that, yes," I said.

"It's because they're extra-dimensional," he said. "Forget outer space, other stars. Too far away. The veil between dimensions is thinner. Ghosts, cryptids, synchronicity, aliens, all that—it's all the same thing."

I felt somewhat dizzy, still caught up on the idea that I was missing my ghosts. Was there something I couldn't see about myself?

Something others saw? I'd barely heard what he said. I nodded weakly, unsure of how to reply.

"This show we do, Laura, it isn't disparate parts. It's all one big extra-dimensional playground. We're really all exactly the same. Dipped our toes in the same water."

"That makes sense," I said, even though it didn't.

"I'm glad you're here," he said. "I think you can help me get back. Help me break out of time."

"I don't know about that," I said, taken aback. I wished for the conversation to be over.

"Sure you can," he said. "You've been out of time, too."

"What?"

"Missing time, it happens all the time in abductions. I bet you experienced it, though you didn't notice it because you were little, and who carries a watch when they're little? You broke out of time. You broke back in. I need to do just that, Laura. Break out and back in, further down the line."

"I can't remember," I said. "I can't remember the abduction at all. I don't think there was any lost time. I—"

"It doesn't matter if you remember or not," he said. "What matters is that it changed you."

To my left, Warner was pretending to shuffle through a yellowed stack of paperbacks, his head slightly turned our way.

"I don't know how to help you," I said. "Judith! Talk to Judith. She is kind of a time person, right? With the future and all that? She'd be able to help you." I was happy to divert the conversation away from me and onto someone else.

"I did talk to Judith," he said. "She said you'd come."

A coldness passed through my body, sickening and electric. "What?"

"She said you'd help me break out of time. She said you'd sing for me," said Marvin.

I looked down at my feet. This was too much for one day. Sylvia and now Marvin—it seemed everyone had a way they wanted to use me. "I really can't help you," I said.

"Judith's never wrong," said Marvin.

We sat in awkward silence. At last, he sighed and pushed himself up off the bench. I didn't lift my head to watch him go.

Even though I knew he was crazy, I couldn't help but repeat his words in my mind: she said I'd come. It could have been another of Marvin's delusions, something Judith never said. But there was something in his face, an openness, a hopefulness, that gave me pause.

What was I meant to do? I closed my eyes and thought of Daddy dying, of the lady begging for an angel. Maybe I could sing Marvin to better health. I rolled the idea about in my head. I could try it, but not right now—not yet. My heart just wasn't in it. My heart wanted something else, and that something was consuming me whole.

I envisioned Sylvia's death a thousand ways before drifting off to sleep.

———

Here's a story about being haunted, about leeches and demons and sickness.

There's a theory that it spreads, like a virus, from person to person. One night you're seeing lights in the sky, dark shapes obscuring the moon, and the next your wife and kids are seeing shadow creatures in the corners of their bedrooms. It's called the Hitchhiker Effect, and it's more contagious than the flu.

There are places on the earth that attract creatures, orbs, UFOs, maybe because the veil is thin there, or because the electromagnetism is just right or maybe just because the water tastes good there, it's impossible to say. Dave visited one such place, observed a strange shape in the sky which filled him with the utmost dread, and then went home to sleep in his own bed.

The next night, his wife woke to see a shadow creature approaching her from the hallway, long-limbed, long-fingered. She screamed out, and it was gone. She'd never seen anything like it before. Not until Dave saw the dark rend across the sky.

The night after, it was his son. He woke them up screaming, kicking and shaking in his bed. The pale glow of blue orbs had woken him, and they flew around his room, skimming his skin with little electric kisses. They disappeared when his mom rushed into the room.

And then there were the sounds—crashings and bumpings from the kitchen downstairs, the sound of chairs being dragged along the tile. No one was down there. No one you could see.

But worst of all was the wolf. It'd stare at you from the yard, yellow eyes intent and unfriendly. And when it had its fill of drinking you in, it would stand on two hind legs and run away into the suburban Virginia night. The Navajo have a name for this creature: *yee naaldlooshii*, Skin-walker.

The poltergeists, the orbs, the creatures—they come for the chosen few who fall out of time, see lights in the sky. They are gifts that cannot be returned.

CHAPTER 35
BELIEF

IT WAS EVENING, but it seemed like a hundred years had passed since the betrayal of that morning. Even though I'd slept, it didn't seem to make the day any shorter. Bad days always linger, drawing on for an eternity.

"You don't believe any of that, do you?" asked Warner.

We were sitting on a picnic table at a little rest stop off the highway. Even though I was reeling, I couldn't deny the sun felt good on my skin.

"Believe what?" I asked, absently examining my arms in the light.

"That shit Marvin spews," he said. "About time and ghosts and things."

"I don't know," I said. I watched Arnold try to rattle a bag of chips out of an obstinate vending machine.

"He's crazy," Warner said.

"Maybe so," I replied.

Warner stomped his foot on the bench below us. "Why are you being so... so flippant about it?" He said the word "flippant" with disgust, like it was a dirty, poisoned thing.

I sighed, looked back at the bus. "Listen, I don't want to talk about Marvin right now. If you haven't noticed, I have other things on my mind. I don't know why you're so hung up on him."

"I just don't want you to get hurt, is all," said Warner. "You can't get invested in these things. End up like him. He's miserable."

"Okay," I said. I was bored with Warner, his cloying concern. I wanted to be alone, dwelling in my hurt like a finger pushed into a bruise.

"I don't get it," said Warner. "Who is she, this Sylvia anyway?"

The sun was red on the horizon, and I squinted into it. "I don't want to talk about it."

"Sure you do. Look at how sad you are!"

I had kept Sylvia a secret—something of my own to hold on to in the middle of the night. But now I just felt foolish. Telling Warner about my blind faith, my love for the wretched old woman would be embarrassing. I'd been such a sucker.

"I just want to understand you," he said.

"Warner, I don't understand me," I said. "I've never known the truth. And the things I think I do know with certainty turn out to be lies. There's nothing to understand. I'm nothing." I imagined myself as a nebulous cloud of atoms, prone to blowing away in the wind. The only thing that could bind my disparate parts together would be the truth, knowing, believing without reservation. It'd be a glue, insolvable and thick. It'd make me whole.

Warner stared at me, a look of confusion on his face. "That's not true," he said. "You're not nothing. You're sitting right in front of me. I want to know that person."

I frowned. "Listen, I don't know who I am. I don't know if the abduction happened. I don't know if the people I thought loved me, love me. All I know is that I've been used, again and again."

Warner shook his head as if trying to get my words out of his ears. "Oh, for Christ's sake, you're insufferable." He offered a weak smile to soften the blow. "Forget about the abduction, will you? You're more than that."

"But you said it happened. You believe."

"Oh, I think it did," said Warner. "But I don't think it means anything. I don't think it matters."

"What do you mean?" The words were short circuiting my brain. It did matter—it mattered a terribly great deal. It'd been with me for so long, there wasn't much else to me. My life revolved around it. I had to know if my life was based on a lie, if I was a con artist, if I had powers. Even my friendship with Sylvia had been formed around The Incident like a clam's pearl shaped around a speck of dirt. It had consumed me, I realized. "I need to know the truth," I said.

He rubbed his head like it hurt. "Sometimes things just happen—car crashes, winning the lottery—and none of it means anything. There's no greater scheme, no riddle to solve. It just doesn't matter. Tell me what your abduction signifies, huh?"

I didn't know how to answer. "Why are you being so *flippant*?" I asked after a long silence.

Warner sighed. "Let's get back on the bus."

"Wait," I said. I couldn't let Warner leave mad. He was all I had now.

Warner had slid off the table, but he turned and looked back at me.

"Sylvia. She was my everything. My only friend before you. I met her when I was young. She's an abductee just like me. When my parents were being horrible, she was all I had. She took me to conventions and helped me earn some money and—" I thought about her books on my convention table. "I helped her. She looks like the nicest little grandma you've ever seen. But she sold me. She's the one who gave my mom the idea to get rid of me, ship me off. She was using me all along." I thought telling him would feel bad, but I instead felt like something had been lifted—a dark veil pulled away.

"That's horrible," he said. "I'm sorry."

"It's whatever," I said, even though it wasn't. "I just feel stupid for loving her so much."

"It isn't your fault," he said. His hair glowed in the dying light, and I could see every split end, every imperfection illuminated.

I climbed down off the table. "I don't know."

"I think you should tell her how it made you feel," he said. "How hurt you are. It would be the truth."

"What? No." The suggestion made me freeze, a deer caught in the lights of some greater machine.

"Why not?" he asked.

A candy wrapper tumbled by on a current of wind. Warner bent over and grabbed it. He stuffed it in his pocket.

"I can't do that. It's not—It's not like me. I don't know how," I said. And it was true. I thought back to the night I ran away into the cold. I'd tried, then. I'd tried to tell my Daddy I was hurting. But that had ended with coffee and blood on the kitchen floor. And the realization of what I could do, if I wanted it badly enough.

He shrugged, wiped his hand on his jeans. "We're going to a library this week. You can email her there."

That night, I composed the letter in my mind. I wasn't sure if I'd send it, but it was interesting, letting all those words flit behind my eyes. For a brief moment, I hadn't wished for anything at all.

———

1897 was a strange year. I've already told you this—can you remember?

It was the first year in which a calculating device was described as a "computer," the only year in which spectral evidence—visions and ghosts—was used in a trial in the United States, the electron was discovered, oil was found on Osage native lands, Amelia Earhart was born; it was the beginning of the end.

But above it all soared a glorious sight: an unidentified airship, metallic and pointed, unlike anything ever seen. It was spotted all over the United States, from California to Texas to Missouri. People everywhere took to watching the sky in hope of seeing the incredible vessel.

It flew low at times, skimming the tops of trees. And inside, through the rounded, smooth windows, beings could be seen. "They were nude," said some. "They were beautiful."

And wherever it landed, stories abounded. The beings asked for water, for oil, for cold chisels. They were a needy bunch. Sometimes they simply pointed at the sky, mouthed unintelligible words. Sometimes they were cordial and joked with the witnesses, at other times they were abstruse, foreign.

On April 26, a group walked home from church in Merkel, Texas. There was a chill in the air, but not so much that you had to wear a coat. It was a pleasant evening. They talked about the sermon, the next day's chores. But they fell silent when they saw the thing—a heavy leaden object being dragged across the road in front of them by a taut rope stretching high into the sky, into the clouds.

They followed. It dragged over ridges and riverbeds, across yards and over cow trails. Eventually it snagged on a rail. At last, the thing had stopped.

And from above descended the airship—the one they'd read about in the papers that very morning, for every morning for the past two weeks. They gasped at the glow that emanated from the windows, heavenly and bright. It was every bit as beautiful as they'd said it would be.

Suddenly, a man came sliding down the rope, a small man dressed in a blue sailor's suit. Seeing the crowd gathered below, he clung tight, halting his fall. He eyed them all suspiciously, then pulled a knife from his pocket. He slashed and hacked at the rope until it came loose from the anchor, and the ship pulled away, the man still dangling beneath it.

They took the anchor and displayed it in a blacksmith shop for all to see. They did not see the airship again in Merkel. Some would wonder how it would ever stop now.

CHAPTER 36
A CHILD

I HAD PULLED a pulpy paperback off the pile that covered the stove. It was hard to read on the bus—I've never been great at reading in cars; my eyes bounce over the lines and get lost with every bump and turn—but I was doing my best trying to decipher the plot about zombies and the buxom women they were chasing. I could tell, despite my haphazard, oft interrupted reading, that it wasn't a very good book.

I sighed, folded the book shut on my lap. We had a long way to go before the next stop, a show in Albuquerque, and I was desperate for some distraction from my racing thoughts. I had long since tired of looking at the passing flat plains of desert. And it hurt my eyes to stare for too long anyway—so bright and unfiltered was the New Mexican sun.

I scanned the bus. Warner was asleep, sitting lounged against the defunct refrigerator, now used to store more lousy books. It seemed most people were napping, having been lulled to sleep by the warm rays leaking through the RV's windows. Only Robichek—ever at the wheel—and Rich and Judith were awake.

I was surprised to see Rich and Judith seated opposite one another at the little round table, engaged in a game of cards. They were silent, laying the cards down, solemnly eying every turn. I'd never seen either do something as trivial as playing a game. Maybe they were human after all.

I pushed myself off of the bench I'd called home for the past two hours and crept toward them. Now was my chance. "Hi," I said, startling Rich. He nearly dropped his fan of cards.

Judith turned her head toward me slightly, said nothing.

"Hello," Rich rasped, eyes downcast.

"What are you playing?" I asked.

"Cards," said Judith. Her voice was cold and low.

"Well, I know that," I said, offended. "I was wondering what game. Can I join?"

There was a slight snapping sound as Judith flicked another card onto the table. Rich rubbed his face with his free hand.

"Can I watch, then?" I asked.

Judith sighed, laid her hand face down on the table. "Why don't you go read your book?"

I recoiled slightly, both hurt and surprised by her words. I hadn't considered that she'd taken notice of me at all. "It's kind of crappy," I said, gathering up some courage. "The book."

"That's too bad," said Judith. She picked up the cigarette smoldering in the ashtray beside her.

"Whose books are they, anyway?" I asked. "Where did they come from?"

Judith shrugged, took a draw of her cigarette. I looked at Rich for an answer, but he was rocking back and forth, studying his cards with apparent rapture.

I felt silly standing there at the table, vulnerable, begging for attention. If anyone were to wake up and see me waiting there, they'd have thought me awfully sad. "Why are you always so mean to me?" I blurted.

Judith's eyebrows raised. Rich stopped his rocking but kept staring at his cards. She exhaled a cloud of blue smoke. "I'm not mean to you," she said. "I simply choose not to interact with you."

My skin tingled with embarrassment. I clenched my fists, feeling my sharp nails against my palm. The shame was dissolving into something more familiar—a resolute anger. "Why?" I asked. "I haven't done anything wrong."

I jumped when Judith laughed—a bark more suitable for Susanna than the dark, lithe woman seated before me. "Sure you have," she said. "And sure you will."

Daddy, laying prostrate on the kitchen floor. A scream building and filling the house. A career built on lies upon lies upon guilt upon doubt upon fear upon a little girl laying broken on the dining room floor, beneath a table, always beneath a table. My mother, sallow and crumbling. I put a hand to the side of my head, trying to quiet the roar inside my mind. Judith's smile widened. Up close, I could see her teeth were slightly pointed, sharp and catlike.

"What?" I gasped, still pushed off-kilter by the storm of images crashing through my mind.

"I have no use for people like that, like you."

Tears blurred my vision. "Like what?"

"Oh, come on now. Don't cry," she said, turning back to her cards. "It's just the truth. Nothing to cry about."

I sniffed. It wasn't fair, I thought, that she could judge me this way, so callously and with such pride. She didn't know me, know the strife and struggle I carried around every second of the day. She—

"Oh, stop it," she said, interrupting my thoughts. "Here." She handed me an unlit cigarette wrapped in brown paper. It smelled of cloves and sugar.

I accepted it into my hand without thinking. "I don't smoke," I said, curt and stiff.

"You start," she said. "Might as well be today."

"Marvin," I said, getting to the real reason I'd approached their table.

"What about him?" said Judith.

Rich raised an eyebrow.

"You told him something about me."

Judith exhaled through her nose. "Did I?"

I squeezed the cigarette so hard it came apart in my hand. "Yes," I said. "You did. And I'd like to know what it was about. Why you told him I'd come."

"Because it was true," she said. "Here you are." She looked me over, up and down. Then cringed at what she saw.

"Stop it," I shouted. "Just stop with your condescending shit."

Robichek slowed the RV, and people opened their eyes, swiveled to look in my direction.

"Oh good, you're gonna cause another scene. My favorite."

Marvin stared at me from the front of the bus, his mouth hanging wide.

"Forget it," I cried. "I don't want anything from you."

Judith laughed. "You sure do a lot of screaming, don't you?"

"I'm not screaming!"

Judith rolled her eyes. I should've stopped. But I was desperate.

"Listen," I said, quiet now, another tactic to try. "I need to know what you meant. What you meant when you said I'd help him get back to his time."

"I never said that," she said.

"Yes, you did!" My voice was a whine.

"Those weren't my exact words."

"Jesus!" I huffed. Judith was impossible. I retreated to my seat, pushed the lousy book onto the floor with a thunk, the sound absorbed by the rolling tires.

Mike leaned over and handed me a yellow sticky note. "What was that all about? How can I help?"

"Mind your business," I snapped.

Mike put his pen back in his pocket, and I immediately felt sorry. But I didn't say that—of course I didn't. I crossed my legs and looked out on the barren landscape.

————

I've had so many things taken from me. I've been violated a hundred ways. Here's someone I sympathize with.

It was best to get the tilling done at night. You could drive your tractor down the middle of the street without anyone to bother you and bask in all that coolness as you furrowed the earth. It was hell to do it in the heat of the day, Antonio would tell you. Besides, he'd never been a heavy sleeper anyway.

He was riding along, feeling the satisfying pull of the dirt beneath him, when a sun floated above him, lit up the path before him in bright, white daylight. The beams of his tractor's lights were nothing, were lost in that wash. Antonio pulled the brake, looked up. There was a luminous egg, thirty-five feet long and shining brilliantly.

It sprouted legs, and his tractor died, engine thrumming into quietness, lights fading.

When it landed, a ladder descended and Antonio swung himself off his tractor, thinking he might need to run. He looked over his shoulder, looked at the dark, and felt their hands upon him, pulling him toward the egg. It was too late.

They carried him up the ladder, placed him in the center of the floor. Five beings in tight suits and strange, bulbous helmets gathered around him and barked and growled and whined like dogs. He shook his head feebly, held up his hands.

They took his clothes, took his blood from a prick on the chin. He lay there naked and bleeding, wondering what would come next.

And come she did. She entered the room with a coy smile, her nakedness nothing compared to her gorgeous lips, and blue, searing eyes. She went to Antonio, stroked his hair, his cheek. She took him, the cold floor grinding into his back with every jolt.

When they separated, she smiled once more, gestured to her stomach and then at the sky.

The doctors who examined Antonio found scars on his chin, purple welts near his groin. Radiation poisoning, they said. But Antonio never found out if there was a child of his among the stars.

CHAPTER 37
NEED-TO-KNOW

WARNER TOOK the library steps two at a time.

"Wait up," I said. Mike, Arnold, and I were close behind. There were only a few of us going into the library. The rest of the bus went in search of a truck stop—they'd get their first shower in weeks. I had been toweling myself off in gas station sinks, dunking my hand-soap-lathered head under the faucet, but Warner assured me that missing a real shower would be worth it.

I was skeptical. Emailing Sylvia was not something I was raring to do. I couldn't imagine how spilling myself out to her, something so vulnerable, would make anything better. Though, it had worked with Warner; I'd told him the truth about Sylvia, and it hadn't killed me. Maybe it was worth a try.

Warner breezed past a librarian, nearly knocking her over. He was heading toward a bank of computers against a far wall.

"Warner," I whispered. A few heads turned my way, and I ducked down.

"We don't have a whole lot of time," he said, flicking the mouse before him. His screen came to life.

I waited for my own computer to boot up. It was old, beige, and boxy. It reminded me of the computer we had at home—the one on which I'd spent so many nights. I suddenly felt a little homesick, and I tried to tamp the feeling down. I didn't want any of that, I told myself. There was nothing there for me.

In the corner, I saw Mike digging through a bin of outcast books for sale and smiled. That would explain the poor selection on the bus. I wondered what Mike's life had been like before he got his new face—if he had a family wondering about him, waiting for news from him.

"Do you know her email address?" Warner asked, eyes on my screen—not his.

I knew her email address, her home address, her phone number. I'd been whispering it into the night and could type it with my eyes shut. "Yeah," I said.

I was finally able to open the browser and type in the website. I waited patiently as the loading indicator spun.

Clicking to open my email I saw three new messages from Sylvia and one from my mother. I highlighted all four and hit "Delete."

"What'd you do that for?" asked Warner.

I shrugged. "I don't want to hear it."

"I'd give anything to hear from my mom one more time," he said, voice wistful.

"Yeah, well, your mom loved you."

"You don't know that," he said.

"Yes, I do. Why would you want to hear from someone who didn't love you?"

Warner scrunched up his face. "I really miss her," he admitted. "I miss having a family. Guess this is as close as I'm getting, huh?" He laid a hand on my knee.

My face flushed scarlet, and I looked away, saw a hint of my disgust in the dead screen next to mine.

"Hey," he whispered. "Why don't you show me a picture of Sylvia? She's famous and stuff, so there'd be a picture of her somewhere, right?"

I hesitated, not immediately seeing the point. Looking at her would be painful. But maybe showing him would make me more understood, somehow. Showing Warner Sylvia was like showing him a part of myself, though messy and stained.

He leaned into me as I typed her name into the search bar.

"One look, and you'll understand," I said. I used to take so much comfort in the way she looked—so normal for an abductee. "I don't know. It gave me hope."

The screen loaded slowly from the top down. First, there were pictures—some unrelated, but some of Sylvia, all seemingly having been taken at conventions. There were some where her hair wasn't as gray—had a brownish hue, and I sighed. She had always been beautiful, had always had a kind face and big, welcoming eyes. How could such a nice-looking woman be so cruel?

"She does look like a grandma," Warner said.

"She does," I agreed, though Warner's mentioning of grandmothers set my mind alight with images of fire, burning.

The page loaded the rest of the way, and my heart stopped. Beneath the pictures, all smiling and golden, were several articles. All recent.

Well-Known Abduction Victim Found to be Fraud
Convention Speaker Accused of Plagiarism
Sylvia Green is a Liar

I made a noise, like a mouse's strangled squeak when the trap comes down upon its throat, and Warner sucked in his breath. "Laura," he said.

I scrolled farther, words flying by. This couldn't be true.

"Laura," Warner said again, laying a hand on my arm.

I shook Warner off and clicked the first link.

"Don't," Warner said, but I ignored him and read, dizzy—my head feeling like a balloon.

Alien convention speaker and well-known abduction advocate Sylvia Green's story came falling apart Thursday when an anonymous source released a seven-page blog post detailing the falsehoods in Sylvia's story. Most prominent among the claims is proof that Ms. Green never lived in Forsythia, the town where the alleged encounter took place. The friends supposedly present during the incident were interviewed and all deny—

"Laura," Warner said, gruffer now.

I woke from my trance with a strangled moan.

"Turn this off," Warner said, reaching for the button on the monitor.

"No!" I cried, pushing his hand away.

I copied the URL for the news story and paged back to my emails. I opened a new message, a field of clean white. I typed in Sylvia's address, pasted the URL, and hit send. I did it all without thinking, a smooth, deft movement.

I stood, and Warner rose beside me.

———

Sometimes we search for the truth and get nothing in return, sometimes we get everything. This story, one of my favorites, concerns curiosity.

Jimmy Carter, 39th President of the United States, was only still governor when he stood before the Leary, Georgia Lion's Club, preparing to speak. He'd been summoned to make some encouraging comments, commend them on their good will. It would be an easy, unremarkable job.

To light applause, Jimmy took the podium. At first, all eyes were on him, but as he spoke, he watched their gazes drift away, up and over his shoulder. Mouths hung open. He turned, looking to see what strange bird or beast had captured their attention.

Instead, he was met with a small moon, hanging just over the horizon. It flashed and changed colors, sometimes moving farther away, sometimes closer. Jimmy watched the thing bounce across the sky until it disappeared. The future president never forgot his meeting with the Lion's Club of Leary, Georgia.

The sighting instilled in him a deep interest in UFOs. When he ran for the highest office in the land, he vowed to declassify whatever documents he could, exposing the American people to the truth behind UFOs and extraterrestrials. However, once he became president, he became quiet on the issue. Many speculate he was shown something devastating, something the people at large couldn't handle. Others propose that the UFO question is discussed on a "need to know" basis and not even the president needs to know, not yet.

Carter did later reveal something interesting: he inadvertently disclosed the existence of a top-secret remote viewing program within the government. Psychics were tasked with attempting to see beyond the Iron Curtain, spying on the Soviets with their minds. It's not exactly aliens, but still within the realm of the paranormal.

CHAPTER 38
HOAXES

SYLVIA. Sylvia. Sylvia. I said her name in my head, sometimes aloud. Sometimes in shame, in grief, in disbelief. Other times in anger. Sylvia. What had she done?

Faking an incident was a mortal sin in our community. There's so little information on phenomenon—aliens, UFOs, Bigfoot, ghosts, faeries—anyone deemed to be telling the truth was seen as a prophet, bringing truth across the great divide of time and space. To fake, to lie, was to demean the entire community, to throw into jeopardy every other victim and witness statement.

I had struggled my whole life with the idea of whether I was telling the truth or not. It was agony not knowing if I was real, if I was contributing to something larger than myself or just laughing in its face, profiting off a lie. For Sylvia to have done it intentionally—to have jumped into these icy waters by her own free will and then perpetuated the lie, especially after meeting me—was lunacy.

Was she mad? I entertained the thought—it would be easier to forgive myself for loving her if she was simply crazy, confused. But nothing else in her life betrayed any reduced facility in thought, in logic. She had meticulously planned out my sale to Robichek, hiding it from me all the while. She wasn't dumb. She knew exactly what she was doing when she told the story of the little girl in the woods, swept away by a light—piercing bright and painful.

I had known fakers in the past, their names whispered in hushed tones around the convention circuit. People no one would hire, have at their talks. They were blacklisted once the truth came out. Ridiculed. Bullied. Forgotten.

I wondered what chasmic hole Sylvia was attempting to fill by creating the story, what aspect of herself found the world lacking enough to require some invention. I had always assumed my life would be better had I not been abducted—no domineering Daddy, no second guessing, no chance for my mother to betray me—but perhaps it would also have been boring, quiet. I longed for that now, but there's no telling how I might have felt had the beam, the spotlight, never shown on me.

"It's going to be okay," said Warner.

But I couldn't reply. I was drowning in my thoughts, letting them wash over me, fill my mouth like cotton.

I had wished for her destruction, but I hadn't known it'd come like this. I hated Sylvia. Hated her with a loathing so complete it was hard to see around it. Yet, I didn't want her to be a liar. I still held myself up against her like a face to the mirror. Even though she'd sold me, I could still say she had always needed me as much as I needed her. We were two childhood abductees just trying to cope. But now, I knew she had always been using me. Using me for money, for credibility, for spite.

We had never been in love. She had never loved me.

When Warner wasn't buzzing about my head like a directionless gnat, Marvin was there, trying in his awkward way to soothe and draw out some scrap of information that would guide him home. In one breath he'd ask me if everything was alright, then ask if I'd given Judith's message any more thought. His words were erratic, all over the place.

"I don't know what it means," I said in response to both of Marvin's enquiries.

"Just think," he said, tapping his head. "Think really hard. I want to go home."

"Marvin, no amount of thinking is going to get me, get us, any closer. Judith's words—have you ever considered that they might not mean anything, might not be true?" I whispered, afraid to be overheard.

"No! Judith's never wrong," he said.

I rolled my eyes. "No one's that perfect. I tried talking to her, and she was rude. Maybe she's messing with you. Have you tried talking to her lately?"

He shook his head. "She just says the same thing every time."

He put his hand on mine and squeezed tight. I tried to pull away, but his grasp was firm. "You are going to save me, Laura."

I gave up my struggling and let the man hold my hand. We sat in silence, and I slipped back into my thoughts. Sylvia had lied, Marvin was resting his head on my shoulder, wanting me to save him. It was all so strange, so ridiculous. I felt like I was in a bleary dream, trying desperately to break through, to wake up.

At some point I was faintly aware that I was on stage, was singing. But it swept by, emotionless and distant. I couldn't remember the show or several after.

I didn't notice that the bus had turned East, was swinging back toward home.

———

Sometimes deception is an art, laborious and rewarding. This is the story of a beautiful hoax.

A plank of wood, rope, a baseball cap fitted with a loop of wire. Doug dumped the things in the backseat of Dave's car. They'd be dirty, damp, and clotted with mud once they were done, but Dave never said anything. He didn't care what the car looked like, always streaked in something unholy, shocks of dead plants sticking out of the fender. No one ever asked where he'd been, and that was enough for Dave.

"Ready?" asked Doug. It was cold, colder than the night before, and he'd forgotten his gloves.

Dave felt for the keys in his jacket pocket. "Yes," he said. He was shaking all over with something more than cold. This was their best nest yet.

The men slid into the car and didn't speak again until they'd found their way back to the main road. It was well past three in the morning, but neither man was tired. They just listened to the tires hum and stared off into the dark.

"When do you think they'll find it?" asked Dave.

Doug whistled, soft and low. "One of that size? Would have to be tomorrow. Farmer checks his plot every day. Nest that big? Can't avoid it."

Dave smiled. He and Doug had been at it for years now. And though it started as something of a gag conceived after one too many drinks at the pub, Dave didn't laugh about it anymore. What they were doing, it wasn't a prank. It was art.

"Where to next?" asked Doug.

Dave shrugged. They'd been all over southern England. Farmers were beginning to expect the cryptic symbols in their fields. "Somewhere else," he said. "Some other country."

Doug clapped his hands together. "But where?"

"America," said Dave. "All those fields... Can you imagine it? We could end up anywhere, some tiny little town in, say, Kansas and—"

"I think we should go to Australia," said Doug. "Back to where it began."

The saucer nests originated there, flattened reeds behind barns and houses. Dave and Doug were inspired, turned them into something monstrous marring the English countryside—geometric wonders gashed deep into the wheat.

Dave shrugged.

"What do you think about the circles over in Avebury?" asked Doug.

"Pale imitations," said Dave. No one could make crop circles quite like him and Doug. In fact, until 1987, no one had made crop circles at all. But it was becoming more popular; more imitators were emerging, trampling misshapen characters into the ground.

"It was quite good," said Doug.

"Copycat," said Dave.

Doug shifted uncomfortably in his seat. "I don't know," he said. "I mean, it was really good. Really."

Dave didn't say anything. The truth was, he hadn't seen the new circles. Not wanting to subconsciously absorb someone else's work, Dave tended to not look at reports of crop circles unless he knew they were his own. If they were his, he'd revel in the reports, laugh himself hoarse.

"Do you think... maybe?" Doug pointed to the sky.

Dave grunted. "How good were they?"

"Pretty damn good," said Doug.

Dave tightened his grip on the wheel. "We'll have to come out soon, won't we?"

Doug sighed, rubbed his thumb across his upper lip. "Maybe so," he said. "If you don't want someone else claiming them first."

The road swam as tears flooded Dave's eyes. To give it all up—to give it up would be hell. Dave not only liked the challenge of creating the complex shapes in the crop, but he liked the feel of the stalks bending beneath his board, liked the way the night air smelled earthy and damp, liked the buoyancy when news of their latest masterpiece hit the radio, the television. It was much, much more than a joke. "Soon," he said, pressing down on the accelerator. "Someday, soon."

CHAPTER 39
HURT

"WHAT ARE YOU GOING TO DO?" Warner asked as we walked lazy loops around the parking lot.

I shrugged. "I wish I knew. Part of me hopes I'll never have to see Sylvia again. Then I won't have to decide."

Warner sighed, pushed the hair out of his eyes. "I still think you should confront her. Ask her why she did what she did. All of it—the lies, selling you—"

"I know what she did," I said. "And I know why. At this point, I'm not sure if I care what she says. And how do I trust her?"

"Fair point," he said. He stared ahead at the woods next to the rest stop building. It was a little cluster of thin, sickly trees, leaves a pale greenish-yellow. I peered into them as well, trying to see what he was looking at, but there were only branches, empty air.

"The bus will be leaving soon," he said. "They're probably waiting on us."

"How long has it been?" I asked, looking to the setting sun. The sky was aflame with luscious reds and oranges. If I hadn't been so sad, I might have relished its beauty.

"Half an hour," he said. "At least."

I followed him back to the RV and climbed aboard to see it full, thrumming with an anxious energy—the feeling of being in one place for too long.

"What the hell were you two doing?" chided Robichek from the driver's seat.

My face turned as red as the sky.

"Walking," Warner mumbled. Someone snorted in the back.

The uneasy feeling on board the bus grew, made a sweat break out across my forehead though the weather was cooler, having left the deserts of the west behind.

Warner and I assumed our usual spots on the little bench near the oven. It felt good to have a place all our own, reserved for us. I had finally carved out my little piece of the show and it was something to hold on to when it felt like the rest of my life was spinning out of control. I wasn't hiding under the table anymore. There was the bench, Warner, my song—I let the images file through my mind again and again, lulling me into a tenuous calm.

I glanced around the bus, and my anxiety returned—something wasn't right. I couldn't put my finger on it, but the air was wrong, vibrating somehow. I shut my eyes, leaned my head against the side of the bus. I was just tired, stressed out—that had to be it.

We merged onto the highway, and the bus shook with speed. Moving farther and farther from that little stand of trees, the limp branches. I rubbed my eyes, unsure why that vision had occurred to me, why the trees mattered at all.

Warner's eyes were shut, as were those of most of the riders. It was the end of a long day of driving, of stopping at rest stops and gas stations and Walmarts and the weariness of the road was heavy.

Susanna and Rich were already asleep, both snoring in gruff little gasps. Judith was reading, though her eyes did not appear to move, did not seem to scan the page. Mike and Arnold both sat at the flimsy table, writing on yellow legal pads, their pens scratching lightly. I wondered if they wrote to each other.

And Marvin—where was Marvin? I leaned forward, trying to get a better view. I scanned the dim interior of the bus, even the little hiding places where only Warner or I could fit, but did not see him. Marvin wasn't on the bus.

I was about to leap up, shout, when something held me back—a faint understanding. If Marvin wasn't on the bus, he was free of the show. He could start over.

Sure, it might be hard at first; he'd have to run into the right people, police officers, doctors, but Marvin was so vocal about his plight, I was sure he'd have no trouble getting help. He may end up in grippy socks, but anything was better than being used by Robichek. I knew better than anyone how painful it was being used. If I didn't say anything, I was helping him.

Break out of time, I thought. Marvin's words. Judith's premonition was coming true, whether or not it was the way Marvin intended. I leaned back in my seat and looked around the bus. No one knew the great deed I was doing. No one seemed to notice I was helping another.

Except for Judith. She stared at me over the edge of her book, her eyes intense, brow furrowed. She knew, was studying me, watching my every move and thought. I smiled, unintimidated, and her expression did not change—she stared, her eyes drilling into mine.

I turned away, toward Warner, and laid a hand on his knee. The jolt of it coiled through him, and he twitched. His eyes opened, and he said, "You're really never going to talk to your mom again? Even with Sylvia gone?"

"Is this all you think about?" I asked.

"Yes."

"What? Why? Besides, that's what Sylvia wanted: for me to talk to my mom. The two are in on it. I'm not talking to either one of them."

"But if you want the truth as badly as you say, I don't understand why you don't at least try with your mom."

He was right, I knew. She was the only way back to the beginning. I picked at the skin on my hand. "I just don't want to give her the satisfaction," I said. I didn't want her to know I needed her, thought about her at all.

Warner looked tired. He said, "All of that, that's for kids. You know that. You should talk to her. You need someone who understands you."

"But I have you," I said, panicked.

"I wasn't there," he said. "I think you should make amends."

"But what about you?" I asked. "You don't talk to your family. You don't talk to anyone."

Warner shrugged. "Everyone's dead."

Judith slammed her book down on her lap with a percussive slap. Heads shot up all around the bus.

"Marvin's not on the bus," she said evenly.

"What?" Susanna asked, blinking bleary eyes.

"Marvin's not on the bus," said Judith again.

"Hey!" Arnold shouted, and now Robichek's eyes appeared in the rearview mirror. "You forgot someone. Turn this thing around."

"Shit," Warner said, turning to look out the window as if he could see the man we'd left ten miles behind.

The bus slowed, pulled to the side of the highway. "What's this?" Robichek asked.

"Marvin," said Arnold. "He's not here. We left him at the rest stop."

Robichek veered back out onto the road. "Goddamn it," he said. "Let me find a spot to turn around. Why didn't anyone tell me?"

I couldn't understand why Judith had done it, notified the bus to Marvin's absence. Couldn't she see that this was for the best? Maybe she couldn't read minds and the future after all. Maybe she was simply doing the inevitable; someone would notice him missing, eventually. At least Marvin had a good head start.

When she felt my eyes on her, she glared so vehemently it took my breath away. I leaned into Warner.

"Poor guy," he said.

The bus was abuzz now, and Robichek finally turned off, steered the bus back toward the lonely rest stop.

"He'll be okay," I said.

Now everyone peered out windows, waiting to catch sight of the stranded man.

"I can't believe it," Susanna said. "We've never left anyone behind."

"We're tired," said Arnold. "It was an honest mistake."

The bus tires hummed along the pavement, lights streaking by.

"I just hope he's still there," rasped Rich.

"Why wouldn't he be there?" asked Arnold. "It's only been twenty minutes. It's not like he'd disappear—back to his time."

There was a faint snicker, but I couldn't tell who it was.

Susanna pulled at her hair, knuckles white. "He has so many weird ideas in his head. He might think we did it on purpose or something. Or he went with the first people to pay him any mind. Oh God."

"He wouldn't," said Warner. "He's smarter than that."

"Is he?" asked Susanna. "The man doesn't even know what year it is, I doubt—"

"Hey, now. We're almost there," Arnold soothed.

We were slowing, the brakes of the bus screeching. A red light bathed the bus, and lit up our faces with a garish glow.

"Great," Robichek said.

I pulled myself up to see what the matter was. A sea of brake lights blocked the highway. The red ribbon stretched as far as I could see.

"There must have been an accident," I said.

"Someone should get out," said Susanna. "Walk the rest of the way to him. Tell him we're coming."

"No one else is getting off," said Robichek, and we crept forward slightly.

"He'll see the lights and know we're stuck," said Arnold. "He'll be waiting."

I could feel Judith's eyes on me, and my skin prickled. The bus moved, making a few feet of progress only to stop again. As we drew closer, inching forward, the red and blue lights of emergency vehicles flashed on the horizon.

"Must be bad," said Warner.

We moved to the front of the bus in tandem, all of us except Judith gathered now around Robichek, peering through the windshield.

At last, we pulled up beside the wreckage, the lights of the ambulances and police cars blinding now.

"It's only one car," said Susanna, shielding her eyes.

"Must have hit the center divider," grunted Robichek.

"Look," gasped Arnold. "Someone's laying there."

A white sheet on the black of the highway, men in uniform gathered around it.

"Someone's been hit," said Arnold.

"Let me out!" Susanna screamed. She leaped down the steps, fell against the locked door. She beat it with her hands. "Let me out! Goddamn it, unlock the door."

Warner looked at me, eyes wide. "You don't think..."

My stomach hurt, was roiling and cramping, and I felt faint. I gripped Warner's arm, scared I would fall to the floor.

"No," I said, unsure if I was answering him or denying the situation all together. "No. It can't be."

Robichek unlocked the door, sending Susanna tumbling onto the pavement. The policemen approached, and horns blared behind us. We were taking up the only free lane. I couldn't hear over the cacophony, but Susanna's face broke into a scream.

"Goddamn it," Robichek said, pulling the bus into the glass and trash-strewn berm. Cars flew past us. "Goddamn it." He turned the key, and the bus settled into silence.

"I'll go," said Arnold. He didn't wait for anyone's response, he was already out in the night air, trying to cross the one open lane.

"I don't understand," said Rich.

"No one else get off this bus," said Robichek. "Stay here." He rose, unfurling the sweaty mass of himself and waddled after Arnold.

We watched the three of them standing with the police, the sheet-wrapped body next to them, Susanna in tears, Arnold pale and holding a hand to his forehead, and Robichek gesturing at the bus.

"Let's go to the back," Warner said, ushering me away from the scene. I resisted, twisting back to the window. I deserved to see it.

"I did this," I whispered. "It's my fault."

"What?" He dragged me to our bench, pulled me down to sitting. "Here, drink some water."

I pushed the bottle away. "Warner, this is my fault." My voice sounded distant, as if someone else was speaking through my lips. The words snagged on every tooth. My body was numb, an effigy stuffed with straw. I was leaving my body, somehow. I was retreating to some guiltless place far away.

"How?" he scoffed. "Besides, we don't even know what happened. It's not him."

"It is," I said. "It's him. He must have been running after the bus."

Judith was looking out the window, but her reflection stared directly at us. I shivered.

Robichek climbed back on the bus. I could see rivulets of sweat streaming down his face even from our spot in the back. "He's gone," he said.

"What do you mean?" Rich asked.

"He got hit by a car. Marvin. He got hit."

"No," Warner said. "It can't be him."

"I saw him," said Robichek.

"Warner," I whispered, voice faint and thin. "I did this."

He shushed me, enveloped my hand in his.

Susanna and Arnold stumbled back onto the bus, and the air was filled with choking sobs. Robichek closed the door behind them, sealing us in with our grief.

"I knew he wasn't on the bus, Warner," I whispered.

He turned toward me, his eyes narrowed. "What?"

"I knew he wasn't here, and I didn't say anything."

"What?" he asked again. "Why?" He glanced around the bus, looking to see if anyone else had heard the nonsense coming out of my mouth.

"I don't know," I said. "I guess I thought he'd be better off without us."

Warner sighed, covered both eyes with his hands. He looked so tired. "You didn't do this," he said.

"Someone *do* something," cried Susanna. "This isn't right."

Mike put an arm around her, pulled her close.

"What can we do?" asked Arnold. "They're gonna take care of him, Suze. We can't do anything else."

"It feels wrong to just leave him," said Susanna.

"Should someone stay behind?" asked Rich.

I stood.

"No one's staying behind!" Robichek shouted. "We have a schedule and a show to get to."

Judith's voice cut through the din clear and calm. "Laura, why don't you sing?"

I shot a dark look at Judith. She knew. She was torturing me, poking at me with her razor-sharp nails.

"Could you?" asked Susanna, eyes wide. She grabbed me by the shoulders, shook me a little. "You call aliens, you cure people! You cure people! I've seen them come up to you after shows. I've seen people say you saved them." Her voice was frantic. "Save Marvin! Bring him back!"

I took a stumbling step backward, wiped her spit from my face. "Listen, I'm not so sure—"

"Sure of what!?" screeched Susanna.

"I've never done anything like this before," I said. The only wishes of mine that had ever come true were the ones that ended in annihilation. My singing only summoned the desperate. Besides, in that moment, I could barely breathe, let alone sing.

"People say you healed them. Fix Marvin!" Susanna screamed.

"Try it," said Rich. "I mean, what's the harm?"

"Yes! Please! Do something!" Susanna was pushing me down the bus steps.

"I don't know if The Incident happened," I said. I had pushed out my elbows, wedged myself in the door frame. "I don't know if I have powers."

The bus was quiet. Susanna stopped her shoving.

The words were rolling out, fast and unstoppable. "It might all be a marketing stunt," I confessed. "I'm not sure. I don't even know if I was abducted. My daddy—I never learned the truth."

I looked up at the sad faces assembled above me. I wiped a tear from my eye. "I'm sorry. I'm sorry I lied, if I'm lying. I don't know! I'm so confused. Always have been. See I have this doubt and—"

"So what?" Susanna gave me one last shove. "Just try."

They piled out of the bus and followed me to where Marvin had died. They were lifting him now, placing him on a stretcher. The door of an ambulance yawned wide before us.

"You can't be here," said a paramedic.

I cleared my throat.

"Do it!" screeched Susanna. "Before they take him away!"

A car honked in the distance. I lifted a hand to shield my eyes from the whirring lights of the police cars. "I don't know," I whispered.

"Please," cried Susanna.

I looked back at them, the ragtag bunch of freaks. They were huddled together, some holding hands, all staring at me, waiting for me. I hurt, looking at them. They had so much to believe in.

I closed my eyes. The first notes of "Ave Maria" came tumbling out of my mouth, and I felt the world still. *Please*, I wished. *Let him live*.

Let him live.

Let him live.

Let him live.

I envisioned Marvin's face, his slick black hair. I wanted that white shroud to rise, to fall away as he sat up. Let him live. Please.

I wished until my head throbbed. I wished until the final words came choking out: *Oh, mother hear a suppliant child*.

When I opened my eyes, the body was being lifted into the truck. The freaks were turning away, wiping their tears, their snotty noses on their sleeves.

It hadn't worked.

I cried for myself, then. And all I had lost.

———

Hurt is universal, as is disease. This piece deals with both.

Ron was driving fast—eighty-five miles per hour. He wanted to get to his brother's house before everyone was asleep. He hated that awkward pause on the doorstep, listening for the shuffle of slippered feet. It'd be better to get there before midnight.

His daughter sat in the seat beside him, saying nothing about the speed or time or how dark the Oregon night was. None of it mattered to her. She had the seat reclined back, and she tried to sleep, but it wouldn't come. Instead, she stared out the window, watching for any signs they might be getting close to her uncle's house. Maybe sleep would find her there.

The fields were dark, inky voids, barely discernible from the sky. It was comforting, in a way, to be surrounded like this. Swaddled. They both thought it, though they did not communicate.

"What's that?" she asked, sitting up straight now.

"What's what?" asked Ron, slowing slightly.

"Blue lights, in that field," she said. And there were—three blue orbs danced in the darkness, floated about each other.

"I have no idea," said Ron.

The orbs flew toward the car, catching up to it with no trouble. Two of them entered the car, flying through the closed windows as if they were nothing but air. Ron pressed the buttons on the door to make sure the windows were up, but they were.

One of the orbs shot through the dashboard and back out into the night. But the second floated toward Ron. It passed through his shoulder, chest, and arm. As the thing entered him, Ron felt a strange stirring in his body—a vibration deep and energetic. But what scared him most was the look on his daughter's face, a visage of pure horror.

The second orb exited the car and hovered in front of them before flying away, disappearing into the obsidian sky. Ron was scared, too scared to stop. And he drove on to his brother's house as fast as the little car would go. Despite the speed, the forty-five-minute drive seemed to take forever, hours.

Ron's symptoms began immediately. Lost hair, swelling, nervousness, and nausea. He'd develop cancer everywhere the orb touched.

CHAPTER 40
SUN SPOTS

THE HUM of tires on asphalt, disembodied wails—the bus was a sepulcher in which every sound was amplified, echoing. But Judith was quiet. I watched her flip through the yellowing pages of a novel. She hadn't cried, hadn't yelled out once. She looked content.

Mike made the rounds passing out tissues and collecting the used ones into a small wastepaper basket.

"Thanks," I whispered, accepting a tissue. My tears came in fits and starts. I hadn't brought Marvin back to life. I hadn't helped him. I was weak and empty and a liar—I'd been fooling myself for too long.

I stared at the top of Judith's bowed head, at the place where her hair parted and cascaded away in perfect tresses. Poised and powerful, she wasn't anybody's fool. She looked up at me and winked.

She read the rest of the trip, only stopping to stretch her arms above her head or reposition her long legs. I stared.

———

"Why didn't you say anything?" I cornered Judith behind the theater in a little alley boasting a dumpster and a few discarded signs.

"Why didn't you?" she shot back. She wasn't even looking at me, was studying the thin strip of sky visible between the two buildings. It was a dusk sky—pastel and golden.

"I thought I was doing the right thing," I said. "I thought he could get help if he was free of us."

"Well, you did the wrong thing." She flicked her cigarette at my feet.

"You knew it was going to happen," I said. "You knew."

Judith shrugged.

I was burning with anger, hot and violent. I wanted to grab her, shake her, break that blank, serene face into something unrecognizable. "You let him die," I said.

"You did," she said. "It was your decision to make."

"Why'd you have to bring up singing?" I asked.

She finally looked at me and blinked, big doe eyes. "I just thought it would be nice. Like saying some words at a funeral."

"You know that's not what was happening!"

Judith's lip twitched as if she were suppressing a smile. "It didn't look like anything was happening, to me. Just like before. Except this time there's no broken pieces to leave scars on your skin."

I choked, my words all clotted up in my throat.

"I know all about that sick trophy on your leg. Now leave me alone. I'm trying to focus before I have to go on. Go put on your prom gown."

I stamped my foot, a gesture childlike and impatient. If Judith was going to make me feel like a child, I was going to act like one. "Murderer," I managed to spit.

"Murderer," she said, her tone betraying nothing.

I spun on my heel and marched back inside the theater. I could hear the clanking of the lights and stage being constructed, muffled talking.

The dressing room, normally a buzzing hive, was quiet and slow with thick, molasses air. Susanna stared at herself in the mirror, comb in hand, and Mike did and redid the buttons of his shirt. I pulled on my dress without even checking myself in the mirror. I didn't bother with makeup—my hands were trembling, and my tears would wash it away.

I had some time before the show since I hadn't done my hair or makeup and went outside to the front of the theater. I didn't want to see sharp-tongued, all-knowing Judith ever again. It was a nice day, early fall, with a warm breeze. I wished I could enjoy it, could feel anything beyond the aching mixture of anger and guilt churning inside me. It wasn't fair that Judith could see through me as if my skin were glass, my thoughts placards, clear and plain.

I leaned against a wall, aware a line had formed at the theater door, and all eyes were on me. I could feel them trying to parse me out—was I a sword swallower, a fortune teller? Maybe they'd read some of the reviews of the show or remembered me from my old life, so far away. They probably already knew all about me—knew more about me in that moment than I did about myself. I ignored them, did not turn their way, and instead watched the slow passage of cars.

"Laura?"

A spark passed through me so violently that I jumped. It was like being stabbed with an electric rod.

"Laura?"

It was her—her voice. From the corner of my vision, white hair and a pink sweater came into view.

I turned, looked her in the eye, and for a moment I was paralyzed. I thought of running, of screaming, of driving my fist into her face. But in the end, I fell into her arms.

"Sylvia," I cried into the crook of her neck.

"I'm here," she murmured, stroking my hair.

———

Here's one about looming destruction.

Señor Bonilla was director of the Zacatecas Observatory in 1883. It was a good job, quiet. He liked coming in before the sun set, when the world was still golden and watching the sky fade into the bruised tones of twilight.

Lately he'd been coming in early. He'd turned his attention away from the sparkling night sky to a closer star. He was mapping out sunspots, examining them for mutations or flares.

He had a nice camera, nicer than the ones down at the university and was proud of his work. The pictures he took were pretty enough to be sold, he thought, put in books and on diaries and cards. He liked looking at them at night, knowing he was one of the few, or only men still gazing upon the sun in those late hours.

It was almost a relief to fall behind the camera, the specially augmented telescope, and lose himself in the bright disc of the sun. It was so familiar to him now, an old friend. He peered through the eyepiece and examined the sphere.

To his amazement, a small luminous object was crossing in front of the sun. He snapped a picture of it to analyze later. He peered back through the apparatus and saw a cluster of fifteen to twenty more of the shapes flying in the same direction as the first. He took another photograph.

He took hundreds of photographs that morning—there were 283 vessels to capture, after all. And the next day he'd see 116 more.

Bonilla had friends in the other observatories across Mexico and he wrote to them, urging them to keep an eye on the sun and to write to him immediately should they see anything crossing the solar field. He never got any response.

He published the photographs, expecting to be lauded for their majesty, but only received criticism. "It's dust," they said. "Birds, bugs."

But Bonilla insisted to his dying day that was he saw was "traveling in space near the earth, but not so far as the moon."

In 2011, long after Señor Bonilla took his last breath, scientists suggested that the specks the astronomer captured were fragments of a billion-ton comet. Had they hit Earth, we would have experienced a mass extinction 3275 times more calamitous than the Tunguska event, which flattened 80 million trees in the Russian taiga. Aliens or comet, Bonilla captured something devastating on his collodion photograph plates.

CHAPTER 41
CIRCLES

WHEN WARNER SAW ME BACKSTAGE, walking hand-in-hand with Sylvia, his mouth fell open, and his eyes grew wide. "Uh, hi," he said. He didn't offer her his hand, nor she hers.

"Warner, this is Sylvia," I said.

"I see," he said, looking from her face to mine.

"She's going to stay for the show."

Sylvia nodded. "I can't wait to see your act."

"Um, well, thanks, I guess," he said. "I have to finish getting ready." He walked away in big, exaggerated strides.

I felt sorry for him. He was so confused. In truth, so was I. I was still hurt by what Sylvia had done, but I couldn't resist her. I had broken when I saw her, spilled all over thick and warm. I needed her. I didn't want it to be this way, I wanted to be angry and vengeful and full of spite, but being so near to her again was like returning to the womb, safe and warm. I wanted to curl up inside her forever.

"Why'd you do it?" I asked as I walked her around to the front of the building.

"Do what, honey?"

"All of it," I said. "Contacting Robichek, lying about your abduction. I just want to know why."

She paused for a moment, chewed on her lip. "I needed the money, Laura. I'm sorry." She had tears in her eyes and her voice cracked, wavered.

Money. That's what my life boiled down to, truth and money. A desperate search for both, riding the current of notes streaming from my body. I'd always been a piggybank searching for my lost cork. "But you had to know I'd find out the truth eventually, that everyone would."

She looked down at her hands. "It was stupid, I know."

"Your book. It was all lies. And you had me selling it alongside mine." I was regaining a little of my indignance. "You're putting my credibility in jeopardy. The show, my book—if people associate them with you, it'll all be over." Truth and money.

"I need you, Laura."

I sighed, and the anger floated away with my breath. Maybe it didn't matter, like Warner said. Maybe the only thing that did matter was Sylvia's love, radiant and hot. I wanted it so badly—maybe more than I wanted anything else. "I need you too," I confessed. "So, you'll stop, then?"

"Stop what?" Robichek waddled by, and Sylvia raised her eyes to watch.

"You know. Trying to spread your story, taking money from him." I nodded in Robichek's direction. "It's over now."

Sylvia frowned, a look so incongruous with her sweet face that I almost laughed. "Oh, I can't stop," she said.

"What?" I asked, ice prickling in my veins. "What do you mean? You have to stop. It's done. Finished. You're here to take me away."

She shook her head, and her white curls bounced. "I need the money, dear. I have to keep on. You have to keep on."

I had already forgiven her, had flung myself back into her arms only to find the arms cold and unmoving. "But—but the truth—" I stuttered.

"What about it?"

"You're a liar," I said. "You lied to me, to everyone, and you're just going to continue on as if nothing happened?"

"Well, not exactly. I'm going on a talk-show circuit to talk about why I lied about the abduction. It's a whole new facet to the story, don't you think? People are dying to hear it. And you have to keep performing, honey. It's been a nice little bonus. I told you, I need the money."

"But it's wrong," I said. "To profit off of a lie."

She shrugged. "You do it every day."

I pushed her then, hard and fast, and she stumbled backward.

"Laura," she gasped, but I was running. I ran through the backstage, shoving past workers and performers. I ran until I found Warner, and I ruined his costume with my tears.

He threaded his hand through my hair, pressed my head to his chest. "It's gonna be alright," he murmured into my ear.

I wanted to protest, to fight—he didn't even know what had transpired, what new pain was unearthed within me—but I was choking. I was falling apart.

"Shhhh," he soothed. He rocked me gently, petted my hair.

"Five minutes, people." Robichek's voice cut through everything.

Warner took a step back, disengaging himself from the tight knot of snot and warmth we'd formed. I wiped my nose on the back of my hand, leaving a snail's trail of mucus there, but Warner didn't see. He was wandering away, pulled toward the group of performers waiting for him, glittering and alive.

———

The show was lackluster. Robichek had been filling in for Marvin, introducing us in an awkward cant, and the energy had gone out of most of the performances. Everyone was mourning and tired, except me. I sang loud and clear. I hit all the notes. Animated by anger, I pushed all my sadness aside. If she was still there, sitting in the crowd, I wanted her to hear me, and I wanted her to know I wasn't afraid. I wanted my voice to haunt her, drive her mad. I wanted her to look at me and see everything she'd lost.

But afterward, when the adrenaline and clarity had burned away, I sat curled on the bus, ruminating. Sylvia had said I was profiting off a lie. That I did it every day. What did she know? Maybe she was just trying to hurt me, to bring me down low. But maybe there was something there.

I needed to speak to my mother. I needed her, I realized, and began to cry again.

Warner crouched down so his face was close to mine and said, "What the hell is going on? What are you doing? One minute I see you're happy with Sylvia and the next you're running through the theater crying. Which is it?"

I wiped the tears from my eye with a clumsy hand. "I made a mistake," I said. "Trusting her, going back to her. It wasn't right."

"I could have told you that," he said, sitting down next to me. "What happened, anyway?"

I told him about how she'd still be profiting from the show, her refusal to change, but withheld her final words—the ones that implicated me. "The truth didn't matter to her," I said. "Just like you said. It didn't matter. Money is the only thing that does."

He sighed, put a hand on mine. "That's not what I meant. That's not what it means."

"What does it mean, then?" I asked.

"I meant, you should live your life regardless of if the abduction happened or not. Stop killing yourself trying to figure out the answer."

I pulled my hand away.

I remember the way his eyes looked in the half-light, pleading and sad.

"Warner?" I asked.

"Yes?"

"Do you really think I should get in contact with my mother?"

"I do," he said. "She's all you have left."

"But I have—" I stopped the words, choked by the truth, remembering how he'd untangled himself from me so swiftly, so easily, there in the dark of the theater. Maybe he was right.

I watched the buildings slip by, the businesses becoming houses becoming fields becoming nothing at all. I shut my eyes. I hadn't spoken to my mother once since I came to the show. I'd replaced her with Sylvia, a liar accusing me of doing the same, and her words stuck into my head like a barbed thorn. I hated my mother still, but she had something I needed. She had the truth.

"Will you help me?" I asked.

"Of course," Warner said. "We'll talk to Robichek. Together."

He smiled, but I turned away, stared down at my feet.

———————

Here's one about love.

You could deny a lot of things, but you couldn't deny The Ring. It was white and glowed, and when you touched it, it felt like your fingers had gone numb from anesthesia. It was the thing sixteen-year-old Ronald Johnson was most proud of, The Ring. It was like it was all his own. He had seen it being formed after all. It was his.

He'd been tending the sheep, and the light was fading fast. There'd be hell to pay if he missed dinner; he knew that. But the damn sheep weren't cooperating, weren't moving none when the dog nipped at their heels. Ronald sighed, waved a stick over his head, trying to look threatening. The things just stared at him dumbly, confused but not intimidated.

And then all at once, the sheep started moving. It was a veritable stampede. They flocked to their pen and stood shivering in the corner. *Real pitiful*, he thought. Something had spooked them.

He turned, expecting to see a coyote in the far field, but his eyes were drawn upward. There, over by the storage shed, only twenty-five yards away, and hovering two feet off the ground, was a glowing mushroom. It flashed with a rainbow of lights. It was a beautiful thing. The sheep cried in their pen.

It rumbled like an old washing machine, off balance. When it took off, it nearly blinded him, so bright were its lights.

He ran inside, still seeing the thing's glow burned into his retinas, and told his parents to come outside. He told them to look up. Sure enough, the vessel was high above them now. Everyone saw it.

And everyone saw The Ring, the strange circle of luminescent crystallized soil where the thing had hovered.

The Ring stayed for a long time. Weeks, in fact, until it started fading. When the snow fell, it didn't stick to The Ring—it melted away wherever it touched. There was time to get lots of important men out there to study it. They scraped away samples, took photographs, and let their fingers trail over the crust of it.

It was found that The Ring contained high volumes of an archaic organism—Nocardia. It thrives off of bioluminescent fungi. And until it disappeared, the sheep steered clear of it, ran in wild circles to get away from the spot. Even the dog wouldn't have anything to do with it, and he loved sticking his nose in everything.

Ronald had touched it, but only once. He felt its hard, crumbling surface, let his fingers grow numb. He held his useless fingers to his lips and pressed them hard against the warm flesh there. He'd have kissed the ring itself, but all those men in suits were watching all the time now. This would have to do.

CHAPTER 42
DISCLOSURE

I MET my mother on the day the trees dropped their first leaves. A flaxen day. We pulled into a gas station just outside town. Warner and Robichek made some sort of agreement—most likely spurred on by the exchange of money—to stop at this specific place at a certain time. That way I could run across the street to the little diner while everyone else got their food, their restroom breaks. I had no idea if we were on time or not—no one bothered to tell me the extent of the plan.

I was nervous. I shook with it, little spasms here and there across my body, my limbs, and Warner tried to calm me down. "It'll be over soon," he said. But there was just so much fear stored in my heart that it spilled over in a great rabid, foaming mass. I had no choice but to twitch, to fizz.

I ignored him, stared out across the road, wringing my hands together with neurotic intensity.

"Well, are you going to go? Do you want me to go with you?" He placed a hand on my elbow, and I shook it off.

"Don't touch," I scolded.

He pulled back, hurt. "Remember, no matter what happens, you're still you. You can do this."

I remember the look on his face—one of both hope and trepidation. I felt sorry for him, wrapped up in my story like an insect trapped in a cobweb. I wondered if I was the spider, or just another bug.

"Thanks," I said. "Really." I knew it was what he wanted to hear. His eyes brightened a bit, and I set off across the street.

I tried to amass some anger—build it up inside of me, push out all the worry and doubt. I needed to be angry to face my mother. I needed her to see that I was hurt, but not diminished. I certainly didn't want her to see me shaking, teary-eyed with fear of finally learning the truth.

"Laura!" Warner called. "I'm proud of you!"

I didn't look back.

When I entered the diner, the little bells above the door rang, summoning me into the hushed world of coffee cups clinking against plates, forks scraping across ceramic, muffled coughing. It was like being underwater. Time was slowing down, diffusing, becoming something tenuous and vague. I needed to sit down.

I scanned the booths, looking for my mother. Perhaps I was early, or too late, and she'd already gone. You couldn't count on Robichek for anything. There were truckers eating hearty meals of eggs and sausage, families sharing stacks of pancakes, but no one I recognized. The smell of all the food mingling made me nauseous, and I started to sit down in an empty booth.

But then a thin hand fluttered through the air as gently as a butterfly, and I turned, saw the small woman there, and knew her for my mother.

She'd changed so much. Her hair was frizzy and cut short, her face thinner than ever, gaunt and hollow. Her skin was a strange shade of yellow. Her eyes, still watery and on the verge of weeping, were bloodshot.

I slid onto the bench opposite her, and I could smell her—an antiseptic smell, the smell of medicine cabinets and rolls of gauze. I wondered what was wrong with her.

"Laura," she breathed. "I'm so glad you came."

She reached out to put her hand on mine, and I didn't pull away. All my anger and fear had fallen out of me the moment I saw her, so diminished she was. I was angry my emotions didn't stick, but it wouldn't have been fair to direct them toward this frail creature. I pitied her the way one pities stray dogs, empathy with a little bit of disgust.

I didn't answer, just looked at the bony knuckles, the loose wedding ring, resting on my hand.

"I've missed you so much," she said. "Look at you, how beautiful you are. You have your daddy's eyes, you know."

My face reddened despite myself.

"I have to tell you something. I—I'm ill. Cancer. I don't know how long I've got left," she said. It was almost melodramatic the way the world was swinging around us now, great spirals of light haloing our heads.

I nodded, couldn't speak.

"I've taken care of everything, so you have nothing to worry about when the time comes."

"Okay," I whispered.

"Okay," she said back, squeezing my hand. "It'll all be okay. I just, I don't want you to be alone in the world. Are you doing alright?"

I shrugged. I hadn't spoken to my mother in so long, it was doubtful her death would make any impact in my life, but I didn't want to tell her that, didn't want her to feel how small the hole was she'd leave. "I have some friends," I admitted.

"That's good," she said. "That's so good."

"Mommy?" I asked, suddenly feeling very small.

"Yes?" she asked, and if I closed my eyes I could see her, hear her at our kitchen table so many years ago. When things were better, brighter. At least her voice was still the same.

"Did it happen? The Incident, I mean. Is it true?"

She sighed, pulled her hand away from mine.

"I need to know the truth. Everything about it. Please, be honest." A frantic burbling was building inside me. It was getting away from me, this moment, this question. It had left my body and was flying free now, above our heads, a gnat she could swat down in a heartbeat.

She looked out toward the windows, toward the street and the RV waiting there. It was taking her forever—so much time to concoct a lie, to build something monstrous. But then she turned back to me, drew herself up tall, and I knew I would believe her. "Of course," she said. "Of course, it happened. It happened just like we said it did. Everything is true, Laura."

Tears ran down my face, a relief so great and pure.

"Except," she said.

My heart was a blade slicing through my chest.

"You weren't singing," she said.

I gripped the edge of the table. The world was coming undone, spooling by like old film. I can see us from above, facing one another. Both so full of wonder, full of fear. I can see us looking in each other's eyes, reaching all the way in, grasping at the raw core of us. I can see us all the way from space. I can still see.

"You were screaming," she said.

It took a while for my breath to come. It felt like I was drowning right there in the diner, dying slowly—silently—among the truckers and pancakes and fluorescent lights. "Does Sylvia know?" I asked at last.

My mother looked down at her jaundiced hands trembling slightly on the tabletop. "She does," she said.

"I don't understand," I said. "Why did you tell her?" It hurt that a person so vile, so willing to play with the truth, knew my reality before I did.

"I needed someone to confide in," she said. "I thought she'd understand. I thought she was like us. But she wasn't. It's all so complicated, Laura. After your father died, there was no one else who knew. It was so scary, the way you were taken. I still have nightmares of you hovering over us, your screams filling the air. Then you were gone. It was horrible."

"You could have told me." I had imagined this moment being violent, being full of shouts and tears, but my voice was level, begging. "I could have handled it," I said.

She looked up, studied my face. "You somehow forgot the whole thing. But I didn't. I remembered. You can't comprehend how horrible it was, Laura. I was trying to protect you.."

"Then why tell me it happened at all?"

My mother shook her head like a dog shaking off water. "Your father," she said. "I was trying to protect you from *him*."

A waitress slid a cup of steaming coffee between us. Neither of us moved to take it.

"All he ever saw were dollar signs. Even as you screamed and writhed, flying up over our heads, he was smiling. Something fantastic had happened to him at last." She sighed, and her shoulders fell. "There was no choice when it came to whether it happened or not. Whether we told the world. Whether you were returned or not. He needed that money. We did. But I could soften it, make it into something else. You were singing. Not screaming in pain, in fright, in terror, in horror. Not screaming loud enough it echoed across the fields and filled my head up like a migraine, like a chasm. But singing."

"All the way up," I said.

"All the way up." She smiled sadly. "I'm sorry, Laura."

I didn't say it, but I was sorry too. I was sorry for the way I'd underestimated her, diminished her in my mind. She stood before me, and I felt ashamed to have spat so much venom at a person so small and frail. I allowed her to hug me before I left.

"You should come home," she said. "It was wrong. All of it." She stumbled, and I thought she might fall.

"There's something I need to do," I said. "Then maybe I will."

"Okay," she said, a smile on the corner of her lips. "I'd like that."

———

This is a revelation.

In 2021 the United States government publicly released a report that confirmed the existence of unidentified aerial phenomenon (UAP).

It was nine pages.

Of the 144 UAP listed in the report, only one was dismissed as a "large, deflating balloon."

Eighteen of the incidents featured unusual flight characteristics such as moving against the wind, staying stationary in winds aloft, maneuvering abruptly, and reaching speeds inconceivable by man with no recognized means of propulsion.

When asked, officials said they currently have no proof that the objects are extraterrestrial. They also have no proof that the objects are terrestrial. They're unidentified, true UFOs.

"We will go wherever the data takes us."

CHAPTER 43

CRASH

I DIDN'T TELL WARNER.

I didn't tell anyone I had been screaming during The Incident. Not until today, until I wrote these words, wrote this book.

I climbed back onto the bus, ignoring the way everyone stared. It felt like my first night, when I was the new girl, scrutinized and ogled; the one they'd heard so much about. My life had been laid out before them a hundred times. I wasn't ready to revise that story. Whether they would see me with pity or as a liar, I couldn't abide either. I needed time.

"Well?" asked Warner. He sat down beside me. He'd told me early on that his story was untrue—that his grandmother didn't spontaneously combust and had instead been smoking in bed. It was so easy for him. I wondered if it would ever be that easy for me or if I had built too much on an insecure foundation to ever be able to tell the truth.

I ran a hand over my arm, looked down at the downy hairs there. "She said it happened, just like they said."

"That's good news, right?" asked Warner. "Do you believe her?"

"I guess so," I said. And I did believe her. We both knew it was the end. I'd visited her, and she'd given me the truth—a small dignity for both of us.

Warner patted my arm. "I'm happy for you," he said.

"Thanks."

He leaned back, put his arms above his head in an awkward stretch. "So, what now?" he asked.

I had known what needed to be done before I even left the diner. It had been whirling through my mind as I embraced my mother, and it carried me through to this moment, this confluence. I looked into his eyes, scared to tell him what came next.

I needed him. He was my only weapon now. The singing, the horrible wishes, none of it was real. People insisted I had the power to do anything; they'd shared their private weaknesses with me, begging for my help, and I thought perhaps I could only bring destruction, death. But now I knew I was just another abductee, screaming in the night, broken and sad.

And Sylvia had known that all along. Sylvia had profited off my lie, off my story, off of who I'd thought I'd was.

I took a deep breath, and the chaos inside quieted. "Would you do anything for me?"

He blinked, surprised by the question. "Of course," he said, equally surprised by the answer.

"Tonight," I said. "We need to go tonight."

"Go?" he asked.

"Run away," I explained, voice low. I glanced up toward Robichek, but he didn't seem to have heard. He was hunched over the wheel, as ever. I wondered if he was like us freaks, and his power was never needing to sleep, always driving, shepherding us along. It didn't matter though, not anymore.

Warner pressed a hand into his cheek. "Why?"

"There's something I need to do," I said. "And I need your help."

"What is it?"

I shook my head. "I'll tell you later. But at the next stop, you and me, we need to run. Bring your show gear."

Warner sat up, looked around the bus. He lingered over Susanna, sleeping slumped over the table. "Laura, I'm not going to agree to do anything with you until you tell me why."

I sighed. Warner was going to take some convincing. He'd attached himself to me so readily in the beginning, but this new phase, this new assertiveness on my behalf, frightened him.

"Sylvia is still taking money from Robichek. I refuse to do this any longer. Not as long as she's in the mix. My mom said I could come home, and I need you to come with me, to help take care of her, to keep me safe."

I hoped he'd believe the lie.

"You want me to live with your mom? With you?" His eyes were wide.

"Yes," I said. "Just until we're on our feet. If we bring our stuff for the show, maybe we can perform a bit at conventions, make some money."

I could almost see the gears turning in his mind. "Your mom. Would she, you know, accept me?"

"Of course," I said.

Warner had wanted a family for so long. It's no wonder he agreed. "Okay," he said. "But Robichek, he'll come looking. You know that. He'll know where to look."

"We'll call the police. We'll get a lawyer. He doesn't matter. Being a family matters. It's worth a try, at least."

He nodded. "Next stop, we run."

———

We got lucky. The bus pulled into a suburban Walmart lot. It crawled with activity even through it was well past sundown. I knew we'd have no trouble getting a ride out of there.

Warner pulled on his backpack, and I shouldered the bag in which I had bunched up my dress. "Just gotta change my clothes," Warner announced as we climbed down the steps of the bus.

"Warner," I hissed.

I could see sweat condensing on his forehead.

"You're acting funny," I said when we were free of the RV. "Just act like you always do."

"I don't know how," he said.

We walked the rest of the way in silence, only speaking again when we'd entered the fluorescent glow of the store.

"We need to find the customer service desk. We can use their phone to call for a taxi," I said.

"Right," said Warner. He kept looking behind him, back toward the automatic doors. Back toward where the RV sat full of the other dispossessed. But the doors stayed still, black and imposing.

He followed me to the counter situated in the corner of the store. The girl there looked up at us with dull indifference. "How can I help you?" she said between snaps of her bubblegum.

"Yes," said Warner, and I shoved him away.

"We were wondering if you had any numbers for a taxi service," I said. "And if we could use your phone."

The girl looked Warner over. "Yeah," she said. She turned, shuffled through a stack of crumpled papers. "Here." She slid a laminated sheet across the counter. "That's the only ones I have."

"Thanks," I said, attempting a smile.

She held out the phone headset, stretching the curly cord straight. I tucked the phone against my shoulder.

"How about this one?" I said, pointing to the sheet at random.

"Whatever," she replied, and took the page. She pecked out the number, and I listened to the shrill ring.

When a man answered, Warner and I both sighed in relief. It was happening. This would work. I told him the address, and he said he could do it, could be at the Walmart in ten minutes. My heart fluttered in my chest.

"Thank you," I said as I passed the phone back to the girl.

She shrugged.

And that was all it took. We left the show as abruptly as I'd entered it.

When we climbed into the taxi, I took a deep breath. A real one that filled me up and made me big. "We did it," I said.

But Warner was twisted around, watching for Robichek in the rear window.

"It's over," I said.

Warner sighed, turned himself the right way. "My contract," he mumbled. "How much longer until we get there?"

"Oh, maybe half an hour," said the driver. He was fiddling with the radio, flipping through stations.

Warner frowned. "But we've been driving forever. How can we still be so close?"

I felt a little sick. The words poured out fast and frantic. "Well," I said. "We were closer to her work than we were our house, I think. And Robichek—he must have gotten turned around. You know how he is."

He cocked his head. "Laura, what if your mom is sleeping? Doesn't hear us knock? What if she won't let me stay? What if she's mad?" He was fidgeting with his pant leg, anxiously picking at the threads.

I shrugged. It didn't matter. I had given the man Sylvia's address.

———

The house wasn't what I thought it would be. It was small, almost dilapidated with loose-hanging siding and overgrown rose bushes crowding the pathway. The windows were dark, unwelcoming.

"So, this is where you grew up," Warner said. He adjusted the bag on his back.

"Well, not exactly," I said. For a second, gazing up at that little house, I considered singing. I could do this the way I'd solved all of my problems in the past. But my heart squeezed around something hollow when I remembered. It had never been real.

Warner's brow crinkled. "Let's go to the front door and knock. I want to get inside as fast as possible. I'm scared the bus will come around the corner at any minute."

We picked our way carefully up the path, avoiding the snag of thorns. When we came to the door, I pulled Warner aside, and we crouched beneath a silent window.

"What are you doing?" Warner whispered. "Just fucking knock."

"Take off your bag."

Warner slid the backpack from his shoulders, plopped it on the ground. "What do you need?" He bent and unzipped the bag slowly, barely making a noise.

"Spread the gas here, at the foundation." I pointed at the spot where the house met the ground. I thought I'd be scared, but I wanted this more than I knew. My heart beat an even, solid rhythm.

"Gas?" His voice was high-pitched, shaking. "Laura? What are we doing here?"

"Take out your fire handling stuff. We need to burn this place down."

"Your mom's house?" Warner was shaking now, and he pulled the bag away from me, toward his chest.

"This is Sylvia's house," I said.

"Laura," Warner gasped. "We can't. I can't."

Annoyance flared up in me like the sudden flush of a fever. "Then give it to me. I'll do it, and your hands will be clean." He stared at me, his eyes wide and unblinking. "Coward," I hissed.

I had wanted him to be the one to set the house afire; I didn't want to get gas on my hands—the smell disclosing my guilt. But it didn't matter. Not really. Sylvia needed to be punished, no matter who did it. If Warner wouldn't do it through fire, and I couldn't do it through song, I'd start the fire myself. I held out my hand.

"No," he said. "No. This is insane." He was standing now, taking quick steps backward.

"Warner, please," I begged. "She never respected the truth. It didn't matter to her. She needs to pay, and I can't make that happen without you. I need to take something away from her."

His mouth opened and closed a few times before a sound came out. "That's not a reason to burn down a house," he gasped.

"You don't understand," I said. I reached out to him, held my hand palm up. "Come back, now. You don't understand. There's nothing else left to do," I said. "My story is done, here." It was true. All that hate and anger and fear, reserved once for Daddy, for my mother, for Robichek, had nowhere else to go. It swirled and built up inside me, waiting for a spark.

He stumbled, got caught up in a rose bush. "You'll kill her," he said.

He was breathing hard—I could see the erratic rise and fall of his chest. He was afraid, but still there, still waiting for me in the dark. There was so much I could have said. I could have started at the beginning. I could have unraveled the tale for him in its entirety, made him see my hurt was persistent and biting and this was the only thing I could do—the only way I could take any sort of real action. I was sick of things happening *to* me, around me. I could have told him I was trying to matter. Maybe I'm saying it all now. But at the time, I just said, "Good. Then she'll die for what she did to me."

His eyes were wide saucers glowing in the night. "You're a monster," he said. And then he was running, tearing through Sylvia's unkempt garden, out into the street.

———

You've been here before, this year, this moment.

The airship of 1897 had cut loose its anchor in Merkel, Texas.

I've already told you that story. I told you how the man slid down the rope, disliked what he saw there, and sawed the anchor free. But I never told you where he went. I guess I'll tell you now.

Aurora, Texas was dying. Bypassed by the railroads, plagued with sickness and foul crops, the little town was reduced to a few shops, a graveyard. But the man in the airship didn't know that. He didn't know much about anything. All he knew was that his ship was floundering, drifting lower, losing speed.

He tried to pull up to avoid the sharp metal spike of the windmill, but he hit it full on, and the ship exploded, raining shrapnel down on the fields and farms of Aurora. He was conscious for the beginning—the rending of his limbs, the awful brightness that cut through everything. He died in midair, just like he lived.

The judge found his torso in the well. Someone else found his arm in their unplowed field. They stacked the pieces up together and determined, mangled as they were, that "he was not an inhabitant of this world."

They buried the body parts in a rough-hewn coffin in the cemetery. The headstone there was etched with a crude drawing of the airship, an oblong shape with round windows.

The marker is gone now, but a large rock, strewn with change and trinkets, remains. Requests to exhume the body have been denied on the grounds that only a relative can give permission to raise the dead.

If you go to Aurora, if you stand atop the man's bleak grave, turn slightly and read what infant Nellie Burris's stone says: "*As I was so soon done, I don't know why I was begun.*"

I was seven when my life ended.

CHAPTER 44
HOME

I STOOD for a while in the quiet dark, looking up at Sylvia's house. Warner had run off without his bag, without his fire-starting equipment. I could see it out of the corner of my eye, black and slumped. He may have been a coward, but he would help me in the end.

I carried the bag to the side of the house where dry leaves had blown and accumulated. I winced as I crinkled through them, the sound deafening in the silence.

Pawing through the ribbons and batons, a wallet, a folded piece of paper with soft, worn edges, the few personal things Warner had carried, I choked back a sob. Grief is strange, welling up when you least expect. I didn't want to feel this way. I wanted to feel angry, resolute. I laid my hands on a plastic squirt bottle of liquid, on a long-tipped lighter.

I stood back and sprayed the top of the mound of dead leaves, then directed the stream higher up on the vinyl siding. I flung the bottle down when the fluid sputtered and coughed.

My hands shook, and I dropped the lighter, had to feel for it against the unmown grass. At last, my trembling fingers closed around the plastic handle, and I took a deep breath in, acrid fumes filling my lungs. I could do this.

I knelt at the edge of the leaves where the fluid hadn't touched. The lighter had two buttons: one on the front to be held with the thumb and another in the back for the index finger. I held the front button down.

I clicked the back button, and my finger slipped off the slick plastic, damp with lighter fluid and sweat. I tried again, and nothing happened. I was shaking so hard, I could barely hold the thing let alone apply any sort of pressure. Tears ran down my cheeks, made dark splotches on my sleeves. I tried the lighter again —nothing.

Grief might be strange, but habit is stranger. I closed my eyes and made my wish. Bright light played in my mind, flashing behind my eyelids. I could almost feel the warmth burning from inside. Quiet and soft, I hummed—an old Disney song.

My hands steadied, my breathing evened out. When I squeezed the lighter, fire erupted from the tip, and I smiled. I lowered the flame to the leaves, watched it eat its way toward the house, toward the gas-drenched center. My shadow danced behind me, joyous and proud.

The house across the street boasted a large oak in its side yard. I walked over, hid myself behind the massive tree, and waited.

The fire crept up the side of the house, lashing at the bubbling siding. It was beautiful the way it moved, the way it played and leapt. I had made something gorgeous, something right and true. Undeniable. Soon the once-black windows glowed, lit from within.

A shrill, but muffled cry—a smoke detector went off somewhere in the house. Goosebumps prickled along my skin. Would she sleep through it? Would the smoke choke her, lull her before she even heard the alarm? I gripped the bark of the tree, some of it coming off in my hands, some of it imbedding itself within me.

A dark shape appeared in the window, and my heart skipped. The silhouette moved away, was lost in the bright conflagration. I squinted to see against all that light.

The door flew open, and the house exhaled a white puff of smoke. I pushed myself against the tree, feeling the rough surface against my face. I breathed into the wood, smelled the damp, mossy scent of life, of living. Then I peeked around the tree, ready to see whatever waited for me there.

A man tumbled down the front steps, and I frowned. I thought Sylvia lived alone. She'd never mentioned anyone else. The man turned back, reached into the house, and pulled out a little girl.

She was in her pajamas, soft patterned pants and a matching shirt. She clung to her father's arm, pushed her face into his bare skin. She couldn't be more than seven.

I covered my mouth with both hands, muffling the scream I couldn't contain. It was the wrong house. I had the address wrong or Sylvia had moved or lied to me from the start, somehow collecting my letters from this strange man. Maybe she'd never gotten them. Maybe they'd been forwarded. Maybe he was her son, the girl her granddaughter. I didn't know. My thoughts weren't making sense. I doubled over, fell onto my knees. The little girl stretched out an arm toward the house, screaming for something within. Her father held her back, held onto her as they watched their house burn.

I scrambled up. I couldn't stay here. I couldn't watch this anymore. The little girl cried and screamed and my insides were a tangled, squeezing wreck. I ran away, zigzagging through yards, tripping over stumps and fences. In the distance, I heard the howl of a fire engine's siren.

My bag slapped against my back as I ran. I had forgotten I was still carrying my dress. I ripped it off my shoulders and stuffed it into someone's plastic trash can. It was weighing me down, making me slow. It was then I realized I'd forgotten Warner's pack and wallet, at the house. They'd find it, I knew. I had left it in the damp grass, too far away from the blaze to burn. They'd find it and they'd find him, and he'd lead them to me.

I had to find him first. The streets were unfamiliar and labyrinthine, always leading back to the same patch of yard, bright with fire and light, but I walked regardless. I was looking for a shock of red hair, pale skin glowing in the pre-dawn light. If I found him, I would start at the beginning. There had to be something I could say that would stop him.

But I didn't find him anywhere.

I slowed. No one had come for me yet. A few cars passed, but none stopped, no one glanced at me. Though my face was streaked with tears, and my body spasmed and jerked with agony, I was unremarkable.

There were a few gas stations along the bigger streets, all closed. At last, I found a pay phone—they were getting harder and harder to find those days—and called my mother. The phone rang and rang. She didn't answer until my third try.

"What is it?" she slurred. "Who is it?"

"Mommy, it's Laura. I need help."

"Where are you?" Her voice was suddenly clear and sharp.

I told her I'd made Robichek mad, and he had dumped me in a random neighborhood, breaking our contract, setting me loose. She agreed to come get me and take me home.

She never asked me what I had done to anger Robichek. Maybe she didn't care. She never was one to demand an answer.

I took care of her until she died in the spring. I watched her wither and curl into nothing. She was gone.

No one ever came for me.

———

Here's the last one. This time we meet in a trivial place awash in lights and confusion. There's something to be seen here if you can hold on tight enough, pierce through all that haze.

Steven would have to tell his mom he was at a strip club. She'd never believe the story if he didn't include the location, the ambiance, the smell of stale beer and body spray. It all mattered, all added up. He opened his phone and began typing.

It wasn't his first time at Sapphire, but it was the first time he'd hung back, shied away from the stages and whirling lights and just nestled himself by the bar. It was two nights before Christmas and he wasn't feeling well. He probably should have stayed at home—Covid wasn't over—but it was unbearable there in the dim light of his apartment, watching the cars pull in and out of the lot. He needed to be around people or he thought he'd go mad. So, he drove into town. He walked down the Strip. He passed the tourists taking selfies in front of the half-scale Eiffel Tower, the dancing Bellagio fountain. He needed a drink.

Sapphire wasn't the most affordable place to grab a pint, but he knew it would be crowded on a night like this, with everyone on vacation for the holidays, and he could lose himself in the throng. That's how Steven found himself in the corner of the world-famous gentleman's club, listening to the staccato barks of two men striving to be heard above the booming bass, the cacophony of laughter.

"Listen," the one man yelled. His voice was thick, a New York accent. "There's something outside."

"It's a UFO!" shouted the other man.

"Somebody, come look at this thing." The first man looked around him, arms outspread. No one was listening. A girl ambled by, lost her shoe, bent over, slipped it back on. "Hey, you. Come on outside. Someone's gotta come look at this thing."

"You're gonna have to stop yelling in here," said a man in a black button-down. "You're gonna scare somebody."

The first man shook his head. "You don't understand."

"I'm gonna have to ask you to leave if you keep yelling that way in here, is all."

The second man looked panicked, a little shaken. "Let's just go, Stu. I want to look at it again anyway."

"No way," said the first man. His face was red and glistened with sweat. "I want everyone in here to know what's going on. There's a UFO outside!"

"Okay, that's enough," said the man with the black shirt. He put his hands on the two men's lower backs and pushed them toward the exit.

"I'm not doing anything wrong!" yelled Stu.

"Let's just go. Come on," said the second man.

"I dunno what you guys are on, but it's not welcome here, okay?"

"There's a goddamn UFO. Right above the club. I'm not shitting you, man. Just come out and look."

The bouncer steered them toward the door, and Steven hopped off his seat, trailed along behind them. It was interesting, this exchange. He wanted to see where it went.

"Are you going to look?" asked Stu as the man pushed him onward. "I think you should see this."

"Leave him alone, Stu. We don't even know if it's still there. It could be gone. It could be nothing."

"Yeah, well," said Stu.

When they reached the door, all four men—the bouncer, Stu and his friend, and Steven—walked a few paces into the tepid desert night and lifted their eyes.

"There! It's still there!"

"I'll be damned," said the bouncer.

"What is it?" asked Steven.

"A UFO," said the quieter man. "It's been there for at least fifteen minutes. It was there when we came in."

Three red lights, a strange streak of gold, the ship hovered behind in a wispy cloud. Steven squinted, could imagine something solid between all those lights.

"It's a drone," said Steven. "Gotta be."

"That big?" asked Stu. "That still? No blinking lights—no nothing?"

"Maybe?" said Steven, feeling unsure. He'd never seen anything like it.

"Maybe it's, like, a reflection in the ice crystals way up high," offered the bouncer. "All these gold buildings? A few red spotlights? Gotta be something like that, right?"

Stu scoffed. "What are you, a meteorologist?"

"Look," said the quiet man. "Watch those beams."

Spotlights spun and raced across the sky—a hundred of them converging and falling away again. This was a normal Vegas sight, and the bouncer sighed, turned to go back in.

"No, man. Just wait. Watch those beams when they hit the craft. Just watch."

It was only a few seconds before a beam flashed across the cloud, across the lights. The thing hidden there glinted—metallic.

"See!" shouted Stu. "It's solid! That ain't no ice crystal!"

Steven felt the ground drop out from beneath him, his stomach rising to his throat. Whatever hung there in the sky was substantial and real. He pulled out his phone.

"What are you looking at?" asked a woman in a glittering dress.

"It's a UFO," said Stu. "Look!" And she did. The longer they stared, the more people congregated. All held their phones aloft, zooming in and out on the object on their screens.

Steven stayed until the cloud blew apart, taking the craft with it.

"Ice crystals," said the bouncer. He'd abandoned his post completely to stare at the lights. "I'm telling you."

"Can't be," said Steven. "It's got to be something more." And he truly felt that way—felt changed by the experience somehow.

He slid his dying phone back into his pocket, patted it once, and went home. He watched the videos again and again, posted them on Twitter for everyone to see.

"I saw this too! Right above Sapphire," said @GOATMan36.

"This is interesting," said @MUFON, the Mutual UFO Network.

Soon thousands of people had retweeted and commented on Steven's post. Other videos were popping up as well, shaky and dark. "I'm at Sapphire Gentleman's Club!" yelled a man with bleach-blond hair. He spun the camera around, focused on the lights. There they were, just as Steven had seen them—three red lights in a triangle, a few brushes of gold.

Steven couldn't look away from his screen. He refreshed his feed again and again, desperate to see new clips—each one an affirmation.

"Dude!" Steven texted his only real friend. He wasn't sure he'd be up—he lived in Massachusetts—but he had to share this with someone he knew, this feeling, this revelation. "Look at what I saw tonight." He sent a link to his tweet. He could have just sent the video, but he wanted his friend to see the momentum, the excitement. He wanted his friend to know that he'd finally stumbled across something rare.

Steven went back to his Twitter feed, refreshed it over and over. Now there was something new. "This is a marketing plot," said @gterryolive.

"Has to be," tweeted someone else. "Every single one of these posts mention Sapphire."

"Kind of genius, if you think about it."

"Even Sapphire has shared this shit."

"DEFINITELY a stunt," they said.

The tide had turned—now the consensus wasn't a general haze of amazement, but rather a cruel dissection of what Steven witnessed. He'd seen it with his own eyes, he typed. It was real.

"Yeah, sure," said a man.

"How do we know you're not on team Sapphire?" asked another.

"Because I'm not!" He typed and swiped, frantic.

"Maybe he did see it. Maybe Sapphire projected something into the clouds. All it'd take would be a few colored spotlights, right?"

"Nah," tweeted a girl with bubblegum pink hair. "Doesn't explain why literally every tweet talks about Sapphire."

"People had to have seen this all over Vegas, but there's no video from, say, Trump International."

"lol," tweeted a random man.

Steven turned his phone off. He couldn't take this, this denial, this lessening of the revelation he carried. He needed to talk to someone who'd believe him without reservation.

He needed to talk to his mom.

CHAPTER 45
TRUTH AND MEMORY

MY MOTHER LEFT everything to me, the house, what was left of the money I'd made her, but it didn't last. Within a year of leaving the freak show, I took up a job as a waitress, just as my mother had and served people their slop eight hours a day. Soon that wasn't enough either.

So I got married.

Louis was boring, ordinary in every way. He had only dimly heard of my past and knew next to nothing about UFOs. We lived in soft apathy. I was able to play house, pretend at normalcy. Let the freak show, fire, and The Incident fade into the background and pretend it all happened to someone else.

That is, until Louis was drinking and took to swinging a chair around in my direction. I dodged his lunges with swift side steps, but something in the doorway caught my eye. A flash of red, a flicker of something otherworldly. And I turned. Nothing was there. Louis caught me in the leg, bringing me down, then was atop me.

I didn't sing or wish or burn my husband dead. He slipped off a ladder while cleaning the gutters. A common, blameless accident. Something no one at the insurance agency questioned.

Am I a monster?

All I ever wanted was the truth—sacred and concrete. A truth to share with others like me. Something to hold on to. I wanted the truth to carry weight, and I wanted to punish those who disrespected it, profited off lies, off me. Is that so wrong? I have only ever killed through inaction, through indifference. There's no song ringing out in the night. I had no power, in the end. I was a weak little girl with no memory of the night that took her, rearranged her, and made her incredible, improbable.

But there is one night that stays with me, the one I can't wash out of my mind—the little girl clutching her daddy's arm as her life blistered and burned. They held each other, supporting each other, loving each other. Everything turned to ash around them—two figures huddled together in a sickly snow globe—and no one was sold, no one was used.

I remember that.

Robichek never came for me. Sometimes it hurts. I almost wish he tracked me down and begged me to come back. Told me the show was nothing without me. That I was the star.

I sought out the playbill online not long after and read I'd been replaced by a girl who was exorcised, purged of all her demons. There wasn't any mention of Warner. If he was found, if the authorities had found the wallet, he never told them about me.

Warner had said my abduction didn't matter. At the time, I was appalled, but realize now what he was trying to tell me was that—cosmically—it was just another thing that happened. A bruised knee, a dent in the fender. A story like all the stories I collected and then repurposed in this book. My story did matter, it did affect me, but it didn't mean anything. It didn't say anything about me, just like how the dog attack didn't say anything about Mike. Bad things happen, as do good things, regardless of who we are. Luck, at once both cruel and wondrous, is an uncaring, random facet of the universe. But I was too young, too dedicated to feeling sorry for myself, and I ignored Warner.

Maybe I did do something monstrous.

Knowing and accepting the truth are two different things, and they're getting closer all the time.

A house is burning down. A child is wailing.

The truth matters.

The truth matters so much it makes you cry and shake and ache all over. It makes you scream.

AUTHOR'S NOTE

I have always found beauty in stories of alien and UFO encounters. Amid the blurry pictures and clinical lists of times, dates, and places, humanity shines brighter than any strange star. I am drawn to the wonder, the raw fear, the incomprehension. Basically, I had a lot of UFO knowledge and figured I'd better do something with it. I considered putting together a podcast or YouTube channel, but fiction is my home.

I set out to write a book that subverts the "typical" abduction story; our abductee is a child, human nature dwarves any evil that aliens might do, Laura is told she was singing. Much of this is informed by my own benevolent experiences with the unknown. My first UFO encounter came when I was four, hunched over a mound of dirt in the yard. I was digging a hole when I felt my hair stand on end, the peculiar feeling of being watched. I looked up and found a large cigar-shaped object hovering over me. There have been several more episodes, some more intense than others, some shared with my sister, and never have I been scared. I've always felt lucky afterward. Chosen.

I want to thank Pete for encouraging me to follow my trail, wherever it may lead. I want to apologize to Naomi for the hours I spent locked away working. I am indebted to the beta-readers who so generously donated their time and knowledge to this project. I don't even know where to begin when thanking Theresa and Sarah; they believed in me and that alone changed my life. Their expertise is so appreciated.

There were many books, shows, and podcasts that inspired and educated me as I wrote. If you're interested in ufology, I recommend the following:

Flying Saucers from Outer Space, Major Donald E. Keyhoe, 1953

Passport to Magonia, Jacques Vallée, 1969

Mysteries of the Unexplained, Reader's Digest, 1982

Communion, Whitley Streiber, 1987

Skinwalkers at the Pentagon, James T. Lacatski, Colm A. Kelleher, George Knapp, 2021

Unidentified: Inside America's UFO Investigation, History Channel, 2019

That UFO Podcast, Andy McGrillen

Extraterrestrial, Parcast

Odd Ball, WJCT Public Media

THANK YOU FOR READING!

If you enjoyed this book, don't forget to leave a review on Goodreads, Amazon, or wherever you purchased this tale.